CLEVER BLACK

IMPLICIT

A NOVEL
BY

CLEVER BLACK

Greetings all. It is never an easy thing, writing these acknowledgements, as I tend to get a little emotional. I start to reflect on the moment I began writing a story and become anxious over the accomplishment; but it is always a wonderful journey. I always worry will the readers love it, did I put all I could into the story, is the plot tight? I am never sure until I hear from you all, but one thing is certain, I gave it my all. And as some of you have heard before, may I do right by you.

When I first began publishing, all I had was my blood family and a few friends to acknowledge, as of this date, the names can fill up an entire chapter in a book and I am so humbled by the reception I have received. Thank you all. Of course I can't go without mentioning Black Faithful Sisters and Brothers, my first home. Thank you all so much for giving me that air needed to takeoff. Just Read Book Club, the hottest club on Facebook, a hearty thank you. Building Relationships Around Books, salute. United Sisters, My Urban Books, Sisters into Reading and Reviewing, all down-to-earth clubs who've shown me some love. Thank you all.

And last but most certainly not least, The Holland Family by Clever Black Group. Man, what fun we have, and there's always something to discuss about that series, fam. I love you all like you were my own kinfolk. You all already know the deal, you know who you are, and where I stand. Much love family. I had to break away from the series for a minute though, and hopefully our family will increase by leaps and bounds with this book here; but that is not the main purpose for writing this story. The main reason is that this was a story I felt needed to be told as these things within this tale do happen. People really do live this way. May you enter into this world and become just as enthralled in reading this story as I became involved in writing it. I want you to be hit with that wow factor upon realizing what exactly is going down. I want you to be blown away. I want you to be taken away from this real world of ours into this too-close-to-real-life make-believe world and see how others live. May you enjoy the read, and again, thank you to everybody who has ever picked up a Clever Black novel and gave me a chance. Thank you very much. Enjoy.

CLEVER BLACK

ISBN: 978-0-989-2445-4-1

This is strictly a work of fiction. Any references to actual events, real people, living or dead, or actual localities, is to enhance the realism of the story. Events within the novel that coincide with actual events is purely coincidental.

All material copy-written and filed on site at the Library of Congress.

CHAPTER ONE
THE FIRST THREE

"...Some people are made for each other...some people can love one another for life...how 'bout us...some people can hold it together...last (through all kinds of weather)...can we...how 'bout us...how 'bout us baby..."

"You like it?" Kree asked sweetly as she lay flat on her back with her legs spread wide. "Your wife doesn't feel this good does she?"

"I love it, baby," her lover moaned before he tongue kissed her passionately while stroking her long and deep inside a dark and luxurious hotel suite as Champagne's song *How 'Bout Us* played lowly in the background.

Two men over the past two and a half years, minus the guy she was with on this spring night in March of 2007, had been twenty-three year-old Kree Devereaux's lover. All three had entered her life at crucial times and had served specific needs. The first guy she was ever with was named Alonzo Milton. She'd met him in Fox Park, her old neighborhood, in November of 2004, when she was twenty years-old. The then twenty-three year-old young man was out hustling that day. Kree had seen the guy once before up to the store, but she was in and out so quick she really didn't pay him any mind.

"What's up, lady?" twenty-three year-old Alonzo said in a smooth voice as he eyed Kree, who was wearing a thick, waist-

high bubble jacket, a pair of jogging pants and ankle-length fur booths with a scarf covering her head.

"Good evening," Kree responded kindly as she neared the store's entrance.

"Look, I know you get hit on all the time and all that, but I'm out here tryna make a honest living, you know what I'm saying? You wanna help support a brother by buying his music?"

"I can respect your hustle," Kree responded kindly. "But all I have is five dollars and much isn't gonna be left after I get what I want out of this store."

"I'm tryna eat. You going eat. You just gone leave me out here on this corner starving, huh, girl," the guy chided. "Let's split the five then. You need to cop my cd I'm telling you, it's gone be better than whatever you buy outta there."

"I'm going to get my Edy's butter pecan and sunflower seeds," Kree laughed as she reached for the door handle leading into Kirk's Corner Store.

Alonzo clapped his hands together and laughed himself. "Alright, mami," he said. "You got a man, though?"

"No," Kree responded coyly before entering the corner store.

Kree wasn't in her best apparel and appearance and she knew it; yet the guy standing outside of the store seemed interested. She paid for her items and was glad to see he was still outside the store when she emerged from the building. She wasn't going to make the first move as she was just too shy, but her smiling at the guy had subtly hinted at her interest, at least in her mind it did.

The guy smiled back and nodded his head towards Kree, who waved quickly and rounded the corner, walking back to her apartment. Kree wasn't feeling real good about herself in November of 2004. She was trying her best to attract a man, but being new to the area and not sure of herself, any form of rejection, for her, was devastating. She tucked her hands into her jacket and bowed her head as she trekked back to her *home in the cold air, feeling a little downtrodden over the entire encounter.*

"Yo," the young man called out to Kree, who turned around in time to see the guy walking towards her. "What's your name, shorty?"

"I go by Kree."

"I'm Alonzo. Alonzo Milton. I was checking you out when you walked up. You look nice."

"In this?" Kree asked as she wrinkled her face and looked down at her apparel. "This is around the house stuff, and I just threw these crazy looking boots on because it's cold and cloudy."

"I'm talking about your face. You pretty."

"You think I'm pretty," twenty year-old Kree Devereaux asked through a bright smile and wonderment. "No one has told me that in a long time. Thank you."

Alonzo scanned the block at that moment, making sure no one was out before he asked for Kree's phone number. She obliged and she and Alonzo began texting and talking on the phone that very day. Kree told Alonzo all about herself the second day after their meeting, the two having spent a couple of hours on the phone.

"I'm not like most girls as you now know, Alonzo."

"I already knew what it was," Alonzo responded. "That shit don't even matter because I just wanna be with you."

"So, me being a virgin and all doesn't bother you?"

"That's what's turning me on, shorty."

"How many times have you done this, Alonzo?" Kree asked over the phone as she sat on her bed in her upstairs apartment polishing her toe nails.

"Shit, I been fuckin' since I was fourteen years old."

"You know what I mean, man." Kree said seriously. "You say you don't have a woman and all, and if we gone be together I can't have you running around behind my back. I

don't play those kinds of games."

"So long as what we do stay under wraps we good. I'm down for you, ma."

"We'll see," Kree responded. "I know how this works, but you have to show me that you wanna be with me better than you can tell me."

"That ain't a problem. What you doing next week for Thanksgiving?"

"My girlfriend Jessie coming over with her two friends and we gone have dinner and just kick it."

"Oh, she bringin' a couple of dudes over there, huh?"

"Now, I know you ain't gettin' jealous," Kree laughed. "Is this what I'm gonna have to contend with if you and I get together?"

"Hey, I was just asking," Alonzo chuckled. "I mean, you talkin' to me about not going behind your back, but you got friends coming over and all. I wanna know if they male or female."

"These are all females, okay? I don't hang out with men. I only need one man to hang out with and I'm taking applications if you're sincerely interested." Kree said matter-of-factly as she leaned back and clicked on a blow dryer to air dry her toe nails.

"I'm definitely interested," Alonzo replied as he sat in his bedroom inside his mother's home. "Okay, you got friends coming over for Thanksgiving. Let's set a date to spend Christmas together, just you and me. And we talk on the phone and text each other until then? Let's let it build up and see what happen."

"We can definitely do that," Kree responded as her heart fluttered with anticipation. She now had what she viewed as a man for the first time ever.

A month or so later, on Christmas Day of 2004, Alonzo was parlaying inside Kree's apartment for the first time. She'd fixed a baked ham, turkey dressing and potato salad and had served him wine. When dinner was done, she went up under the Christmas tree and handed Alonzo three gift boxes before sitting beside him on the cushy sofa.

Alonzo opened the first gift and four plastic packages came into view. "Kree," he said in amazement as he stared at what lay before his eyes.

Alonzo had been telling Kree that he needed new USB cords and MIDI cords along with a DVD burner in order to transfer the beats he was creating from his drum machine to his computer so he could produce an album the times they'd talked over the phone in the weeks leading up to Christmas. The cost of the cords and the DVD burner wasn't cheap, over a thousand dollars, and Alonzo couldn't afford to make the purchase.

The weeks she'd spent talking to Alonzo had won Kree over. She'd fallen in love with him just by talking to him over the phone. He was kind, sincere in his interests, and was determined to make something of himself, not to mention he was the first guy that had ever shown any real interest in her for an extended period of time. With the full understanding that her future man could use some help, Kree had gotten all the things Alonzo said he would need in order to produce his album.

Alonzo opened the second box and leaned back in shock. "You got the DVD burner," he smiled as he leaned forward and kissed Kree's cheek.

Kree was expecting more than just a kiss on the cheek. And a simple thank you would have been nice in her mind. She eyed Alonzo with a smirk on her face, believing he was just as nervous as she about the possibilities that lay ahead. The love-struck twenty-year-old felt comfortable with Alonzo. She knew he appreciated the gifts, but she was only just beginning. She was really trying to get ahold of the guy by seducing him.

While Alonzo was looking the DVD burner over and explaining to Kree what he was planning to do with his music, she opened the third gift. "Look what I have, Alonzo," she said in a sweet voice, really caring not to hear what Alonzo had planned. He'd gotten what he asked for; she now felt that it was time for her to get her dessert.

Alonzo looked up and saw Kree resting on her knees before him with a white silk negligee draped across the upper portion of her body. "Would you like to see me in this?" she asked as she stared Alonzo the eyes.

Alonzo licked his lips and smiled. "You gone do it up for a nigga?" he asked as he sat the DVD burner aside.

"Yes. I'm going to get more sexy than what I already am for you," Kree said in near whisper as she crawled over to Alonzo and neared his face as U2's song I Still Haven't Found What I'm Looking For played lowly on her stereo.

"I have run...I have crawled...I have scaled...these city walls...these city walls...only to be with you...but I still haven't found...what I'm looking for..." *Kree sang along with the music as she leaned forward and hugged Alonzo. She really wanted to kiss him on this day as it would be the first time she'd ever kissed a boy. And what better way to cap off Christmas than with a sensual kiss from the man who was quickly capturing her heart was her reasoning.*

It didn't take Kree long to discern that Alonzo was either not interested, or reluctant to kiss her, however, given the way he'd refused to move his lips nearer to hers. She reached out and ran her hands across Alonzo's wavy hair before kissing his neck, refusing to go any further with her attempts to kiss his lips as she leaned back and stared into his face.

Alonzo was a handsome man to Kree. He was caramel-skinned with a neatly-trimmed goatee, wavy hair and thin side burns with thick eyebrows and snow-white teeth. Not only was he handsome, he was tall and sexy.

Kree knew Alonzo understood fully what she was expecting, and despite his refusal to kiss her, she went on with the rest of her plans because she believed Alonzo was willing to give her the very thing she'd been craving ever since she'd landed on American soil a year earlier. She pulled her gym shorts down and moaned the instant Alonzo's hands touched her bare flesh.

"His touch feels good," Kree said to herself as she began gyrating her backside in Alonzo's calloused hands. Filled with lust and moaning softly, she turned around and knelt face down in the carpet and spread her cheeks, putting all of herself on full display for Alonzo as U2's song ended and the room grew silent, only the faint sounds of an NBA game on the TV on the opposite side of the living room stirring the atmosphere.

Alonzo had stiffened the moment he gazed upon what lay before his eyes. Kree had a backside that was near perfect; round and protruding, and soft to the touch. Her virgin opening was pink and smooth, begging to be penetrated if Alonzo had to tell it. "Damn, girl," he said as he licked his lips and leaned in for a closer look. "You doing it like that?"

"Only for you. You like what you see?" Kree asked as she made her cheeks jiggle before Alonzo.

Alonzo wet his middle finger and pressed it in between Kree's cheeks and rubbed his thumb across her entrance. "You want some dick, don't you, bitch?" he asked matter-of-factly as he reached over to the wooden table beside the sofa with his free hand and grabbed the blunt he'd rolled just before Kree presented him with gifts.

Alonzo's finger had just penetrated Kree the moment he'd called her a bitch. It was a term she had always resented, but she gave it up to the act that was about to go down rather than verbal abuse; she was willing to do just about anything to get Alonzo to penetrate her. "Daddy," she moaned as she slowly rotated her hips on the tip of Alonzo's middle finger.

"Umm, hmm, you wanna be fucked," Alonzo said as he took a deep toke off the blunt he'd lit up and sat it back down. "You want me to fuck you, girl," he asked as he unzipped his jeans.

"I do. I do," Kree moaned as she eased back on Alonzo's finger. "Fuck me," she pleaded as she began rotating her hips wildly on Alonzo's extended extremity.

Alonzo was behind Kree before she could finish her plea. He pressed the head of his phallus to her opening and drove forward.

"*Alonzo, wait.*" *Kree protested all of a sudden.* "*Let me get it wet, baby.*"

"*It's wet enough for me,*" *Alonzo retorted as he rubbed his shaft up and down Kree's crevice and drove forward again.*

Kree shrieked at that moment. Her eyes watered from the pain and she fell forward onto her stomach. "*Alonzo,*" *she panted. Kree was unable to catch her breath before Alonzo was on top of her again. He drove into her once more and hovered over her backside.*

"*Chill out,*" *Alonzo commanded as he began pistoning back and forth.* "*You gone have to let me fuck it right if you wanna get used to this dick, girl.*"

"*How many times you did this,*" *Kree cried as she lay flat on her stomach with her hands tucked under her chin. Alonzo drove deeper into her and she shrieked again.* "*You're hurtin' me! How many times have you done this?*" *Kree cried as she lay underneath Alonzo's slender, six foot frame.*

"*Quit all that fuckin' noise, bitch,*" *Alonzo hissed as he lay flat atop Kree on the floor in front of the couch in between the coffee table.* "*I told you this was my first time. You gone take this mutherfuckin' dick straight like this here. You know this what the fuck you want.*"

Tears began forming in Kree's eyes as she felt Alonzo sinking deeper into her. The dream she'd had concerning her first time with a man had been shattered. Instead of being made love to in her bed like she'd always envisioned her first time being, she found herself getting fucked raw on her living room floor. Alonzo was neither gentle nor kind when it came to sex. He called her a bitch repeatedly and kept one of his hands on the center of her back to prevent her from squirming away. "*Don't hurt me,*" *Kree pleaded as she stopped struggling and let Alonzo have his way with her body.*

"*I'm not gone hurt you. Tell me this dick don't feel good.*" *Alonzo huffed as he began pistoning in and out of Kree, sinking deeper and deeper with each stroke.*

"*It do. Just go slow. Let me get used to it. Ahh!*" *Kree*

screamed as Alonzo began pounding her furiously while breathing uncontrollably.

"Take it out when you come! Take it out when you come! Oooh!" Kree shuddered over the sensation.

"Yeah, you love this dick! This my pussy now! Who this pussy for? Huh? Say this my pussy, bitch!"

Deep down inside, twenty year-old Kree felt as if she was being taken advantage of on this Christmas Day because this was not what she wanted, per say. Yes, she'd wanted to have sex with Alonzo, but she figured he would be gentle knowing it was her first time. Instead, he was calling her names and sexing her mercilessly on her living room floor. "It's yours, daddy! Your pussy!" Kree cried out.

Alonzo creamed inside of Kree a couple of minutes into the act and jumped up immediately and pulled his jeans up. "Girl, you got that fire," he said through laughter as he fell back into the couch and reached for his blunt.

Kree said nothing as she turned over and looked Alonzo in the eyes. There was nothing sensual or rewarding about what the two had shared other than the fact that Kree had found a guy that was willing to be with her for the first time ever. She was hoping for much more her first time out. It just wasn't meant to be though, she surmised. Her first sexual experience had left her disappointed and confused instead of love-struck. She pulled her gym shorts on and picked up her negligee. "What now, Alonzo?" she asked meekly.

"You mines now," Alonzo remarked before jumping up and taking the gifts Kree had bought him. "You wanna get together call me. But it's between me and you, aite?"

"Okay," Kree responded through a faint smile that hid her disappointment.

Alonzo had left Kree's apartment without so much as a thank you for the sex or the gifts on Christmas Day of 2004. She couldn't help but to feel played, but she couldn't deny the fact that she loved the way Alonzo felt inside of her. He was worth keeping around in her eyes; he just had to mature a little more and she was willing to wait. A couple of days later, she went to her doctor and had a complete blood exam run on her; she was tested for every sexually transmitted disease known to man and had come back with a clean bill of health. She'd skated her first time; but she vowed never again to have unprotected sex unless it was with a man with whom she would give her heart to, and as of the date of her test results, Alonzo Milton was not that man.

The two spent New Year's of 2005 together and had sex again. Alonzo was rough as usual, but Kree had gotten him to refrain from calling her out of her name. More importantly, she had asserted herself and demanded that Alonzo use a condom lest the two not have sex. It took Kree only a week to learn that she did have a say so in the way men treated her and they weren't going to abuse her in any way. As time wore on, what started as mere sexual encounters had blossomed into a relationship between twenty-three year-old Alonzo Milton and twenty year-old Kree Devereaux.

Kree's career as a beautician was accelerating, and Alonzo seemed to be doing okay with his music throughout 2005. By spring of 2006, however, Kree began to suspect that it was much more to Alonzo. She'd given him five thousand dollars to press up CDs for his album, but he'd only ordered maybe a hundred CDs. The math wasn't adding up for Kree, and she began to suspect that Alonzo had pilfered the money and did otherwise. The two had been involved for eighteen months; and whereas Kree saw herself growing financially, Alonzo hadn't made any progress in her eyes. He lounged around her apartment waiting for her to come home to cook and she was tired of the monotony. All she and Alonzo ever did was have sex inside her apartment. All was well in the bedroom; it was the things transpiring outside of the sheets that ailed Kree.

Alonzo didn't help keep the apartment clean, didn't pay any bills, never took her anywhere and stayed high most times. The potential she had seen between her and Alonzo at the outset had faded into her life's memory. She was glad she'd decided to continue to use condoms with Alonzo because he had proven to be nothing but a bum in her eyes. She loved him, though; Alonzo was her first sexual partner and her first love.

And it was for those two reasons Kree found herself having a difficult time letting go of the guy. She ended up remaining in what would turn out to be a dead end relationship headed nowhere fast.

Alonzo wanted to keep Kree behind closed doors because he was on the verge of becoming a major music producer was his story and she believed what she was being told at the outset. Alonzo had showed her some equipment he owned and had even played instrumentals he'd created not too long after she'd agreed to be his girlfriend. Kree had put over $6,000 dollars into Alonzo to help support his dream, but it seemed as if he was more interested in spending the money rather than using it to propel his ambitions forward.

In March of 2006, Kree discovered that Alonzo had a cocaine addiction. One of the neighborhood drug dealers came to her apartment looking for Alonzo, stating that he owed her two hundred dollars after she'd given him seven hundred dollar's worth of powdered cocaine for five hundred dollars. Kree wasn't sure what to believe, but she knew the young teenager and had smoothened things over by telling her she had to talk to Alonzo first before she paid her the money owed.

Kree was leaning more towards believing the young drug dealer based on Alonzo's previous actions. She had given him five hundred dollars to pay her car note and insurance the month before and had allowed him to use her new car to make his moves on the streets while she was at work. The day before she was approached by the young drug dealer, Kree had received a notice of termination from her insurance company and a past due bill on her brand new 2006 Nissan Maxima. Now she had some young drug dealer, who couldn't have been no more than fourteen or fifteen years-old, standing before her looking for $200 dollars she claimed she was owed. Kree surmised right away that Alonzo had taken her $500 dollars and bought drugs, and had been given another two hundred dollar's worth up front. Her eyes were opened even more on that day. Not only was Alonzo a lying, lazy bum, he was a powder head.

When confronted, Alonzo denied everything, saying he paid

the bills, but he'd paid them late. The following day, Kree received confirmation that her insurance was in good standing and her car note was up to date, late fees included. She soon found out from Alonzo himself that he was selling drugs to earn more money for his label and she was shocked over the entire scenario. She couldn't understand Alonzo's method of operation. She'd given him more than enough money to get started, but all she ever saw was freshly painted cars with big rims and loud music. That's all Alonzo was really about in her eyes now, clothes, cars and getting high. Every dollar he obtained he spent on himself or some car he was riding around town in.

Kree was saving most of her money and spending some on her apartment. She was always buying new curtains, other accessories and decorative towels. She rearranged her furniture often and kept a clean house. She was really a home body searching for that one special man she could give her all to. She thought she had that man in Alonzo, but by April of 2006, after eighteen months of trying to help him get on his feet, twenty-two year-old Kree Devereaux realized it was time to move on. She was to the point to where she was only going through the motions of the day when she left her job at the hair salon. Alonzo was making her home life miserable; she was no longer comfortable nor happy and really saw no future for the two of them.

The last straw for Kree came in the same month of April of 2006 when Alonzo had stolen a blank money order she'd set aside for her light bill in order to get high. It was a test she'd put on Alonzo and he'd failed tremendously. Kree was outdone after that incident. She left her job, said fuck Alonzo and the apartment, and went out to have a few drinks before returning home to her apartment just before two in the morning. And that was the night the two's relationship had reached its climax.

Alonzo was sitting across the street in the darkened Fox Park playground when he saw Kree pull up in front of her door. Since she'd taken her key back a couple of weeks earlier, he now had to wait on Kree to get home before he himself could enter the apartment.

Kree was unlocking her apartment's front door when Alonzo ran up on her. "Where the fuck you was all day?" he yelled as he grabbed Kree's arm and pulled her close.

"I was at work, boy! Then I went and had some drinks— alone!" Kree snapped as she snatched away from Alonzo's grip. "Where is my money for my light bill?"

"I told you I paid that shit a week ago! If they fucked up that's on them!"

"You got high with my money and you know it! I can't live like this, Alonzo! Look what you doing to us, man! I'm supposed to be your woman, but you treat me like shit!"

Alonzo backed away from Kree and wrinkled his face. "What the fuck you tryna make this shit out to be?" he complained. "I have to get high just to deal with this shit! You should be glad I'm even dealing with your ugly ass! Dick sucking, ass-licking, bitch!"

Kree covered her heart as her jaw dropped open. "Is that all I am to you?" she asked as her eyes filled with tears.

"That's right," Alonzo scoffed. "Nah go 'head and cry with your ole bitch ass! I'm the man in this shit!" he yelled in Kree's ear.

Alonzo was high out of his mind and Kree knew it; all she wanted to do was get inside her apartment where she had something waiting for him. She turned around, never bothering to engage in any more conversation and unlocked her door and entered her apartment. She tried to close the door quickly, but Alonzo pushed it open and stepped in behind her.

"Get the fuck out! This isn't your apartment and your name isn't on the lease!" Kree yelled as she trotted upstairs.

"You gone come back and talk to me! I wanna know who the fuck you was with tonight!"

"I went out and I had a couple of drinks by myself, Alonzo! I don't say nothing about all the dirt you do around here!" Kree said as she reappeared at the top of the stairs with her hands behind her back.

Alonzo was preparing to climb the stairs until Kree pulled a chrome .380 semi-automatic handgun from behind her back and aimed it at his head. "You're not gonna hurt me anymore!" she screamed as she pointed the gun at Alonzo.

Alonzo turned and ran for the front door, where he was greeted by the Saint Louis Police Department upon exiting the premises. Six officers had responded to a domestic dispute call at Kree's address. Alonzo was taken down to the ground and handcuffed. After officers heard both sides of the story, Alonzo was taken to jail for unlawful trespassing. It was the authorities' way of defusing the matter.

That April spring night of 2006 was the last night Kree had ever seen Alonzo. She'd tried to call and apologize the days following the argument after learning he'd been released on his own recognizance, but Alonzo never bothered calling her back. Kree shut off her phone after seven days of trying to apologize and went and rented a hotel for a few weeks until she found another place. She still thought of Alonzo often and even missed him to a degree. She didn't think he would harm her ever; things had simply gotten out of control that night. She wouldn't mind seeing the guy again, if only to apologize. He was her first after all, and he still held a special place in her heart.

Kree's second lover was a forty-six year-old Caucasian lawyer named Sean Bradsworth. She had met the guy inside a river boat casino lounge three weeks after she and Alonzo had went their separate ways. She was in between apartments at the time and had grown tired of laying around her hotel suite watching TV and ordering in. She got off work one Saturday night and made herself up and hit the town alone, despite her friends' attempts to take her out to cheer her up.

Twenty-two year-old Kree Devereaux went back to her suite inside Embassy Suites hotel after getting off work that night and soaked in the Jacuzzi for about an hour. She'd laid out a beige, loose-fitting pair of silk pants with a matching blouse and a pair of three-inched heeled, leather, knee-length boots. Her hair was made up, lip gloss shining and she was smelling real sweet. She left the hotel and strolled along the streets of downtown Saint Louis by her lonesome.

Kree hadn't felt this free in a long time. She strolled along the sidewalk, mixing in with the droves of people who were out enjoying the night life. After walking through a few clubs, having a conversation or two with other clubbers, she decided to catch a cab to President's Casino. Her boss, Kantrell, had told her more than once to check the lounge out inside the casino while she was staying at Embassy Suites so she'd decided to see what the place was all about as there wasn't anything in the clubs she'd perused that really piqued her interests.

Kree was sitting on a bar stool playing the quarter slots inside the low-ceiled, dimly-lit, cozy casino lounge, enjoying her time alone, when a handsome, older man eased into the stool beside her and introduced himself as Sean Bradsworth. Kree didn't know it at the time, but what she and Sean Bradsworth would share on this particular night would transform her life forever.

"I'm Kree Devereaux," Kree responded through a smile as she extended her hand towards Sean after he'd introduced himself.

"Devereaux," Sean said through a smile. "Are you French?"

"Brazilian and Portuguese."

"Qué hermoso rostro tienes." (What a beautiful face you have.)

"Gracias. Y eres muy guapo." (Thank you. And you are very handsome.)

Sean extended his arms and began gyrating them in a wavy sort of motion. "We are on the same wave length tonight, baby," he smiled under the dim lighting inside the sparsely-filled lounge.

Sean was the first man that had made Kree smile since she'd split up with Alonzo three weeks earlier. She was single and the guy was handsome, so she'd opted to see what he was about and what the night had to offer. "Can I get you a drink?" she asked over the music.

"No," Sean said as he pointed towards Kree and smiled. He closed his eyes and tried to hold back his laughter, but he just couldn't. "I am having so much fun with you, young lady," he said cheerfully. "You are drinking?"

"A lime margarita."

"Okay," Sean said as he wobbled in his seat.

"You okay, Sean?" Kree asked as she placed her hand on his chest to keep him falling forward.

"I'm fine," Sean replied in a proper manner as he righted himself. "I am fine, Kree. It was just a slip in my swag that's all."

"A slip in your swag? I have never heard that one before," Kree laughed.

"Yeah. Sometimes us white guys zig when we should've zagged and we get a little discombobulated, you know? Hey, I'm working on my swag, okay? Just bear with me on the swag."

Kree was tickled by Sean. She couldn't stop laughing. The jovial man had ordered her another lime margarita and a whiskey sour for himself and the two entered into a lingering and leisurely conversation. She told Bradsworth a little about herself and he invited her back to his place in the town of O'Fallon after the two had shared a few more drinks and talked for a couple of hours.

Kree accepted, believing she knew what Sean was expecting, but it didn't bother her as it would be her way of getting over Alonzo. Things didn't work out as expected in the bedroom with Sean, however; the two had fun, but Sean was a kinky individual in her eyes.

Sean had Kree dress up in an all-black leather dominatrix's outfit with the back cut out, exposing her butt cheeks. She had been having her assumptions about him all night from their conversations, and when he told her he wanted her dress up as a dominatrix, she knew her assumptions about him were right. She couldn't help but to smile over the realization at that moment. *Some good lessons did come out of her relationship with Alonzo as she reflected upon it briefly. She now understood that she had the ability to read men and adapt to her surroundings.*

"How do I look, Sean?" twenty-two year-old Kree asked as she stepped out of the master bathroom freshly showered and scented.

Sean eyed Kree's curves and smiled as he stood before his bar in a silk robe and silk boxers with his chest bare. He held a bottle of whiskey in one hand and a glass of ice in the other, the Rolling Stones' song I Miss You, was playing in the background. He gazed upon Kree's small waistline from across the room and made a circular motion with his hand as he held onto the glass of ice.

Kree turned in a quick and awkward manner, being new to this particular routine. "Go slow, baby. Raise one hand and pull that lovely hair of yours up off your neck and turn slowly," Sean remarked casually as he poured himself a glass of whiskey.

Kree pulled her hair up with her right hand and placed her left hand on her hip. She then dipped and rose slowly as she began to turn away from Sean in a slow and seductive manner.

"You are gorgeous. Show me that lovely ass of yours," Sean said as he sat down before his bar to enjoy the show.

Kree walked around in a circle in her black, knee-length leather boots, sashaying across the marble floor inside the extravagant master bedroom with her hands on her hips. She kept her back turned to Sean as she did a slow and sexy impromptu dance routine to the rock song, bending over to expose herself on occasion.

The song ended and Kree walked over to Sean and ran her hands across his muscular thighs. "You liked it?" she asked while smiling into his handsome face.

Sean handed Kree a stem glass and grabbed a bottle of champagne. "That, my lady," he said as he poured Kree a drink, "that by far was one of the sexiest routines I have ever seen."

"For real?" Kree asked apprehensively. "I was really nervous. I'm going to need some time to get into this here. This, this is a new experience," she said as she sipped her drink.

"Well, let me help put you at ease, beautiful," Sean said as he leaned forward and nuzzled Kree's neck.

That tickle, man," Kree laughed as she leaned back, still holding her glass of champagne.

"I'm gonna have so much fun with you." Sean said as he leaned back and opened his silk robe to put his tanned and toned physique on display.

"That's nice," Kree smiled as she reached out and grabbed Sean's semi-hard tool and stroked it slowly. "How does that feel?" she cooed as she continued stroking Sean's erect shaft.

Sean laid his head back and relished Kree's soft, manicured hands. "You wanna be mines," he asked through closed eyes. "I'll take good care of you, baby."

Kree was flattered by the offer, but what she believed Sean was going to ask her to do was turning her off to a degree; she didn't want a man that was into receiving anal sex. She wanted a real man, and in her eyes, Sean Bradsworth, although nice, handsome and obviously full of money given the three story condo and 750 BMW he owned, was not the type of man she wanted to be emotionally attached to; she actually measured him as being gay, and that was a real turn off for her. "I can take care of myself, Sean. I really don't need a man to do anything for me financially."

"Is that so? What about these," Sean said as he sat upright and reached out and thumbed Kree's nipples. "You want an upgrade, baby?" he asked lowly while staring into Kree's eyes.

Breast augmentation had been Kree's dream for some time. Alonzo kept her in debt by owing people, going to jail and stealing money. She had a few thousand saved now that they'd split, but she wanted grade A breast implants that looked and *felt natural to the touch. The doctor performing the procedure charged $7,000 dollars, two thousand more dollars than she had saved.*

With her being in between homes and steadily searching for a new residence, Kree was apprehensive about spending all of her savings and then some on implants, no matter how badly she wanted them. Sean had presented her with an opportunity, however, and she was keen on listening to his proposition. "You're willing to buy me breasts?" she asked, a little uncertain.

"Wouldn't be the first time," Sean laughed. "Hell, my, my wife? That was the last thing she asked me to do for her before she ran off with my best friend and business partner."

"I'm sorry about that," Kree said in a sincere manner as she looked into Sean's eyes.

"Aww, forget her," Sean laughed as he eased up from the bar stool. "I'm having more fun now than I have ever had in my life, Kree. She didn't get one red cent either. I have money to do as I please. You want me to pay for your breast surgery I'll do it. But there's a catch to the deal."

"What's the catch?" Kree asked cautiously as she leaned back and looked into Sean's eyes.

Sean walked over to a large walk-in closet and disappeared from sight. He reemerged with a medium-sized box and waved Kree over to the bed and extended his hand, allowing her to sit. He then sat beside her on the bed, pulled the lid open on the box and showed her a strap on dildo. "You have to fuck me with this," he said as he stared Kree in the eyes.

Kree wanted to laugh out loud at that moment. She'd never been involved in anything of the sort. Her girlfriend, Jessie, had a strap on that she used on the women she slept with, so she was somewhat familiar with the device after listening to Jessie recount many of her sexual conquests and how she put the 'Big Dipper' down in the bedroom.

"Why not just get the real thing?" Kree asked as she eased up from the bed and turned and faced Sean.

"Because I like them big," Sean laughed.

"So do I," Kree chuckled as she eased over to the bar and poured herself another glass of champagne. She finished the glass quickly and walked back over to the bed where Sean was waiting with the dildo in his hands and sat down beside him. *"I don't know how this is,"* Kree paused as she grabbed the strap on and looked it over. *"How do you use this?"*

"You mean you have to ask," Sean asked as he lay back on his elbows.

"I know how it goes, okay?" Kree chuckled. *"I'm curious as to why you wanna do this?"*

"The same reason you do it, Kree...because it feels good."

"It's much more to it than that for most of us women, Sean. It's not always about the sex." Kree remarked as she eased up from the bed and began to wrap the strap on around her waist.

"You are most likely right, but, what are we doing here tonight?"

"It's strictly about money if that's what you're asking me," Kree replied as Sean came to her side and gave her some assistance with the belt.

"And that is fine by me," Sean remarked as he tightened the strap on's belt around Kree's waist. *"I want you to stick around, Kree. You don't have to be mines, just be around. And I'll help you with your implants. I'll pay you fifteen hundred dollars if you do this with me tonight."*

"Can I get paid up front, please?" Kree asked politely as she held out her hand and stepped back and tugged on the strap on to make sure it was secure, never making eye contact with Sean. Kree wasn't feeling this scenario at all. It was as if the roles had been reversed. She didn't like this game, but she now realized that Sean was serious about getting her implants; and if it took her having sex with him using a strap on dildo to make that dream a reality, well, that is what she was willing to do.

"A woman about her business," Sean smiled as he backed away from Kree and walked over to his office desk on the

opposite side of the room. He reached into a file bin and walked back over to Kree holding a white sheet of paper and an envelope. "If I pay you today? You will work for me exclusively," he said as he as he held onto the stationary.

"Work for you exclusively," Kree laughed as she walked over to the large dresser and grabbed her handbag. "You want a stick of gum," she asked while fumbling through her purse. Kree had grown nervous at that moment. Sean was coming off like a pimp in her eyes and she wasn't about to succumb to abuse. She placed her hand around the trigger of her .380 and walked over and sat on the edge of the bed with her handbag on her lap and her legs crossed, the gun's barrel pointed directly at Sean, but hidden from sight by the purse itself.

"Yes. This is an offer from me to you to do further business," Sean remarked as he opened the envelope and pulled out what appeared to be money. He walked over to the nightstand beside his bed and spread out fifteen, crisp, one hundred dollar bills before Kree's eyes. "What I will do is record what we do tonight and upload it to my video site where I charge a membership fee. I make maybe, maybe seventeen thousand dollars a month charging thirty dollars for full access."

"That's a lot of money every month," Kree said as she ran numbers in her head. "So that means somewhere around six hundred people will see a video of me every time we do it. How many other people do you do this with exactly?" she asked as she scooped the money up off the night stand with her free hand.

Sean eased the money out of Kree's hand. "I've had dozens of people I've done this with. There are two this month. Two who are older than you," he said as he tucked the money behind his back and presented a contract to Kree. "You have youth and damn good looks about you. I'll pay you more if my business increases like I know it will if you allow me to film you. You agree tonight? And I'll pay you fifteen hundred dollars."

"I don't want my face seen," Kree remarked as she eased her hand off of her pistol's trigger and grabbed the contract. "I mean, we can do a deal of some sort, but if my face has to *be shown, I'm not going through with it."*

"No one's face is ever seen. I use total discretion. It's all about the body, the voice and the act. But yours is a very beautiful face. You would be magnificent in front of the camera completely and could make a lot more money."

"I don't wanna go that far, but I'll do it without my face being seen. At least until I get the money to do my implants." Kree responded as she scanned the contract.

"Good," Sean said as he walked over to his bar and turned on his laptop. "Come here and take a look at this, Kree."

Kree walked over to the bar and looked at the computer screen and saw an adult website advertising home amateur videos. "Amateur dot com is my own private little playground," Sean said proudly as he smiled at the screen. "Now, you can go in there, take a look around, see how I do it, read over the contract and tell me your answer when I return."

Kree heard the water turn on in the shower just as she was entering the website. She soon caught sight of the money on the counter beside her. Sean had left the money on the bar and was deaftly out of sight. She knew she could've just taken the fifteen hundred dollars and run at that moment; she had Sean stop by Embassy Suites to pick up her car and it was still parked out front. That would be a dumb move, though, Kree had surmised. The guy was pretty fun to be with and he was cool and handsome, but the bigger deal was the fact that she knew she could get much more money if she stuck around and kept things professional.

Kree looked at a few of the videos on the site and wasn't repulsed by anything she'd seen. One thing was certain, Sean was no virgin, front or backside. His website was about what she had expected to see and she was fine with it all. She turned her attention away from the computer and began reading over the contract as she eased down from the bar stool. She walked around the spacious bedroom in her black, knee-length, leather boots, the strap on dildo still dangling from her waist while reading slowly. The contract was simple, one informing Kree that both parties would be filmed and the video would be uploaded to Amateur.Com. No faces would be seen and a right-to-sue clause for defamation and fraud was binding for each and every video where a new contract would be signed.

The terms within the contract where suitable for Kree; she walked back over to the bar and grabbed the money and tucked it into her purse. Sean's office desk was on the opposite side of the pentagon-shaped master suite. Kree went and scanned the desk top for a pen and was signing the contract when Sean emerged from the bathroom just off to her right. He was in her peripheral sight, but she felt him staring at her as he stood motionless.

Kree signed the contract and looked over to Sean and had to do a double take. He stood before her leaning against the threshold wearing red high heels, red lip stick, a silky black wig, and a red, silk camisole. She quickly covered her mouth to suppress her laughter as Sean pushed himself off the threshold and started walking towards her with his hands on his hips, trying to be sexy, but he looked about as awkward as a newborn horse trying to walk for the first time in his high heels to Kree, who eyed him with a smirk on her face as she walked back over to the bar.

"You're not the only one in here with a smoking ass body, dear," Sean said, trying to imitate a woman's voice.

"Yes I am," Kree responded as she leaned back against the bar and poured herself another glass of champagne. "I signed the contract and put the money in my purse so I guess we're in business, Sean."

"No, honey, it's Shawna now."

"Shawna?" Kree asked as she sipped her champagne.

"Yes. Shawna is my alter ego. You're familiar with alter egos aren't you, Kree?"

"I am," Kree chuckled. "But I wanna talk to Sean Bradsworth. He's the one I was dealing with on this contract."

"Kree, you're ruining my moment." Sean said in his regular voice as he ceased his feminine charade.

"Okay," Kree laughed. "I'm sorry. You look cute, though."

"Really," Sean asked in delight.

"No," Kree chuckled. "I'm not gonna lie to you, man. You would make an ugly woman."

"What? Look at this ass," Sean snapped as he turned around and looked back at Kree. "Tell me this ass doesn't look good."

Kree fell back against the bar and screamed to the top of her lungs. "Why you got a skull and bones tattooed on both your butt cheeks?" she asked aloud though her fun-filled tears.

"Because this ass is dangerous, girl. You keep mocking me I just opt for the real thing."

"The, the real thing works much better," Kree said as she sat up and wiped her watery eyes. "That tattoo looks like the poison control sign symbol, though. People might take it the wrong way, Sean."

"These ass hats are my signature, Kree. When people see these tattoos online, they know it's authentic. They know it's me getting plowed."

"Glad I don't have any recognizable marks on my body."

"And you have none on your face. You really should be in front the camera," Sean said as he danced before Kree.

"That has no plan in my future."

"Suit yourself, babe," Sean remarked as he snapped his fingers to the rock song playing on his stereo.

Kree nearly dropped her glass of champagne when Sean moonwalked backwards in his heels and turned around and placed his hands on his knees and began sinking to the floor while gyrating his hips back and forth. "Is this a part of your swag," she laughed uncontrollably, leaning over to her side.

"You don't think this is sexy?" Sean asked as he continued dancing.

"Not at all," Kree replied through laughter. "You were undeniably born a man. Here, let me give you some pointers," she said as she stood up and removed the strap on dildo. "I love to dance."

The two danced side by side for nearly an hour, Sean doing his best to imitate Kree's sensual moves to no avail. This was the most fun Kree had ever had in her young life. She was learning something from Sean also. The guy was a free-spirit. He did whatever he wanted to do whenever he wanted to do it in front of whomever he pleased and thought nothing of it. It would become a lesson in one's self that Kree would carry with her the rest of her life.

"This is one my favorites by this band," Sean said as he trotted across the floor and grabbed Kree's hands. "You know this song, honey?"

"Rolling Stones... you can't always get want you want." Kree responded as Sean led her to the center of his bedroom.

"And you're a connoisseur of music!" Sean exclaimed. "**No you can't always get what you want...you can't always get what you want...you can't always get what you want...**" *Sean sang as he intertwined his hands with Kree's and began rocking side to side.*

"***But if you try sometimes...you'll find...you get what you need...***" *Kree sang softly as the song's guitar opening came into play.*

The two stood face to face and danced in each other's arms slowly to the song's opening guitar. This man was so much for Kree. She and Alonzo had never done anything of the sort and she was enjoying every minute of her time spent with Sean. His antics were a delight.

"Let's shower and get down to business, Kree," Sean said once the song had ended as he pulled her towards the bathroom.

"You mean together?" Kree asked in wonderment.

"Why not?" Sean asked as he let go of Kree's hand and eyed her.

Kree grabbed Sean's hand and looked him in the eyes. "I'm just, you don't know how much you are turning me on right now. This is something I have always wanted to do."

"I know what excites you better than you know yourself,

Kree." Sean smiled as he led her towards the bathroom. "You'll know much more about yourself before the night is over, too, believe me."

What Kree experienced on that late spring night in May of 2006 was nothing short of exquisite. It was the first time she'd done anything of the sort, but with Sean, she couldn't deny how good it felt doing it for the first time. She was slapping his cheeks with the riding crop and calling him all sorts of dirty names, which was his desire. When she got behind him and penetrated him, she continued talking dirty while stroking his rock hard shaft. Five minutes later, Sean ejaculated all over her hand. The stimulation deriving from her grinding into Sean had excited Kree and she, too, had climaxed.

She backed away and eased into the bathroom and wiped herself clean with a damp towel and reentered the room where she picked the strap on up off the floor and moved around to the edge of the bed. Sean reached out and tapped her hand at that moment, signaling for her to drop the device.

Kree complied and Sean pulled her onto the bed where he lay her flat on her back and spread her legs and lowered his head. Kree's eyes rolled to the back of her skull when the sensation hit her. Sean was licking her with tender loving care. It was another first and the feeling was indescribable. The warmth of Sean's tongue, his strong sucking and gentle licking of her most private parts was sending waves of pleasure throughout her body. She was feeling as if she had missed out on so much with a man having dealt with Alonzo because he had never serviced her in such a sensual manner. She laid her hands back in the pillows and pushed her hips upwards, grinding into Sean's face. "You like that, Sean," she asked softly with her eyes closed before she licked her lips. "That feels so darn good," she moaned.

Kree raised her legs and grab the back of her knees, exposing herself fully. She didn't think Sean would do it, but when she felt his tongue on her sphincter, she screamed out in delight. Another first had been conquered. Sean wasn't a man Kree could ever see herself being in an exclusive relationship with, but he was definitely a man she would be willing to see *from time to time as he was teaching her a lot about herself and paying her for her services at the same time. It was a perfect and even exchange in her mind.*

Kree's life was now going along smoothly in March of 2007. She'd learned a lot about herself and men in general the two and a half years she'd been involved with them intimately. Curtis Morrow, the guy who lay atop her on this steamy spring night, was what she'd been looking for ever since she and Alonzo had parted ways nearly a year ago. This man had everything she was looking for in a man; he was masculine, sensitive, compassionate, and ambitious, but just like the previous two men she'd encountered, thirty-four year-old Curtis Morrow came with some baggage, serious baggage.

Curtis was a married man with two kids and a wife who adored him. Kree knew all about his home life from their first ever meeting, but this particular man was a hard man for her to stay away from because she saw what could be. She lay underneath Curtis with her arms thrown back over her shoulders into the silk-laden pillows and arched her back. "Yes, Curtis," she moaned before she thrust her head forward and drove her tongue down his throat.

Curtis was the first guy that had ever French kissed Kree. That carried a lot of weight with her because it made her feel vulnerable and wanted. She loved the sensations her body gave off whenever Curtis held her close, another first she'd experienced. Neither Sean nor Alonzo had ever cuddled with her; but Curtis made it happen. He treated her in ways she'd only been dreaming about for so long. And it was for those many facets of their relationship that Kree found it hard to stay away from this man whom she knew had a wife and kids.

Kree wrapped her legs around six-foot tall Curtis' back and placed her arms under his shoulder blades and extended her legs, pulling him in closer and allowing him to sink further into her entrance as Champagne's song *How 'Bout Us* continued playing low on the stereo.

Curtis' back was hunched, his cocoa skin glistening with sweat as he stroked Kree in a rhythmic, circular motion while grabbing her ass cheeks and kissing her wildly. "Damn, baby," he groaned, as he made slow love, pistoning back and forth in and out of Kree's snug entrance in a slow, sensual and steady motion.

Thirty-four year-old Curtis Morrow had met Kree a few months back inside a small boutique in Saint Charles, Missouri in August of 2006. He was in the boutique picking out perfume for his wife and had sought Kree's help after overhearing her discussing the latest fragrances with the salesclerk.

Kree obliged and introduced herself and started helping Curtis by pointing out various perfumes. He was genuinely grateful for the assistance, but he was also checking Kree out the whole while and she knew it. She soon suggested a fragrance created by Oscar de la Renta that she knew most women would adore. Curtis thanked her kindly as the two stood at a counter in the rear of the boutique.

"You know? And I hope I'm not offending you by saying this, Kree," Curtis said on the day of he and Kree's chance meeting back in August of 2006, "you are a very beautiful young woman. If I weren't married with kids, I would definitely ask you out."

Kree smiled as she scanned items on the counter inside the rustic boutique situated inside the historical district of downtown Saint Charles, Missouri. She'd seen Curtis eyeing her subtly and had to admit the man was handsome, but he was married. Kree, however, had taken his statement as one of allowing her to choose. She picked up a small crystal jar of scented powder and removed the cap.

"What if I said I would go out with you knowing you have a wife and children at home? Would you still date me?" Kree asked, never making eye contact with Curtis.

"Are you interested in going out with me knowing I have a wife and children at home?" Curtis asked as he stared down at Kree curiously.

"Maybe. But it all depends on what you want to do with me," Kree hummed before sniffing the perfumed powder.

Curtis was intrigued all of a sudden. The young woman

before him was gorgeous, young and willing. The two were inside a single story Victorian-style home that had been renovated and transformed into an expensive boutique in the heart of town in the mid-morning hour on a weekday. Curtis Morrow, although known by many in Saint Charles' business community, now saw an opportunity. No one would know of this meeting. And he was only planning on taking this young woman to lunch to show his appreciation was what he'd told himself.

The two left the boutique and walked a short ways to a Greek Deli where they sat and had goat gyros and chatted. Kree was new to the area. She really just wanted someone to talk to, namely a man. She hadn't seen Alonzo in nearly five months and hadn't seen Sean since the month before, after he'd taken her to get her breast implants. She viewed Curtis as a friend in the beginning. The two would meet at least once a week for lunch at the same Greek Deli. The more the two talked over lunch and got to know one another, however, Kree realized that Curtis was really interested in her despite his being married. She was genuinely flattered. Neither of the two men she'd been with before had ever treated her in the manner in which Curtis treated her. She was willing to be with him despite him being married, but she had to tell Curtis all about herself first.

Once Kree told Curtis about her previous two lovers and how she shared her intimacy, she was expecting him to become angry and leave. To her surprise, however, Curtis told her that he was intrigued and wanted to see more of her, but in a more private setting. The two soon started meeting back over in Saint Louis on Fridays for drinks after work inside the lounge inside of Embassy Suites.

They were enjoying a bottle of Dom Perignon and listening to a live jazz band in the dimly-lit lounge inside of Embassy Suites in late October of 2006, two months into knowing one another, when Curtis asked, "What you say we get us a room here for a couple of hours?"

"Are you sure, Curtis? I don't want you to have any regrets." Kree said over the band's soft music as she stared

him in the eyes.

"I had an opportunity to do this once down in Miami, but I couldn't go through with it. This time, I won't let the moment pass me by."

"What's different this time?"

"You're very beautiful. And a young woman like you deserves to be made love to. That's what you been missing, right?"

"I have, been missing that, Curtis. It's been a while since I've been with a man that makes me feel like a real woman," Kree smiled while gazing into Curtis' eyes.

Curtis lowered his eyes and smiled sexily at Kree before leaning forward. "Be right back," he whispered into her ear as he inhaled her Oscar de la Renta perfume, the same brand she'd picked out for his wife two months earlier.

Curtis slid from the booth and had Kree wait. He returned several minutes later with a key card to a top floor suite inside the hotel. The two entered the luxurious suite and Kree went and showered while Curtis sat in the living room sipping champagne. He'd called his wife and told her he would be late getting in because his meeting with his new clients was lasting longer than anticipated. He hung up the phone and stared at it afterwards with the full understanding that he was now about to engage in an extra-marital affair for the first time ever; he sat quietly sipping champagne while imagining the things to come.

Kree soon returned with a towel wrapped around her waist with her small, perky, newly-purchased breasts on full display. She stood before Curtis and danced sexily to Xscape's song Do You Want To with her back facing him. Curtis was in awe of Kree's body and the way she moved. He was stricken with lust over the beautiful smile on her yellow-skinned, brown-eyed face, a face enhanced by pearl white teeth that made her real easy on the eyes. Her curly, black hair was shiny and silky and cascading down just above her shoulders, adding to her natural beauty.

Curtis sat rubbing his stiffening rod as he continued enjoying the erotic performance. Just before Xscape's song ended, Kree turned around and faced him and slowly began pulling the towel away from her body. She then walked over to Curtis in the nude and stood before him. "You like what you see," she asked sexily as she turned around and leaned forward slightly.

"Does it feel as good as it looks," Curtis asked as he grabbed Kree's cheeks and rubbed them gently.

"Taste as good as it looks, too, my love. You wanna taste it?" Kree asked, rocking her hips from side while during an alluring dance routine she'd learned to perfect the few times she'd been with Sean.

Bolts of pleasure shot through Kree when she felt Curtis' hands wrap around her waist. He pulled her back to him and placed a hand on her back, nudging her gently. She leaned forward and moaned the moment Curtis' tongue touched her center. The man had exquisite tongue skills. She'd never felt nothing like that ever. Sean wasn't this good ever, and Alonzo had never even considered. Curtis had taken her to a place she'd never been before with a warm, stiff tongue that slid back and forth over her opening as gentle as a slow and cascading heated waterfall that was pouring down her crevice. She began moaning and was really getting into it; sliding back and forth across his face as she reached back and held herself open.

"You're gonna make me cum all over your face," Kree sighed as she eased forward, turned around grabbed Curtis' hand, pulling him up from the suede couch. "Let's go to bed. I want to take my time with you, baby," she said softly.

What Kree and Curtis experienced that night had driven the both of them over the edge. Kree had fallen for him completely, and Curtis had accepted the fling he was getting himself into to the moment he and Kree slid into the sixty-nine position inside the bedroom of the suite where they now regularly meet. He'd gotten Kree off quickly with his tongue their first night of being intimate and next sat her down on his thick tool and could only call out to a higher source as Kree slowly slid down to the base of his shaft and engulfed him fully. Up and down she went, hands planted on his muscular chest, and slightly bent forward to allow him maximum penetration.

Kree could feel Curtis breathing on her neck as she rode him slowly, and she knew he wanted to kiss her; but she also understood that particular act would be too personal. It was the very thing she wanted, however, that first lovemaking kiss; because in her mind, Curtis was doing nothing less than making love to her, sweet love at that. Her willing to be with him despite him being married would be all worth it in her eyes if Curtis was to kiss and profess his love for her. Maybe she could have this particular man all to herself one day was her thinking.

Kree ran her delicate hands through Curtis's short, wavy hair and rubbed her face to his as sweat began to form in between their bodies, slickening their skin, and intensifying the pleasure. Her lips slowly began kissing their way up and around Curtis' neck to the front of his face, but he'd turned away. Kree started over again, kissing his neck and earlobes as she continued working up and down on his tool, flexing her muscles and milking him slowly at first. "Feel good," she moaned into Curtis' ear as she rocked back and forth.

"Incredible," Curtis groaned as he reached out massaged Kree's breasts.

"Fuck me," Kree cried as she moved up and down on Curtis' rigid rod.

Curtis grabbed Kree's waist and started rocking her back and forth as she sat atop him. He was thrusting upwards into her now, his back arched and eyes closed. Kree knew she was having a major effect on Curtis; she knew she was taking him all the way there. The two had a perfect rhythm going, rotating and thrusting hips in a perfect, circular motion. When the pleasure became too intense for Curtis, he rose up on one arm, grabbed her waist with his freehand and began thrusting upwards as his head tilted back. "Ohh, sweet baby. What're you doing to me," he moaned though closed eyes as he palmed Kree's ass cheek.

Kree wasted no time. She immediately leaned forward and kissed Curtis on the lips, seizing the moment. This time, Curtis didn't resist, instead, he moaned like a mad man, releasing all his pinned up passion as he pulled Kree down to his chest and drove his tongue down her throat with force while moaning aloud in to her mouth, completely out of control and stroking for all he was worth and no longer caring that he'd crossed the threshold into the forbidden. "I love you," he growled just before he thrust deep inside Kree and released into the condom while tugging on her hair.

Kree had erupted herself; she was gripping Curtis' head tightly as she sat astride him as his rigid rod convulsed deep inside her pleasure passage. She lay her head beside his, rubbing her face alongside his while smiling inwardly at that moment. She continued flexing her muscles to milk Curtis dry, believing in her heart that she'd just earned herself a man, a real man in her eyes.

"I love you too, Curtis," Kree stated lowly as her eyes watered. "I really do love you," she ended as the two held one another.

After ten or so years of laboring to get their lives on the road to success, his wife's editorial career in full swing, and his home construction business practically a household name throughout the Saint Louis vicinity, Curtis Morrow found himself bored in his marriage. He wanted a younger love as well in order to reinvigorate himself and make up for the time he'd lost during his twenties—time spent away at Missouri State University studying architecture and starting a family early on in his life.

Curtis had numerous opportunities to indulge in extra-marital affairs during his rise to prominence and prosperity, but he was able to remain focused throughout his progression. With financial success came more freedom, however, and the opportunities to step outside the binds of holy matrimony increased and Curtis' resolve therein began to falter.

A business party down in Miami where he'd secured a contract to renovate the mayor of Saint Charles' second home had brought Curtis into contact with some interesting people to say the least. Women of all shapes, sizes, and colors were everywhere down in South Beach. Curtis had never been exposed to such beautiful women in all his years; he was a country boy from Thayer, Missouri, a small town on the Arkansas-Missouri border and hadn't seen much as far as city life was concerned. Miami was only the second city he'd been to besides Saint Louis and a small city in the state of Vermont, but he'd soon discovered that there was a lot that he loved about traveling, namely the freedom to explore his mounting and inquisitive appetite when it came to sex.

Curtis had attended a formal after sunset dinner hosted by the mayor of Saint Charles in one of the Ritz Carlton hotel ballrooms after securing the contract and he was hit on by several women. He was tempted on a couple of occasions to engage the women in something more than just conversation, but upon realizing he was on the verge of stepping outside of his marriage, he left the dinner early and opted for a sit in the sauna, his way of avoiding the temptation that was all around him.

After changing into a pair of swim shorts, Curtis left his hotel room and headed to the workout station on the top floor of the hotel with a towel draped across his broad shoulders. Upon entering the sauna, he noticed a short, tan-skinned young woman with brown, curly hair sitting on one of the top benches with a towel draped over her body. She opened her eyes and smiled at Curtis and gave him a friendly wave.

"Good evening," Curtis said on that warm January evening in 2006.

"Happy New Year's," the petite young woman responded in kind as she watched Curtis walk through the orange-hued steamy room headed towards the bench.

"Same to you, miss," Curtis said lowly.

"You were at that dinner in the ballroom weren't you?"

"I was. Were you in attendance?" Curtis asked as he sat on a lower bench across from the young woman.

"I worked the room for a minute, but I decided to take off on

my own because there wasn't much action."

"Okay. You were helping to cater the event I take it?"

"You can call it that if you want," the young woman grinned as she stared down towards Curtis, her slender, brown eyes gazing his muscular biceps and the imprint on his swim trunks. She licked her lips and tilted her head to the side and said, "I am a caterer by nature."

"How long have you been in the business?"

"Not long. Two years maybe. Are you interested in my services?"

Curtis laughed lowly. "What kind of services do you offer, young lady," he asked as he scanned the young woman's body.

"For three hundred dollars I'm all yours for the night," the young woman replied as she pulled the top portion of the towel down to reveal her breasts.

Curtis thought this young woman was one of the most beautiful women he'd encountered since he'd been down in Miami. Her curvaceous physique was obvious despite the towel covering most of her lower body. Her eyes were alluring and her smile was captivating. Her breasts were, in a word, perfect, just a tad smaller than cantaloupes with tan nipples that sat upright.

"You like what you see?" the young woman asked as she began tweaking her erect nipples.

Curtis watched as the young woman pulled one of her nipples into her mouth and began sucking, making low smacking sounds as her hand slid down underneath the lower end of her towel.

"I'm enjoying the show," Curtis smiled. *"Are you going to charge me for watching,"* he asked, laughing lowly as he rubbed his chin and licked his lips.

"Not for this," the young woman responded, *"but I do charge for everything else,"* she said as she slowly removed the towel, putting her nude body on full display. *"Are you interested?"* she asked while staring Curtis directly in the

eyes.

Curtis wasn't expecting this from the young woman. He eyed her body, but was turned off all of a sudden. "You are a very beautiful person, but this isn't my preference. I'm a married man here on business," he stated as he stood up from the bench.

"Oh, you're involved," the young woman replied with a smirk. "Don't worry, no one will ever know. I'm totally discreet. We can go back to your room if you want," she said softly.

"I'm moved by the offer," Curtis replied as he stared at the young woman's body. He was in admiration of her appearance; but he couldn't find it within himself to go through with the act. "I'm, I'm not interested," he spoke up, never removing his gaze from the young woman's body.

"Your mind says one thing, but your body is sending an entirely different message," the young woman chuckled as she pointed towards Curtis' tented swim trunks. "A man as fine as you are? I'll do you for free. You wanna have some fun on your trip before you go home to your wife? You wanna fuck me?" she asked as she lay flat on her back and began rubbing herself.

What lay before Curtis' eyes was very tempting. He'd been lured into the point of near seduction. "As much as I would like to, I'm not going to go through with this," he said as he backed away from the young woman.

"You were caught off guard by me and my actions. I understand," the young woman replied softly.

"I'm sorry," Curtis remarked as he gathered his towel and started for the door.

"You don't have to apologize," the young woman replied as she scooted up to rest her back against the wooden wall. "But just to let you know, you wouldn't be the first married man that I've been with. Some have taken me up on the offer."

"I don't doubt it based upon first appearances," Curtis stated before he turned and exited the sauna.

The day he boarded his flight back to Saint Louis, Curtis was left wondering what could've been, if only for one night. He felt as if he'd let an opportunity slip through his hands. Kree reminded him of the person he'd met inside the sauna down in Miami. From her looks to her demeanor, save for Kree having lighter skin and jet black hair, they were the same person in Curtis' mind. He never intended for things to end up so deep between he and Kree, however; but the two actually started having feelings for one another their first night of being intimate.

Now, eight months later, Curtis and Kree both were caught up in a lurid web of unintentional desire that had spun out into a full blown love affair that neither wanted to end.

"You like it?" Kree asked through closed eyes in a sexy voice as she rubbed her cheek against Curtis' face.

"I love it," Curtis moaned as he lay flat atop Kree, his phallus planted deep inside her opening, stroking her deeply.

"Make love to me," Kree cried as she clinched her muscles and met Curtis' deep, powerful thrusts. "Oh my, god. I love when you do this to me," she whispered as she moved her arms forward and began running her hands all over Curtis' muscles.

Saint Louis' skyline and the Mississippi River Bridge could be seen off in the distance from the lovers' top floor penthouse suite and the two silhouettes operating in perfect harmony on this cool spring night were in a world of their own and the loving was superb.

"You like this dick, baby," Curtis asked, his nostrils nuzzling Kree's neck, inhaling her lavender perfumed oil.

"Oooh, I love it, Mister Morrow," Kree moaned.

"Oh shit, baby. Let me get off into this pussy," Curtis moaned as he placed his arms behind Kree's knees and pushed her legs forward.

"No, Curtis," Kree cried out in protest, but it was what she loved the most. She thrust upwards and engulfed Curtis completely and moaned as if she was possessed as he slid deep inside.

Curtis had ignored Kree's mocked protest and impaled her completely and let his brick-hard rod rest deep inside her as he flexed the muscles in his member, all-the-while grinding her slowly.

Kree gasped aloud and her eyes rolled to the back of her head. The feel of her lover's sack resting against her ass while being filled completely was like a drug that had no cure, a cure she had no desire to discover as she'd had a drug that was definitely worth keeping in her mind and heart.

Curtis was grunting and clutching Kree tightly as he drove deep into her, kissing her hungrily as he worked up a continuous sweat while doing his best to please this young woman who had an alluring effect on his psyche.

"Vas a hacerme venir esta!" (You're going to make me come like this!) Kree exclaimed as she began gripping the sheets, her eyes now open and focused in on her lover amidst the darkness.

"Talk that Spanish, baby! Come for me, girl!" Curtis groaned as he began stroking Kree in a rapid, circular motion, driving ever deeper into her insides.

"¡Dios mío! Se siente tan bien para mí, Curtis! ¡ ya voy!" (Oh my God! It feels so good to me, Curtis! I'm coming!) Kree moaned huskily as she spread her legs wider and rotated her hips on Curtis' thick tool, the two joined at the hip as smoothly as a key inside of a lock.

Curtis picked up the pace. Hearing Kree moan aloud in Spanish was the ultimate turn on. His rotations began to accelerate and his need grew more urgent. "Mutherfucka," he growled as he gripped Kree tighter. "Kree, you gone make come!"

"¡Dámelo!" (Give it to me!) Kree pleaded as she wrapped her arms around Curtis' back and picked herself up from the mattress and kissed him deeply. "Give it to me!" she cried.

"You want it, baby?" Curtis asked as he began pounding Kree at that moment, stroking her fiercely in a rapid back and forth motion. "You want it?"

"*¡ Sí! Quiero que todos ustedes!*" (Yes! I want all of you!) "Jesus," Kree moaned as she spread her legs wider. "Come for me! Come for me, baby!"

"I'm coming, I'm coming!" Curtis yelled as his body began convulsing with his shaft planted fully inside of Kree. "Baby! Baby, yes!"

It was the manner in which Curtis screamed aloud for her, as if he was in awe of the sensations she was bestowing upon him while convulsing as he ejaculated into the condom that had sent bursts of joy throughout Kree's body as she came without being touched. The twenty-three year-old got off on pleasing this man eleven years her senior and having him unable to resist her loving.

"You liked it," Kree asked as she stared up into Curtis' eyes with a smile on her face, both their bodies being silhouetted by the full moon.

Curtis stood on his knees before Kree and removed the condom and reached over to the nightstand and grabbed a towel that was soaking in a heated bowl of water. He rung the towel and wiped himself with the warm, damp cloth and lay beside Kree where he pulled her into his arms and began rubbing her clean with the towel while kissing her tenderly. "You ask me that every time we're together and I tell you what, Kree?" he asked through a smile inside the darkened room.

"That you loved it," Kree said while pulling the silk sheets half way up over the two.

"Well, there's your answer. It's always good. You can't tell?" Curtis laughed.

"I just wanna make sure you're happy with me, that's all."

"And I am. Always," Curtis responded lovingly as he kissed Kree's hand and eased out of the bed. "I'm hungry. You want anything while I'm in the kitchen?"

"Yes, please. You can warm up my Alfredo. I'll change these sheets and find us a movie to watch while you're doing that." Kree responded as she turned on the lamp on her side of the bed and placed her feet on the floor.

"Be back shortly," Curtis said as he left the bedroom suite. The two lovers went on to eat while watching a movie and conversing about everything from sports to politics before falling asleep in one another's arms for a couple of hours. Curtis arose around one in the morning, showered and returned home to his family while Kree slept soundly inside the penthouse.

CHAPTER TWO
HOMEGIRLS

Kree's eyes snapped opened upon hearing the alarm clock on her phone go off; her phone was also ringing as it vibrated across the night stand. She sat up and grabbed her phone and shut off the alarm and answered the call, knowing who was on the other end.

"Jessie, what I told you about messing with the alarm on my phone," Kree complained as she stretched.

"I *knew* your ass was gone oversleep, Kree! I *knew* you was gone be late so I set your alarm before you left the shop last night. Ole boy supposed to meet you at Bangin' Heads so you can braid his hair, remember?" Jessie replied in an enthusiastic tone.

"I know what you really want. That boy ain't gone fall for that, Jessie. I'll braid his hair—but I'm not playin' with that man like that. You know that ain't my style. What time is it?" Kree asked as she looked at the time on her phone. "Damn," she sighed.

"That's right. It's seven 'o' clock in the a-m. We got an hour to get up to the job," Jessie said over the phone, knowing Kree had checked the time. "But back to the subject at hand."

"No," Kree snapped as she threw the covers off her legs.

"Kree? Any nigga that want you to braid his hair, the nigga

down for that shit."

"Thanks for making me feel like I know what I'm doing when I'm working. Everybody is not like that, Jessie. That man might just want his hair braided by somebody who actually knows what they're doing."

"I ain't buying that shit," Jessie countered. "Eh, but that nigga look familiar, though. Either way, we need to get to work."

"Right. Work," Kree said as she hopped out of the bed. "Work and no games."

"Whatever," Jessie replied as the two went silent.

For the last week, twenty-two year-old Jessica Suede, whom everybody called Jessie, had been trying to get Kree to approach a young man who was an up and coming music producer over on Saint Louis' south east side in a section of town called Soulard. Ever since the day he'd walked into *Bangin' Heads Beauty Salon* on South 14th Street a week ago looking for someone to braid his hair, Jessie had been plotting on the man because the two times he'd visited the salon, she'd witnessed him riding up in two different cars—a black, four door 2006 5 series BMW, and a red four dour 1996 Impala on twenty-six inch chrome rims. The jewelry that was draped around his neck and hanging down to his diamond-crusted belt buckle alerted Jessie to his baller status and now she wanted to set the guy up to blackmail him, which was one of her methods of making money outside of cutting hair and playing in basketball tournaments.

Kree was visiting her gynecologist for a bi-annual checkup and shots and had a dental appointment the following day, so she was out the two days the guy had come through the shop. Jessie was the one who'd told the guy that Kree was the best at braiding and gave him the price. Kree, when she got the info on the client, understood that the young man was only looking for a hair technician and nothing more. To her, the guy was just another customer. She wasn't about to entertain Jessie and her foolishness.

Kree was still doing pornography with Sean, but that was her secret. What she did on camera was all business, she rarely if ever got any joy out of the acts. It was her way of preparing for her future, not a way to blackmail people. Sean was now paying her $3,500 dollars each time the two were together as she was in high demand. Kree's face had never been featured to date, and when she'd started filming, Sean had around six hundred subscribers. When she debuted on his website in June of 2006, however, membership increased two fold the following month. Now there were nearly two thousand men on the website who wanted to see her in action. She would sit and watch the video when done to make sure only her body was on display before signing off on the video. Kree may have loved Curtis, but she had goals to accomplish that her married lover couldn't fulfill at the time, but everything she did, it was with the sole intent of being with Curtis and Curtis only.

"Eh, Kree," Jessie spoke aloud, shaking Kree from her thoughts, "you might be right about him just wantin' his hair braided, but that nigga got some cake and I want it. The least you could do is find out where that boy stay and let Sweet Pea and Loopy break in his crib."

"Jessie, are you bonkers? What are you on?" Kree asked as she headed for the bathroom.

"Shiit, I'm on the last of this good ass herb right now," Jessie laughed as she coughed off the weed she was smoking. "I'm just fuckin' with you, girl. Come scoop me up before you bounce over to Banging Heads. We gone be late so you already know it's gone be some shit with Kantrell this morning."

"What are you sayin'," Kree sighed. "I know that she is going to trip, but I'm not even trying to rush this morning, okay? I'm going soak in the Jacuzzi and I'll see you in a couple of hours at the latest." Kree said as she turned the water-jets on inside the Jacuzzi.

After a lingering forty-five minute spa bath, Kree dried herself and coated her skin with watermelon lotion. She went and stood naked in front of a full-length mirror, staring proudly at herself while reminiscing about the night before; Curtis had handled her body aggressively and she loved everything about it. It made her feel proud to have a man 'adore her', 'worship her', Curtis' own words spoken the previous night as he held her tightly in his strong arms as the two drifted off to sleep. Kree was really feeling herself this morning. She was on a natural high as she stood smiling at her 5' 4" one hundred thirty pound frame imaging back at her in the full-length mirror.

Kree's family was all from the city of Sao Paulo in Brazil. A Portuguese father and Brazilian mother had created a yellow-skinned child with baby doe-like brown eyes, jet-black hair and pearl white teeth. Her mother, aunts, uncles and cousins were all involved in the coffee industry and were very prominent in her Brazilian homeland.

Kree, however, had broken the rules of the game as far as her family was concerned when she revealed her plans for her life and future; and for her perceived deviance, she was shunned by all of her conservative kin. Only her mother stood by her, but even that solace and support was from a distance and insulting to Kree at the very best.

Kree's mother had taken her to be evaluated by a psychologist at the age of eighteen. After a year of unsuccessfully trying to convince her child not to go through with the plans, Kree's mother sent her to the United States, far away from the family at the young age of nineteen. She'd given Kree $20,000 dollars to basically fend for herself and told her to never contact the family again lest she change her deviant ways.

Kree quickly obtained a degree in Cosmetology from a local beauty college and bounced around from salon to salon until she and her best friend Jessie landed at their current place of employment in the latter part of 2005. Now four years removed from Sao Paulo and completely out of touch with her family, twenty-three year-old Kree Devereaux had her own house, a new car and two well-paying jobs. She was doing okay for herself and her family was a mere afterthought given the way she'd been treated during her teen years. She was glad to be away from them so she could just be herself.

Naughty thoughts of the night before forced Kree to blush as she donned her skimpy bikini underwear. She then pranced over to the bed and slid into a pair of olive green Capri pants and a tight-fitting cream-colored silk blouse. She placed her cream three inch heels onto her pedicured feet and donned a short-sleeved olive green short jacket and headed out the door with a medium-sized cream-colored handbag tucked under her arm.

Kree stepped off the elevator and strolled through the lobby of Embassy Suites with confidence. Public stares were a thing of the past for her, unless it was in admiration; but her now-normal day-to-day life hadn't always trouble-free. Throughout her growth, Kree had been haggled, laughed at, and mocked by strangers here in America and back home when she was younger. She'd embarrassed herself with false assets, stuffing her bras with tissue and buying pants with pads in the rear to enhance her appearance. It wasn't too long after becoming involved with Alonzo Milton, later Sean Bradsworth, and now Curtis Morrow, that things began to be put into perspective for Kree. She'd learned many things from these men, namely to just be herself and not act stereotypical. She knew she had natural beauty—all she had to do was conduct herself in a lady-like manner and everything else would fall into place. With lessons learned, Kree had ridden her beliefs to a life of glamour and contentment. She stood under the hotel's canopy waiting for her car to be brought up from the parking garage while powering up her cell phone.

After tipping the valet a twenty dollar bill for bringing her car around, Kree hopped behind the wheel of her 2006 white on white four door Nissan Maxima with dark tint and chrome 22" wheels and set off to see what the day had in store. She turned on the radio and reached for her phone just as Soul For Real's song *Candy Rain* began playing on the radio as she texted Curtis, thanking him for the night before as she climbed the ramp leading to Interstate-70. *You were wonderful, baby. I love you.*

Kree sat her phone down and began bobbing her head to the music as she sang aloud while cruising down Interstate-70 on this clear blue spring Saturday morning in March of 2007, "*My love...do you...ev-er...dream of...candy coated rain drops... you're the same...my candy rain....*"

Kree sang out loud with uninhibited joy inside her car as she opened her sunroof and continued traveling down Interstate-70/55 and merged onto Interstate-44 headed west while jamming to the music. Just as she was nearing her exit, she received a notification. She picked up her vibrating phone from her lap and opened the screen and read the message. *I can still taste you, lady. Until we meet again.*

Kree was bursting with joy as she exited the highway onto Jefferson Avenue, where she made a left turn and cruised pass a McDonald's and entered a neighborhood called Fox Park. A few blocks down, she made another right turn onto Russell Boulevard and cruised through her old neighborhood, blowing her horn at a few people she recognized that were waving at her car. She made a left turn and headed south on Ohio Street until she approached Armand Place, where she made a left turn and pulled up in front of a grey-bricked townhouse quad-plex that resembled the brownstones in Philadelphia and New York. She blew her horn a few times as she opened her handbag.

Kree wasn't new to Fox Park. She'd lived here once; Fox Park was one of the roughest sections of Saint Louis, an area just south of Interstate-44. There was a drug gang in the area, two drug gangs in fact, that were run by Mexicans. Killings were common and sporadic shootings seemed like a daily occurrence along with the armed robberies. The fight Kree had with Alonzo nearly a year ago had actually proven to be a blessing in disguise. She was able to move away from her often rowdy previous place of residence into her own home after securing a fist time buyer's loan through contacts of Sean. The move had opened up doors in her life she'd only dreamed of once upon a time.

"Senorita," an older man spoke out to Kree as he walked by her car. "I haven't seen you in a while, no? Where've you been?"

Kree recognized the guy. He was a mid-fifties crack head who owned an old Buick her girlfriends sometimes rented.

"Hey, Dibble," Kree smiled as she turned down her radio. "I moved off Saint Louis Street. I don't stay back here anymore."

"Yeah, I heard. After you and that crazy guy you was with got into that fight," the pale-skinned slender Hispanic laughed lightly. "*¿Viste Donatella y Guadalupe?*" (You saw Donatella and Guadalupe?) he then asked as he knelt down and made eye contact with Kree.

"*No en un par de días. ¿Déjame adivinar, tienen su auto nuevo?*" (Not in a couple days. Let me guess, they got your car again?) Kree chuckled.

"*Si,*" Dibble sighed as he shook his head. "*Ahora tengo que coger el autobús para trabajar.*" (Now I have to catch the bus to work.)

"You want me to drop you off?"

"Not really. Could you just let me hold a couple of dollars and I'll catch the bus?"

"You just want to get high don't you?" Kree laughed as she looked down into her opened handbag.

Dibble laughed and said, "Look, I'm needing a little bump right now, Kree? Just something to hold me to Sweet Pea and Loopy get back, no? They gone pay me and I'll pay you back out my money, okay?"

"You going off what Sweet Pea and Loopy say," Kree chuckled as she shook her head in disapproval. She came up with a five dollar bill and stuck her arm out the window and said, "I don't know when I will see you again, Dibble, so keep that. Don't worry about paying me back."

"Thank you," Dibble responded though a surprised smile as he folded the money. "Hey, if you see Sweet Pea and Loopy, tell them to bring my car, or at least drop me off some money or something else maybe if they're going to keep using it, okay?"

"Okay," Kree replied before she blew the horn again.

After another minute or so, Kree's best friend, Jessie, emerged from the four unit duplex wearing a pair of baggy indigo jeans, a white, loose-fitting silk tee shirt and a pair of white Air Force Ones. Her long, black hair was neatly pressed, hanging just below her chin. She locked her door and began walking towards Kree's car, holding on to a small black satchel as she looked around the neighborhood.

Kree and Jessie had been friends for the past three years. The two met in beauty school and formed a tight friendship over a short period of time. They'd even shared an apartment in Fox Park for a few months until Kree got her own place in the area. Kree and Jessie were the total opposites in looks and sexual preferences. Jessie was a connoisseur of women. She loved females and everything about them. She stood five foot eight inches and weighed one hundred and thirty-five pounds. Milk chocolate skin with radiant, dark brown eyes and long, black hair was her makeup. Jessie could jump sexy real quick whenever she wanted as she had a banging body and stunning good looks; she also had a real nice wardrobe to show off her sexy physique, but she really didn't like getting hit on by men so she dressed and acted like a tomboy in public most times.

"Eh, bend the block right quick and hit Saint Louis Street. I need to pick up some kush off your old block before we go in," Jessie said to Kree after climbing into the car and giving her a brief hug.

"Who you going by? Pepper 'nem?" Kree asked as she cruised through the neighborhood.

"Yeah, girl," Jessie said as she leaned the seat back little further and scanned the block. "Pepper and Simone done made it back in town since that shit that went down with Toodie and them people from 'round your way done cooled off."

"I don't see how Toodie gone win that battle. Those people around my way look like they really mean serious business."

"Yeah," Jessie replied as she rubbed her chin, her left leg posted up on Kree's console. "Toodie and her click ain't nothin' nice either, though. I'm just glad I'm not involved in that shit right now."

"Get your feet off of that," Kree snapped as she knocked Jessie's foot off the console.

"My bad, girl, shit," Jessie said through laughter as she looked down at her tennis. "You touch my new 'Forces again we gone fight, homegirl. My bad for real, for real," she joked as she brushed the side of her tennis shoe and leaned back in the passenger seat.

"Don't you hang with Pepper kinda deep, though, Jessie?" Kree asked as she turned onto Saint Louis Street and cruised beneath the oak tree-lined, shady street. "She supposed to be beefing with Toodie, right," she inquired.

"They slick-beefing," Jessie replied as she opened her satchel and pulled out a fresh pair of dark-tinted Gucci sunshades and placed them over her eyes while brushing her hair out of her face. "Whoever get caught slipping first gone get got, but them two bitches is up on they *shit*, Kree," she said in admiration of two opposing clicks. Jessie had respect for both drug gangs, but she was only loyal to one. "At the end of the day I side with Pepper and Simone, though. They down for the 'hood big time, man. Them my fuckin' girls."

"I'd side with Pepper, too. I like her, she's cool."

"Eh, how you know Pepper?" Jessie asked as Kree pulled up the trap house. "Hold up before you answer. Let me run in and get this weed right quick."

"Tell Pepper I said hello," Kree said, rising up through her sunroof.

Jessie waved back at Kree and walked up to the door and tapped a few times. A minute or so later, the door opened and she was let in. She gave Pepper a fist pound as she walked through the threshold. "What the deal," Jessie asked, turning to face Pepper.

"Gettin' that paper," Pepper responded in a sassy tone as she bumped fists with Jessie.

"All day, huh? Yo, my girl Kree said hello."

"Kree," Pepper questioned as she ran her index finger across the side of her chin while locking the door.

"She talkin' about that red muthafucka used to live two houses up," Pepper's friend, Simone Cortez, replied as she reclined back on a light grey, plush velvet sofa.

"Oooh, Kree," Pepper laughed. "She was funny as hell! She still fuckin' with that powder head Alonzo?"

"Nahh, they split like a year ago." Jessie looked to the floor at that moment and had an epiphany. "That's where I know that nigga I was tryna get set up from!" she said aloud as she snapped her fingers.

"Good! I'm glad they split up," Pepper chimed in as she sat down on her sofa and reached over into the cushions and pulled out a large Ziploc bag filled with small packets of envelopes. "And somebody *oughta* set Alonzo ole bitch ass up," she added.

"Yeah. That was foul how he treated, Kree." Jessie said as she handed Pepper a twenty dollar bill.

"I thought Alonzo was gone kill Kree that night I called the police, girl," Pepper laughed as she handed Jessie a twenty dollar sack of weed. "I shoulda stayed out it, though. I ain't know Kree be packing. Shit, she probably coulda aced ole boy that night. Tell my friend I said hola," she told Jessie as she let her out of the apartment.

Jessie left Pepper's apartment and hopped back into Kree's car. "Yo," she said as she began flipping through Kree's CDs, "Pep say what up."

Kree let down her window and blew the horn while waving at Pepper, who was standing in the doorway waving happily as Kree's car eased up the block.

"Now, how you and Pepper met?" Jessie asked as she slid Ludacris' Release Therapy CD into the stereo and selected the song *Runaway Love*. "All this time I never knew how y'all met," she said as she turned the volume up a little and leaned back into the seat.

"Remember when Alonzo messed up my car note and insurance last year?" Kree asked as she nodded her head to the music.

"That was right before y'all broke up."

"Right. Pepper knocked on my door the day after I got those notices telling me that my bills were past due. She was like,

'Alonzo owe me two hundred dollars, and since his ass nowhere to be found, I need to get that from you'."

"Her li'l young ass told you that?" Jessie laughed.

"I know, right? Not to mention Alonzo had placed me in the middle of his mess, girl," Kree sighed as she pulled up to an intersection.

"So what went down?" Jessie asked as she pried the small envelope open with her finger nails.

"Pepper looked like a fifth grader or something, girl."

"I know that's what you thought—but your ass found out something different about Pepper real quick, huh?" Jessie laughed as she sniffed the contents of the envelope, savoring in the potent scent. "This that good herb," she added.

"You ain't lying about Pepper," Kree said as she made a left turn into Jefferson Avenue and headed back towards Interstate-44. "That li'l girl had a look in her eyes like, 'Bitch, I want my fuckin' money right now', had on these little loose jean short shorts and a tank top with a new pair of Nike's with the tag still on 'em trying to be grown. But Jessie," Kree laughed, "she was standing there eating these Skittles like they were going out of style. And then she had a can of Pepsi in her other hand taking sips and staring me down. It was like she was on the playground at elementary school or something collecting recess money—but I didn't laugh." Kree quickly added.

"I bet your scary ass didn't." Jessie chided while smiling at Kree. "What else happen?"

"I told Pepper I didn't get paid until Friday and I had to talk to Alonzo first, too. She stood there licking her fingers while looking off to the side. Talkin' about, 'Umm, hmm. We gone see Friday, miss thang'—and then took another sip of her soda before walking off."

"Ohh, that was when the bank Kantrell deal with fucked our checks up when she was holding our money that one time," Jessie said, snapping her fingers as she recalled Kree's reference to the time frame.

"Right," Kree said as she cruised under Interstate-44 headed north. "I knew I didn't have the money. I ain't had nowhere else to go and wasn't gonna run anyway. Pepper came over at about ten that Friday night."

"Wait," Jessie said laughed as she raised her left hand in protest, "you sat there waiting, knowing you owed Pepper two hundred dollars and didn't have the money?"

"It was an honest mistake, Jessie. I figured Pepper would understand." Kree said in a high-pitched voice.

"What you think the game like Peabody Energy or something? Like you can just ask for an extension and they gone give you that shit," Jessie laughed as she tilted her head back into the headrest.

"Well, technically I did get an extension. I had till Friday and it was a Wednesday when I asked Pepper to come back on Friday."

"So what happened when Pepper came back on Friday?"

"I opened the door and saw Pepper and this heavy-set girl with a low hair cut standing behind her staring me down."

"Okay, that was Simone. What they say?" Jessie asked as Kree made a right turn onto Lafayette Avenue and cruised down the sunny boulevard.

"They didn't say anything. I let them in and they stood in the center of the living room and asked me about the money. I told them about the discrepancy with the bank and said I'll pay them on Monday."

"So after they drawed down their guns on you what you did?" Jessie asked matter-of-factly.

"They didn't draw any weapons, Jessie," Kree said through laughter. "But they did start looking around my apartment. I was like, 'oh no, are they really going to confiscate some of my furniture?'"

"What they do? 'Cause I know they ain't take none of your stuff." Jessie said as she grabbed her cell phone and began texting.

"Pepper was like, 'Kree your shit is laid the fuck out. Where you shop for furniture?' I told her about Sweet Pea and Loopy and how they was hooking me up when I first got my place, so she was like, 'turn me on to 'em'. She told me if I turned her on to Sweet Pea and Loopy the next day, I wouldn't owe her the two hundred dollars."

"That was the day you fixed them steak enchiladas and burritos and shit. Had that Spanish party for Loopy and Sweet Pea," Jessie laughed. "You a slick somebody."

"Girl, I had a piñata filled with Skittles and a whole case of Pepsi in there for Pepper I was so scared of her short ass," Kree laughed. "I knew what she was about the time I opened my door and I didn't want any trouble with her."

Jessie kept shaking her head as she heaved in her seat. "I can't believe you threw a party just to get Loopy and Sweet Pea to come over to your house so they could meet Pepper," she said through laughter as she removed her sunshades and wiped her watery eyes. "Kree, you are something else."

"Maybe so," Kree said as she tapped Jessie's leg. "But that was two hundred dollars I didn't have to pay. So there."

"That's all that matter out that deal. I see you already know what's up," Jessie said as she eyed Kree, realizing she'd taken another route to work.

"Gotta feed the beast," Kree sighed. "Oooh, Jessie," she then quipped. "They had a special chef inside Embassy Suites last night and me and Curtis ordered these crab legs and shrimp Alfredo that would make you slap somebody. We got full, oooh, we had a good time."

"Oooh, Kree," Jessie said with mocked cheer. "I took this lady out to the movies last night and introduced her to the Big Dipper afterwards!"

"Now you're making fun of me," Kree laughed.

"Nah, I got up with a woman last night and we had a good time. She was married herself—but I ain't worried about her because I know she ain't leaving her husband and I don't want her to. I'm really worried about this ole fraudulent, married ass nigga *you* dealing with, though," Jessie sighed as she turned and looked out the passenger window. "Why y'all don't just hook up?"

"It's not that easy, Jessie. He *is* obligated, you know?"

"He should only be obligated to you and his kids. Y'all like man and woman and shit around here. I know he got a wife and all, but, if he really saying all the things you say he be saying to you? He should leave his wife and be with you then, Kree. You don't have to be *nobody's* side piece, homegirl."

Kree said nothing as she cruised down the street. Jessie would always remind her of her current position with Curtis, but it wasn't meant to come across as ridicule or envy. Jessie simply believed that she deserved much more than what she was getting from Curtis, the man she professed to love.

Kree understood her friend's concern, but it was her life to live. "Right now," she said somberly as she pulled over to the curb down the street from *Malik's Grill*. "Right now? I'm content with the way things are, Jessie. Curtis said he needs time, and it's time I can spare. I'm willing to see what becomes over time, but my heart says we'll always be together."

"I hear ya'. But the heart can be a liar," Jessie said as she eyed Kree seriously while opening the door. She placed one foot on the sidewalk and looked straight ahead and said to Kree, "It just seem like because, you know, to me it's like Curtis know you willing to stick around until he get that divorce. I don't think he gone do it, though. He gone just keep stringing you along for as long as possible and end up keeping his wife in the end."

"I don't feel the same way," Kree said seriously as she stared Jessie in the eyes. "Curtis may be married, but when I'm with him? He makes me feel as if I'm the only thing that matters in his life. And as of right now? That's all I ask for." Kree said as she turned the car off and wiped subtle tears from her eyes. "I really am in love with that man."

"Here she go gettin' all sentimental on a bitch and shit," Jessie said as she eased out of the car. "Come on! Let's get these orders so we can head over to Bangin' Heads."

"I can't help it!" Kree laughed as she hopped out of the car and ran up on the sidewalk. She grabbed Jessie's arm and laid her head on her on shoulder. "You're my best friend and you should understand my feelings as a woman," she pouted.

"I understand, I just don't wanna see you make a fool of yourself," Jessie said as she hugged Kree, the two walking side by side towards the grill's entrance.

After picking up their call-in orders from *Malik's Grill*, the pair made their way back across Lafayette Avenue onto South 14th Street where their job was located. Kree and Jessie both knew they were late, but they were hoping a giant omelet stuffed with ham, cheddar cheese and all the veggies would calm their boss's nerves.

****

Thirty-three year-old Kantrell Luckett was owner of *Bangin' Heads Hair Salon*. She'd been styling hair all her life. It was all she had ever wanted to do since she was able to walk. She'd opened her first business in New Orleans' Lower Ninth Ward section back in 1996 shortly after obtaining her Cosmetology license and a Bachelor' degree in Business Administration from Southern University of New Orleans. She'd borrowed $25,000 dollars from her parents to get the business going and it began thriving upon its inception.

Nine years later, Kantrell's salon was destroyed completely by Hurricane Katrina and she was forced to leave the city and her former life behind, which was actually a blessing in disguise for the quirky, fun-loving, yet very business-oriented young woman. Insurance money and FEMA had paved the way for a new business for Kantrell, which she'd established just over two years ago on South 14th Street in a retail space provided by Cochran Community Center.

Bangin' Heads lay in a highly populated neighborhood filled with numerous apartment complexes. Heavy vehicle, and even heavier pedestrian traffic abounded in this area that lay just south of downtown Saint Louis.

Kantrell had a boisterous and prosperous salon back in New Orleans before Katrina struck and she'd merely picked up in

Saint Louis where she'd left off in her home city and had quickly returned to what she was used to doing before the storm, which was shit-talking, minding everybody's business and gossiping while she made her money and ran her business. Lots of characters came through Kantrell's happening spot; no one ever knew what to expect on any given day up to *Bangin' Heads.*

Kree and Jessie entered the salon quietly and Kantrell started up right away. "Well, look who decided to show up for work, everybody," she said aloud over Alicia Keys' song *You Don't Know My Name* while shampooing a client's hair.

Bangin' Heads was laid out like a penthouse. Luxurious, brown, leather C-sofa sectionals throughout and wall-mounted plasma TV's in every corner. Two thousand square feet of tan, ceramic flooring and white plastered walls engulfed ten chairs, eight sinks and eight dryers and an array of accessories were sitting atop a white marble counter that ran the length of the salon's work area.

Kantrell often entered hair shows in Atlanta, Miami and the DC area and took home a trophy every time she did so. She may have been a young and rowdy thirty-three year-old, but she knew her profession inside out. She was a cool boss to work for as well; it was really hard for her to get mad at a person because she had a naturally bubbly spirit and it was hard to burst her happy bubble—but people knew when Kantrell meant business.

Kree smiled and walked over to Kantrell and sat the styrofoam plate with the large omelet inside near her station along with a large bottle orange juice. "Malik said good morning."

"Yeah, he told me that when I woke up beside him this morning and got my ass here on time." Kantrell snapped, never making eye contact with Kree.

Kree shrugged and turned and waved her first customer over to her station and began setting up for the day.

Kantrell pat-dried her customer's head with a large towel and turned and flipped open the container and scanned the contents.

She then closed the lid and went about her business as if she wasn't fazed.

Kree and Jessie thought they were in the clear until Kantrell asked aloud a few minutes later, "You two scallywags think a couple of eggs spit out by a chicken and heated up on a rusty ass stove gone stop me from saying what I gotta say today?"

Kree and Jessie both rolled their eyes and sighed.

"For the last three Saturdays y'all two have been coming in two, three hours late and shit and it done wore thinner than a mangy ass dog tail." Kantrell said as she backed away from her chair and eyed Jessie and Kree.

Kree asked her customer what her preference was for the day and Jessie already had a customer in her chair and had just clicked the clippers on; both were silent, ignoring Kantrell, in fact, because they just knew she was about to slide into one of her rants.

Kantrell picked up on the two's nonchalant attitude and smoothly walked over and unplugged Jessie's hair shredders. She then skipped past several more of her stylist chairs and turned off Kree's vanity lights. "I'm not done tal—king— bitches!" she snapped as she tapped her hand on the marble countertop.

"Quit playin', man," Jessie whined before she went and plugged her clippers back in.

"We came in and went straight to work. Didn't say anything about it," Kree stated calmly as she turned her lights above the mirror back on.

"You couldn't say anything about it, Kree! The clock speaks for itself, baby! The hell you gotta say about strolling in here two hours late?"

"I'm sorry it'll never happen again?" Kree asked as Jessie began sniggling.

"See, now you being facetious," Kantrell said as she nodded her head up and down. "And you," she then said to a sniggling Jessie, "you gone be the one to get fired first. And then I'm gone let that ass sit home for a good week or two and let Kree scary butt witness your sorrow and despair before I fire her shysty ass."

Everybody sitting in the salon knew Kantrell wasn't going to fire Kree and Jessie. They were her top earners and they never missed a rent payment on their chairs. Besides Kantrell herself, Jessie and Kree were the only stylists who'd been with *Bangin' Heads* since its inception in late 2005. The other seven seats were in constant rotation even though they stayed rented out. The problem with a chair being in constant rotation was that Kantrell would lose clientele from time to time, and by the time it was reestablished, the chair would become open again. Kree and Jessie were money in the bank so they got a little freedom, but it came with a price, usually that of being made fun of by Kantrell.

"You been firing us for the last year and a half," Kree said with a smirk planted on her face. "Go on and fire us and watch we sue you for discrimination."

"I wish your mix-match weave-wearing ass would take me to court," Kantrell snapped as she cut her eyes at Kree and sniggled.

"All natural, baby," Kree remarked as she placed her hand on her hips and flipped her hair. "This is all natural. Ask your man. He knows 'cause he was running his hands through it last night, okay sweetie?"

"Your hair may real, but you got your titties outta catalogue, you stank cat heffa." Kantrell snapped as her client chuckled, heaving in the chair. "That was a good one?" she leaned over and asked her customer through laughter. "I got her ass good one time?"

"You got her, girl," Kantrell's customer replied through laughter. Kree took that last jab from Kantrell, laughing herself at the snap as she returned to tending to her customer, the day now in full swing.

CHAPTER THREE
HUSTLIN' AND FLOWIN'

"…You wanna know what we play in the club…ay bay bay… white folks, gangsters and thugs…ay bay bay…stuntin' with a stack for them gurls…ay bay bay…riding in the lac with a mug…ay bay bay…I'm in the club hollarin'…ay bay bay…ay bay bay…" Rapper Hurricane Chris' song *Ay Bay Bay* blared from a black 2007 Durango Citadel sitting high upon 26" inch black aluminum Foose Nitrous rims that was slowly cruising through Cochran Community Center's parking lot headed towards *Bangin' Heads,* its custom black paint job and dark tinted windows gleaming in the afternoon sun.

Everybody in the community center, including administrators who were working this Saturday, knew what time of day it was and they all began reaching for their wallets and purses and making phone calls. *Bangin' Heads* now had over two dozen clients waiting to get serviced and they, too, were checking their financial status as the music blaring from the Durango grew louder and louder until it began vibrating the windows on the front of the salon as it came to halt right in front of its front doors.

Twenty year-old Donatella "Sweet Pea" Cruz and her cousin, twenty-year-old Guadalupe "Loopy" Cruz, were the neighborhood saleswomen. Whatever the people in and around Cochran Community Center needed or wanted in the realm of furniture, electronics, clothes, DVDs and CDs, Sweet Pea and Loopy would bring it into their lives. The two females had thievery down to an art form. They'd known Jessie since high school, having played on the same basketball team over to McKinley High School for two years before Jessie graduated two classes ahead of the two after the three had won back-to-back state championships.

Fox Park was where Sweet Pea and Loopy met Kree back in the summer of 2004 when they'd met up with Jessie to drop off a Mac Computer she'd ordered. Kree had asked Sweet Pea and Loopy if they could get her a big screen TV for her new apartment and a deal was made. Upon delivery, Sweet Pea and Guadalupe, both natives of the Oriental Republic of Uruguay, that had gained legal citizenship fifteen years earlier, took an immediate liking to Kree. The rapport now established between the four friends was genuine and held no strings. Kree, Jessie, Sweet Pea and Loopy were just four individuals who got along well in life.

Twenty year-old Sweet Pea's 5'9" slender, one hundred and thirty-five pound tan-skinned frame eased out the passenger seat. She pulled her blouse down over the top of her tight-fitting Capri pants and opened the back door of the Durango and grabbed a milk crate full of CDs and DVDs in white envelopes off the backseat and turned to waiting customers. Donatella had earned her nick-name because she often wore her auburn hair in a single, tightly-woven ponytail. Her face was an even oval—perfectly round and flawless. Big, round, gorgeous green eyes and a wide mouth that never ceased smiling had earned her the name Sweet Pea, after the cartoon character from the Popeye cartoon.

Twenty year-old Loopy slid out from the behind the steering wheel of the Durango, her five-foot ten, one hundred and forty pound skinny physique carrying a natural swagger as she shifted the platinum Virgin Mary chain that draped her neck into its proper place and shifted her baggy jeans. Loopy was the rougher of the duo. She was a thin-faced young woman with small, sunken, opaque eyes, high cheek bones and jet black hair with a wide mouth that curved downward slightly.

Loopy often sported a Saint Louis Cardinals baseball cap most days, and she could give off an angry demeanor at times; but she was actually fun-loving and laidback at heart. Her sometimes goofy behavior was not be taken for granted, however; the pale-skinned Uruguayan, who could easily pass for being Caucasian, had bodied a man over in East Saint Louis who'd robbed her aunt's taco shop two years ago and had never even been questioned about the homicide; although many people in their neighborhood over in East Saint Louis knew she was responsible.

Customers walked up to the Durango at random as the cousins were setting up and they began looking over what Sweet Pea and Loopy had to sell on this day.

****

Kree had gotten her order of movies and music from Sweet Pea and Loopy earlier in the week. She sat in her rental chair with her legs crossed eating the remnants of a seafood platter Jessie had bought her earlier for lunch as she bobbed her head to the music blaring from Sweet Pea and Loopy's Durango. She couldn't help but to chuckle at the Cruz cousins as they went about their business, dancing to the music booming from their ride while counting money and checking any and everybody that tried to short them on a sale. She'd just motioned for the remote control and was about to change the plasma TV facing her chair inside the nearly empty salon when a young man walked in and asked aloud for someone named Kree.

"That's me. How can I help you?" Kree responded as she sat the remote down and stood up and straightened her attire before turning to face the young man.

When the guy locked eyes with Kree, both their hearts fluttered. A few patrons had reentered *Bangin' Heads* at that moment, so neither Kree nor her potential client had shown any emotion. The guy was still good-looking to Kree. Medium-built with a muscular physique, standing about six-feet tall and he was caramel-skinned, just the way she'd remembered him, only he was a little more muscular and had braids.

"Your coworker told me about you. You braid hair," the guy asked as he eyed Kree.

"That I do. I charge seventy dollars. Did she tell you that?"

"Yeah. I want like a ziz-zag pattern close to the scalp and flowing to the back, ya' feel?"

"I got you. Come on and have a seat and let me get set up."

"Been a while," the guy managed to say lowly as he sat down.

"I know. You look nice." Kree said in a near whisper as she lowered her chair and eased it back slightly.

"You do too."

While Kree was setting up, Loopy walked in holding a thin cardboard box and a basket full of movies. She handed the basket over to a couple of customers and walked over and bumped fists with Kree while speaking to the rest of the hair techs on duty. *"Necesitas algunas películas más. ¿Kree?"* (You need some more movies, Kree?) she asked.

"Soy bueno. Vi Matute vuelta en Parque de Fox. Dijo que traiga su auto o al menos dejar algo de dinero con él" (I'm good. I saw Dibble back over in Fox Park. He said bring his car or at least drop off some money to him.)

"Ese coche caliente ahora," (That car hot right now). Loopy replied calmly as she briefly side-eyed the guy sitting in the chair and shook her head. *"Sé que no estás con él."* (I know you're not back fucking with him.) she leaned in and asked Kree when she got near her station.

"No y sólo estaba transmitiendo un mensaje." (No and just relaying a message.) Kree replied nonchalantly, as she gathered a few items, never making eye contact with Loopy.

"Okay," Loopy said, a little unsure of Kree's reply. "Hey," she then called out to a woman sitting in the lobby area. "I got that for you," she said happily as she skipped over towards the lady while holding the cardboard box out slightly away from her body.

"What you got in that box, Loopy?" Kantrell inquired.

"It's a laptop," Loopy replied as she went into the lobby and handed the box to the lady.

"I don't know if I'll have enough to pay for it," the woman told Loopy as she looked the computer box over. "How much is it again?"

"Three hundred. The same price I told you last week when we talked. How much you got today?" Loopy asked as she eased the box from the lady's hands.

"Just enough for my hair. I didn't think you were comin' today."

"*Esto rompió perra jugando conmigo hoy.*" (This broke bitch playing games with me today.) Loopy said as she turned and held the lap top up over her head. "Who got two hundred and fifty dollars for this laptop?" she asked aloud. "Brand new laptop for sale!"

Another customer got up from her seat and asked to see what Loopy was selling. She took the laptop out of the box and went and plugged it in and Loopy went to telling her about the computer as it powered up. "This here a Dell seventeen inch screen with two point four gigabytes. You can save a lot of data on this one here and it's fast. It has a touch pad so you don't need a mouse. It cost five hundred dollars in the store, but you can get it for half price today. I was selling it for three hundred—*but somebody ain't bring they money!*" Loopy said loud enough so the lady could hear her. "It come with a free download for Windows, too," she stated as she turned back to her potential customer.

"This is exactly what my daughter needs for school," the woman said happily as she went into her Burberry handbag and handed Loopy thirteen twenty dollar bills. "That's two sixty, go ahead and keep the rest. I can't pass this up. Kantrell, I'll be back," she ended as she left the lobby.

"You know half that sale go to the house right, Loopy," Kantrell said as she peeked from around her chair.

"For what?" Loopy asked as she tucked the money into her front pocket.

"You done took one of my customers, girl. Her ass ain't comin' back no time today," Kantrell smirked.

"That's a woman with priorities," Loopy laughed. "She gave me ten dollars extra. I'll get you some dinner from Malik's down the street."

"Y'all hoes is gone stop acting like the only things that make me happy come in a styrofoam box outta Malik's," Kantrell yelled aloud as she came up from behind her chair. "First it's Kree and Jessie this morning with a omelet the size of a dumpster and now you tryna offer me a token dinner."

"You need to appreciate what you have more," Loopy said through a straight face. "They have people around the world wish they had somebody to buy them food every day."

Kantrell stared back at Loopy from across the room with a blank expression on face. "Don't preach that hungry people bullshit to me," she snapped before turning her back on Loopy. "This doesn't have anything to do with starving kids. This is about everybody thinking food is the only thing that makes me happy around here."

"You want the meatloaf again when we go up there, though?" Loopy asked aloud.

"Yes, please. And tell my man Malik if he's in there? Tell 'em I say put a extra slice of meatloaf in there for me. He know that code," Kantrell said as she laughed lowly.

"You're nasty," Loopy chuckled as she threw up a peace sign. "We got clothes, music, books, movies, shoes—ask for what ya' want!" she said aloud as she turned around and reentered the lobby.

"Them two cousins got it sewed up around here, huh?" the young man sitting in Kree's chair asked.

"All the time. I'm gone let these braids down, give you a wash and let it dry a little before I start."

"Do what you do. If I fall asleep like I used to do, don't wake me up."

Kree smiled to herself and quickly reminisced over times

past while noticing the matching tattoos on the guy's hands that looked like a microphone laid across the letters AMP. "I think I know what the first two initials are," she said lowly as she began taking the braids out of the young man's hair. "What's the P for?"

"Productions."

"You finally got your thing off the ground? How're you doing with it?"

"I'm doing okay. I'm 'bouta do something big over in the ATL with this label Dirty Deeds."

"They're pretty popular. They have that singer Narshea with them don't they?"

"Sure do. I'm working on producing tracks for Narshea and a couple other people they got on the roster. Nothing on the radio yet, but this compilation I'm producing for Narshea 'nem gone be hot. I'm gone have some tight album cuts on the radio after while, but I got a mixtape called Midwest Wildin' I just put out and it's doing okay on the streets. I came a long way from that corner where I first met you."

"I'm happy for you."

"Yeah. The music is taking off for me."

"And the cocaine?" Kree asked as she backed away from the chair and eyed the back of the young man's skull with her lips pursed and her hands on her hips.

"Take your hand off your hip and wipe that look off your face, girl," Alonzo laughed lowly.

"You think you know me still, huh?" Kree laughed as she resumed taking down Alonzo's braids.

"Shit, I was with your ass for about, what? Two years?" Alonzo said in a near whisper.

"You were so high most days you don't even remember the times we shared I bet." Kree said lowly.

"It was eighteen months. Eighteen months solid and I could never forget those days. The good ones especially, and I can also proudly say I'm done with that habit. I got too much going to ruin it over snorting powder."

"Well, you deserve it. You really do deserve it. I been meaning to tell you that I'm sorry for what happened over in Fox Park," Kree said in all sincerity. "You treated me okay, but those drugs had you—"

"Say no more," Alonzo interjected. "You was right the whole time. I was trippin' big time and you deserved better. I apologize, too. Let's leave that in the past."

"Thank you for apologizing. That really means a lot to me. Sit back and let me hook you up."

Kree was absorbed in her task of taking down Alonzo's braids when Sweet Pea entered the shop holding a milk crate full of DVDs and CDs.

"I have this movie called Lakeview Terrace and it ain't even out yet, everybody!" Sweet Pea yelled aloud inside the bustling business.

"Bring it here I wants that! Sam Jackson my dude!" Kantrell yelled back while organizing her station.

"Y'all ain't tell me about that movie the last time," Kree said from behind her chair.

"We got it yesterday." Sweet Pea responded as she threw Kree a copy. "On the house!"

Alonzo caught the DVD and said, "Yo, let me see what else y'all got. Y'all got some music?"

"Got all the hot shit, homeboy," Sweet Pea responded as she walked over to the young man and handed him a stack of CDs. "You look familiar," she said before walking off.

Alonzo flipped through the CDs, smiling at first and selecting a few CDs himself, until he came across copies of his own Midwest Wildin' mixtape.

Sweet Pea was walking around the chairs before the work station making sure she didn't miss any sales and wasn't really paying any attention to Alonzo. He looked his CDs over and grabbed all seven copies from the stack he was holding and threw the rest on the floor. "Alonzo Milton Productions and the Midwest Wildin' Click," he said matter-of-factly as he eyed the CD. "This *really is* some hot shit y'all got."

"That cee dee right there is tight. I give you three for ten." Sweet Pea said, turning her attention back to the man. "Hey, why the rest of the music on the floor?" she questioned as she looked at the scattered CDs.

When Alonzo held up the CD cover with his picture on it next to his face, Sweet Pea caught on. "Oh shit! That's your joint! I know your ass from Fox Park!" she said through laughter.

Alonzo wasn't laughing nor smiling, however; he didn't take kindly to the fact that his music was being stolen. He separated the CDs into each of his hands and cracked them on the armrests of Kree's chair, startling Kree in the process. "Bitches ain't gone be stealing my shit!" he snapped as he jumped up from the seat. "How much money y'all makin' off my shit?"

"Enough to pay the bail after I fuck you up today!" Loopy snapped as she emerged from the lobby and ran up beside Sweet Pea, who was picking up the rest of CDs off the floor.

"Whoa! Whoa! Whoa, nah!" Kantrell snapped, freezing everybody in their tracks. "Look like to me you was about to buy some shit, nigga—and now you done flipped the script? At least people hearing your shit!"

"Nahh, fuck that! Don't nobody put my shit out like that!" Alonzo said as he went for the milk crate Loopy had set down on one of the tables situated across from the work station. "I want all my music up outta here!"

Sweet Pea and Loopy thought Alonzo was tripping. The whole thing was funny to them. In their eyes they couldn't understand why Alonzo was getting so irate. He and Loopy got to the milk crate at the same time and began arm wrestling over the plastic tote.

"Come on, nah! This is our shit!" Loopy snapped.

While laughing, Sweet Pea ran over and kicked Alonzo in the back of his knee, buckling him to the floor as she held onto the burnt CDs she had picked up off the floor. Loopy then grabbed the crate with the burnt CDs and movies and she and Sweet Pea ran out the front door.

Alonzo picked himself up off the floor and ran towards the doors, but by the time he emerged from the building, Sweet Pea and Loopy had already hopped into their Durango where Sweet Pea was peeling out.

"Lame culo, Alonzo!" Sweet Pea and Loopy yelled repeatedly as the Durango sped out the parking lot with both cousins inside laughing aloud. *"Lame culo, Alonzo,"* they kept yelling as they disappeared from sight.

CHAPTER FOUR
IT BE THE VIBES

"What I'm suggesting is that we go with the sequoia—the Coastal Redwood variety which is native to the state of Oregon. This wood will last a century or more with proper care. And with the type of weather up in the Ozarks? The Redwood is perfect for the humid conditions because it's durable and can withstand the moisture in the air."

"We'll go along with whatever you suggest, young man. After looking over your portfolio and receiving three outstanding references from our trusted peers? We are certain that the construction of our third home will be in good hands."

"Three homes," Curtis smiled. "I'm still purchasing my first. You people will have to tell me your secret," he said as he sat behind the desk inside his quaint, early twentieth century office located on Main Street in downtown Saint Charles, Missouri. It was just over a week after the events had transpired inside *Bangin' Heads* in the month of March.

Curtis's reputation in the field of home construction was unmatched in the greater Saint Louis area. He'd built million dollar homes for politicians, a couple of top physicians and several professional athletes in and around the area based off his reputation. The middle-aged wealthy couple meeting with him on this day had presented him with architectural designs for a log home and wanted to have the home built in the Ozark Mountains of Arkansas. They were deciding on what type of wood to use and Curtis had won them over with his suggestion of Redwood and the couple was all ready to sign a contract and pay the ten percent down payment on the soon-to-be built two and a half million dollar luxurious getaway.

"Now," Curtis said once the contracts were signed, "what I'm going to do is take a trip out to Oregon in a couple of weeks and hand-pick your lumber from the mill. This home we're building will have the best of everything and I wouldn't hesitate to use the word perfect."

"And the flooring? It's a hard to find variety."

"That's why I can say I'm the best at what I do," Curtis said in a confident tone. "I've sent the specs on the granite tile to my associates up in Vermont and cutting will get underway in a week or so. By the time the wood arrives, everything, the shingles, windows, brick and cement will be ready to go. Lady and gentlemen? Your new third home is on its way."

The couple stood up and shook Curtis's hand and exited the office just as his phone rung. "Morrow Construction how can I help you?"

"Hey, dear." Curtis's wife, Denobria, spoke cheerfully.

"Baby. How's everything? All set for lunch?"

"That's why I called. I'm going to have to reschedule."

"Everything okay?"

"Fine. Just some exclusive stories here at the station. I have to do several additional editorials for our evening broadcasts. It's nearing deadline time and everybody has waited until the last minute to make changes to the upcoming broadcast. That's not even considering the *scheduled* work I have to do. I'm working through lunch."

"Okay. You know you'll have to make it up to me now, right?"

"What'd you have in mind?" Denobria asked as she smiled brightly.

"Something mind-blowing, baby. I'm going to Oregon in a couple of weeks. What say we get your sister to watch our boys and you and I just up and go? No luggage. We'll shop when we get into town."

"Aww, that is so sweet. But I can't, baby. I'm sorry." Denobria cooed.

"This trip is the perfect get-a-way. It's what we've both been needing, Denobria. I mean, I'll have to conduct business, but that'll last only a couple of days at the most. We would still have three days left. Why not take me up on the offer, baby," Curtis asked, somewhat disappointed over his wife's innocent decline.

"I'll make it up to you, alright? I just can't right now, Curtis. I, I haven't the time of day. Look, these phone lines are ringing like crazy, baby, and I have unedited stories all over my desk. Let me call you, we'll, we'll talk over dinner tonight, okay? I'm real busy," Denobria ended abruptly as she hung up the phone.

Thirty-four year-old Denobria Morrow was a somewhat socially conservative 5'5" one hundred and fifty pound, voluptuous, light-skinned woman with short, brown hair. She and Curtis had been lovers since their sophomore year in high school when they'd met while trying out for the track team. It was Curtis' friendly smile and humble attitude to match his handsome features and ambitiousness that had attracted her to him early on. Almost two decades later, Denobria now found herself in a stable relationship with a well-paying job and two wonderful sons aged three and five, who were the spitting image of their father, the only man she had ever loved in her life.

A two-story 3,500 square foot home and three luxury cars were some of the Morrow family's possessions. Private school and tutors for the children, the occasional nanny and maid services, along with a few other amenities, including bi-annual trips abroad, were the family's makeup. The Morrow family enjoyed some of the best life had to offer and was the ideal household before the eyes of many in the community, but things aren't always what they appear to be as those involved in this tangled web of love would soon come to discover.

Curtis looked at the phone a little befuddled. He understood his wife's refusal to join him on his trip to Oregon, but he felt she'd given up an opportunity to spend time together that the two were really in need of sharing. He leaned back in his high-backed leather chair and reflected on his wife's neglecting of his needs. Needs that, coupled with Denobria's unwillingness to step outside of the comfortable confines of their home nowadays, was the reason that had led to his having an affair.

Blaming his wife for his own discretions with Kree, however, was not fair to Denobria, Curtis knew, so he brushed those thoughts aside, refusing to hold his wife in contempt over his own selfish desires and transgressions against their marriage. His mind then drifted off to times spent with Kree and he smiled. He smiled every time he thought of his mistress, which was quite often throughout each and everyday. With pleasurable memories of times past running through his mind, Curtis picked up his cell phone from his desk top and dialed a number he knew from memory.

"Hello?"

"Good afternoon," Curtis said through a smile upon hearing the soft voice on the other end.

"Hey, baby. How're you doing?" Kree asked as she sat in her living room watching Maury while giving herself a French manicure and pedicure before she relaxed for a couple of hours.

Just hearing her voice made Curtis throb; and reflecting on their past rendezvous only made him long for her more now that he'd called. "I'm okay. Just thinking about you," he said lowly.

"I'm surprised you call so early. You're still working aren't you?" Kree asked as her pet dog, Riley, jumped up on the couch and lay beside her.

"Yeah. But, I'm about to have lunch over to the Greek Deli. Relax and read the paper."

"Can I join you," Kree joked, knowing Curtis wouldn't agree to meet her in Saint Charles now that the two of them were having an affair.

"You know you make me feel guilty every time you ask me that, don't you?" Curtis remarked as he leaned forward in his chair and looked towards the floor.

"I don't mean to. I just wish for it so bad, Curtis. When will you take me out?" Kree asked through a wide smile as she leaned back into her sofa. She didn't ask but once before, but the first time she did ask, Curtis had told her that the two of them would go out together one day, he just didn't know when. That was in late January, about six weeks ago and Kree had decided to ask again on this Monday afternoon in March of 2007.

"When the time is right? We'll do something very special together, Kree. You know my situation and what's on the line with me. But I don't make promises that I can't keep, baby. But even without that, aren't we good when we're together right now?"

"I only want to do something special with you, baby. I was kidding about lunch, but I really would like for us to do something together outside of Embassy Suites."

"Just give me time, Kree. We'll do it, okay? I promise." Curtis said with a hint of frustration in his voice. "Are you going to ask me that every time I call?"

Kree rolled her eyes and was immediately turned off with the way the conversation was beginning to go. She was sorry she'd even begun joking with Curtis as it was beginning to morph into a tête-à-tête she cared not to have. "This was only my second time asking," she asserted. "So there! I'm going to hang up now, Curtis, because I feel myself getting upset. It was good talking to you."

"Look," Curtis reasoned as he stood up from his seat and elevated his voice, "If I say we're going do something, we're going to do it. Just let me maneuver things so there won't be any interference!"

"You don't have to raise your voice I can hear you just fine," Kree snapped.

"It's too early in the day for this. And this isn't what I called for," Curtis said, lowering his voice. "I called to see how you were and to tell you I missed you."

"I'm missing you, too. But it doesn't change the fact. I understand your situation, okay? But something, anything—I don't care if we ride to the park and just sit and talk. I just wanna do something with you outside of a hotel room. Bye, Curtis." Kree said somberly before she hung up the phone, her eyes beginning to well up with tears.

Curtis hung up the phone understanding Kree's feelings fully, but he was unable to do anything to remedy the situation right away. He really wanted to be with her openly, but he was a married man with a lot to lose—his kids, his home, his wealth, a possible change in social status in the eyes of his peers, one that could possibly diminish his thriving business in conservative Saint Charles. He wasn't certain just how he was going to break the news, but Curtis was really planning on telling his wife that he wanted a divorce so he could be with Kree openly as he'd fallen deep in love. The only problem for Curtis, which was a major problem, was the fact he couldn't let it get out that he was having an affair, and he had to have grounds for divorce of his own, lest he lose everything he'd ever worked for in life.

Curtis knew Kree would rather be with him every day of her life, and by all means did he want it also; but it was just not possible at the time. This rift was the only mechanism that caused problems in Curtis and Kree's affair at times, but their making up would always lead to some of the best lovemaking ever. A thought soon entered Curtis' mind as he eyed a map of the United States on his wall. He went and poured himself a cup of coffee and sat back down behind his desk and began searching for airline tickets on his computer.

****

Irritated over the conversation she'd had with Curtis, Kree jumped up a few minutes after she'd ended the call and went into her kitchen. She was in the process of gathering items to make a strawberry margarita when her cell phone rung, leading her to believe that it was Curtis calling her back. She thought about ignoring the ringing phone because she was mad at him at the moment; but then she remembered Jessie had called early in the day and had invited her out to dinner with her, Sweet Pea and Loopy later on so she went and checked just to make sure it wasn't Jessie or one of the Cruz cousins calling.

Upon seeing the number, Kree, picked up the phone and said, "Mister Milton."

"You ain't gotta be mistering me, girl, you know we closer than that—at least we was once upon a time," the raspy, baritone voice remarked.

"We were. But you had some issues back then, Alonzo. The drugs, remember?"

"You still on that? I thought we was past that."

"Yeah. I am still on that, Alonzo. I mean, I'm really not into games."

Alonzo laughed and said, "Okay. I respect that to the fullest. I'm not fucking with them drugs though."

"What about other girls?"

"I am. Nobody like you or nothing, though."

"Thank you for being honest. I hope you're using protection?"

"Always. What about you? You been with anybody else?"

"I have. I've only been with two other guys besides you and I use protection each and every time. But only one of them can get it now. And he's still getting it."

"That's a lucky man."

"Thank you. I care about him—I love him to be more accurate. He just has some things he has to work on outside of the bedroom with other people in his life."

"That mean that nigga married. Look, Kree," Alonzo said, getting to the gist of his call. "I'm not gone beat around the bush. I sent you those flowers with that card and my number a few days ago because ever since you ended what we had a couple years back I been thinking about you. I can't put into words how happy I was to see you that day I walked in that salon. I was like, 'I found her again'. I was glad you called me after you got them flowers"

"Awww. That's so sweet."

"I mean that shit. Can I see you tonight?"

"I'm having dinner with my friends around nine."

"Not them two crazy ass cousins."

"Them and my girl Jessie. Who I think is responsible for all of this?" Kree sassed.

"I ain't recognize her at first, though. When I did, I kinda figured she was talking about you because y'all been tight. I ain't got nothing against Jessie, but I hate the hell outta Sweet Pea and Loopy. Them two ain't right."

Kree laughed and said, "Boy, you was about to buy some of what they had until you saw your own cee dee laid up there."

"I was," Alonzo chuckled. "But that's beside the point. It's different when you see your own product gettin' hacked like that."

"So y'all not gone beef?"

"Nahh, we good. Tell 'em we cool, just ease up on the bootlegging."

"I'll let 'em know."

"Alright. So you comin' through or what? Put this address in ya' GPS. I want you to come through and check out the studio I built."

"That's right you do music," Kree quipped as she turned the blender on and mixed her margarita.

"You got jokes. You gone take this address down or what, though?"

"Give it to me. I'll stop by for a minute before I meet up with my girlfriends." Kree responded as she began searching for pen and paper.

****

"*Thatt's una azada de tres puntero!*" (That's a three pointer hoe!) Loopy yelled out to her opponent, calling the shot before the ball had even sailed through the nets while trotting back to the top of the key, just that certain that her shot would fall, which it did.

While Kree sat home pampering herself, back in the city, Fox Park's basketball court was packed with onlookers. It was just after six and still hot out, but Earth's star had nothing on Jessie, Sweet Pea and Loopy. Whoever the three chumps were that thought they could ride over into Fox Park and beat the three friends in a first-to-fifteen tournament for $3,000 dollars on a court where they balled on a regular basis were in for a rude awakening. Everything short of dunking on their opponents, two females and a male around the same age and height as the three, had been accomplished. Long jumpers, left-handed lay-ups, the blocking of shots and several steals were completed. Money was circulating around the court and most of the crowd, many belonging to the two Mexican drug gangs that controlled different parts of the Fox Park neighborhood, was betting on Sweet Pea, Loopy and Jessie.

To add insult to injury, Loopy and Sweet Pea quickly picked up on the fact that their opponents couldn't speak Spanish and the two were going to town with the trash talking as they neared victory to close the deal on the challenge and take home the $3,000 dollars.

"*Le disparo que perra ojos que acaba de hacer, Loopy!*" (You shot that bitch eyes out you just did, Loopy!) Sweet Pea chided as she defended the inbound pass by stretching her arms wide and moving side to side.

Sweet Pea stole the inbound pass and passed it to Jessie, who'd been taking her opponent to school repeatedly with a murderous cross-over that kept tripping the guy up. She made the move again and rushed towards the rim for the final score, but instead of laying the ball up to end the game, she ran under the goal and circled around and waved one finger in the air, calling for an isolation as she pulled up her gym shorts.

Sweet Pea and Loopy walked off the court leaving Jessie alone with her opponent. Two dribbles between the legs, a fake to the left then a spin to her right sent Jessie speeding towards the rim where she jumped with all her might and barely—just barely—dunked the ball. The shot was more of an extended finger-roll, but Jessie's grabbing of the rim gave the impression that she'd slammed the ball home through the chain-linked net. The onlookers erupted into a loud ruckus as Jessie swung from the rim yelling aloud, "Go home and get some game, mutherfuckas! Fox Park!"

Money began exchanging hands and the three friends walked off the court and hopped into Sweet Pea and Loopy's Durango after collecting their winnings.

After showering over to Jessie's apartment and changing into a fresh set of clothes, the three friends sat around in the living room smoking blunts and talking before they went out to have dinner with Kree. "Yo, after we leave the rib place," Loopy said before toking on her blunt. "After we leave the rib place, me and Donatella gone need you to drive the Durango back on this side from East Saint Louis for us."

"What's up?" Jessie asked.

"We used Dibble car to break in a furniture store in Granite City last week," Loopy answered. "We hid it over in the old warehouses by the river after we ducked the police. It was hot for a minute, but we think we can move it now. It's been a week almost."

"Y'all had that man car for damn near a week?" Jessie asked as she shook her head in disbelief. "I know he was pissed with y'all."

"We just kept breaking him off with rocks we got from Pepper," Sweet Pea said. "Shoot, that's our hustle car. Dibble don't care what we do with that car long as we get him high."

"I feel ya'," Jessie said. "Eh, yo, I was thinking about

inviting this woman I been dealing with for a while out with us tonight. I changed my mind on that shit, though," she said before she lit her blunt.

Sweet Pea laughed aloud at that moment.

"What's funny," Jessie asked as she smiled at Sweet Pea before toking.

"We was talkin' about this when you was getting dress," Loopy chimed in. "First you had on one of your designer pant suits and some heels, that meant you done pulled something nice was planning on doing something with her."

Jessie looked away and laughed. "Y'all done picked up on my routine," she stated matter-of-factly. "Y'all some nosey ass folks."

"No we not," Sweet Pea laughed. "It was just something we noticed about you. And when you wear the baggy jeans and tennis like you have on now that mean you either going solo or don't wanna be bothered."

Jessie blew smoke out her nostrils and laughed. "Y'all a trip. I be pulling some tight women when I dress up, though. Professional women. Bankers and managers and shit."

"How you do it?" Sweet Pea asked.

"I got the Big Dipper, girl. What you mean?" Jessie laughed.

"No. I'm like, how you be pulling all those different women? And they be acting all uppity and stuff, too, sometimes in them videos you showed us." Sweet Pea said seriously.

"It's like a slow seduction in the beginning," Jessie replied as she leaned back and looked up at the ceiling. "When I get them vibes I just start laying down my game. Talking. Depending on what type of woman you dealing with, you can either be direct or hint around at it. Me I'm direct. Ain't no sense in not speaking up and asking for what you want or expect."

"I thought Kree was wild. You wild, Jessie." Sweet Pea chuckled as she toked on her blunt.

"Kree ain't wild," Jessie sighed as she sat upright. "She really be with all lovey dovey shit. That's my girl and all, but she fall for a man way too easy. She going meet Alonzo tonight before she get up with us. She text me that right after the game."

"That guy," Loopy sighed as she sunk into the suede chair and pulled down on her Saint Louis Cardinals fitted baseball cap. "When I saw him sitting in Kree's chair I was like, 'man, I hope they ain't back together'. She should just stick with Curtis."

"I knew his ass looked familiar but it didn't hit me until I got over by Pepper apartment the day he was supposed to come up the salon," Jesse replied. "By then it was too late because I ain't even have a number to call his ass and cancel that shit. I knew Kree was gone get back with him if he asked her. She loved that no good mutherfucka back in the day. If I could, I'd catch dude with Kree and film his ass on the strength of what he did to y'all a while back in the salon. Blackmail the hell out his ass. He got a li'l money I know."

"Kree won't be down for that," Sweet Pea said as she got up and stretched.

"Not to mention that dude would kick you and Kree's ass for real," Loopy said in a slow, raspy tone as she shook her head from side to side and relit her blunt. "If he clowned like that behind seven cee dees?"

"He'll do worse to both y'all for tryna expose him. Dudes like that feel like they have to live up to a rep," Sweet Pea added as she got up and checked her eyelashes in the mirror.

"See that's that low down ass shit right there what dudes like Alonzo be on," Jessie said in an aggravated tone, getting a little exasperated over the entire situation involving Kree and Alonzo. "Let's be out. Kree gone meet us over to the Iron Barley. Fuck that nigga Alonzo." she ended as the three friends began getting ready to head out to dinner.

CHAPTER FIVE

OLD HABITS DIE HARD

Kree had just pulled up in front of Alonzo's studio over in Soulard, having called a few minutes earlier to make sure he was alone inside. She exited her Maxima and tapped lightly on the single, dark tinted glass door and Alonzo opened soon after. He looked up and down the street casually as Kree stepped inside before he closed and locked the door behind his self. Kree went and stood in the middle of the small carpeted lobby, two money green couches were on either side of the room with a wooden desk sitting straight ahead to the left of two wooden doors and she began looking around the nicely furnished, pristine dwelling.

Alonzo walked past Kree, his hand sliding gently across her lower backside. "This here where the magic happens," he said as he opened the two wooden doors and walked down a long hall laced with pictures of himself with various rappers from the south.

"You know all them?" Kree asked casually as she trailed Alonzo down the narrow corridor while eyeing the pictures on the wall.

"Did a li'l sumthin' sumthin' with 'em. But my real work over in Atlanta," Alonzo answered as he led Kree to the last door at the end of the hall on the left where he opened the door and stepped back proudly, watching in silence as Kree stared at the state-of-the-art studio in obvious wonderment.

The recording studio inside Alonzo Milton Production's office was high tech in Kree's eyes; but she had not a clue what she was staring at. What she deemed was a large computer was straight ahead. It contained a bunch of small screens across the top, and numerous, seemingly hundreds of small knobs. Speakers were all around the white-walled room and a large window was behind the computer, the obvious place where musicians would stand and record their music. "This here is nice, Alonzo," she said as she as she entered the room and went over to the large mixing board to have a closer inspection.

"Thanks. I put a lot into it." Alonzo said as he stepped into the room.

"I see. I don't know what I'm lookin' at, but I can tell it's worth a lot. This studio is awesome," Kree responded as she stepped forth and ran her hands across the massive mixing board.

Alonzo sat down in a leather chair and slid forward beside Kree and fired up his equipment. "Check this out," he said as a melodious tune began playing.

Kree began nodding her head to the rhythmic tune, which had an R&B appeal as it reminded her of Li'l Wayne's current hit song. "That sound like that Lollipop beat," she said upon becoming familiar with the melody.

"It is. I sampled it and reworked the baseline. I'm working with Narshea on a couple of tracks on this compilation and I think she gone feel this one here."

"I'm proud of you. Go boy," Kree said through a smile as she tapped Alonzo's shoulder lightly.

"Yeah," Alonzo replied as he eased up from the chair before the mixing board and went over to a small table that sat before a low-lying couch where he grabbed a half-smoked blunt out of an ashtray and lit it up. He took a few tokes and then offered the blunt to Kree.

"You've never known me to smoke ever," Kree sassed, the

bass from Alonzo's Lollipop remix steadily thumping in her ears.

"Thought your crew rubbed off on you some after all this time."

"No. Not at all like that, you thought wrong." Kree said as she bobbed her head to the music while flipping through the pages of a XXL magazine she'd found resting in another one of the chairs inside the studio.

"Kree," Alonzo then said as he went and turned the volume down on the music, "when we talked on the phone earlier you told me in so many words you didn't like the way I treated you back in the day. I wanna know if could get a second chance?"

Kree set the magazine down atop the mixing board and stood before Alonzo staring at his tempting six foot frame. He looked good to her, his caramel skin and ripped body. The braids she'd styled in his hair a week earlier were still fresh along with a neatly trimmed beard and mustache. Kree was feeling exactly the way she felt on Christmas night back in 2004. It was the same loving feeling she had before her and Alonzo had sex and it felt good to her, good enough to hold her in place as she stood silent for a few seconds, gazing into Alonzo's eyes as the beat played on. "What will be different this time around, Alonzo?" she asked curiously over the music.

"I'll be gentle?" Alonzo said with a smirk on his face.

Kree was taken aback. "I thought you would've gotten more sensitive and maturer by now," she sighed as she stepped back from Alonzo and folded her arms while shifting her weight. "Is that the best you have?"

"I got a rep out here, Kree," Alonzo said lowly. "I mean, something like this—"

"What? The truth about us?" Kree asked dispirited. "I don't hide who I am from no one. Neither should you, man."

"I ain't tryna hide nothing," Alonzo protested. "I came in Bangin' Heads hoping it was you. I been looking for you ever since you left your old place."

"You could've asked my friends how to reach me," Kree

said in all sincerity as she stared at up Alonzo.

"I wasn't gone ask them shit! I ain't want nobody up in my business!" Alonzo snapped as he looked away from Kree and toked on his blunt.

"You think people in Fox Park didn't know about you and me, Alonzo?" Kree asserted as she took one step forward and pointed back at herself, pressing her finger to her heart. "People were out there when you went to jail that night, remember?" she professed with a hint of bitterness in her voice.

"But you told them way before then," Alonzo accused. "Nobody didn't know what was going on until you said something," he then added as he took a stronger pull off the blunt he was smoking.

"I didn't have to say a thing," Kree responded softly, not wanting to argue with Alonzo. "You had a key to my place, you were driving my car, and you spent nights with me inside the apartment, baby. What did you think people were thinking about us?" she reasoned as she stepped closer to Alonzo inside the dimly lit studio.

"Shit, that we was just kicking it."

"See? That's why things between you and I didn't work," Kree confessed as she snapped her fingers and placed a hand on her hip. "You were, as you say, 'kickin' it'. It was more than that for me, Alonzo. I remember all of the things you told me when we first met and it was hard to walk away from what we had because I loved you—but we weren't ready back then. And I don't think we're ready now," she stated as the song came to an end.

Alonzo had a certain kind of lust for Kree that he couldn't control. It wasn't about love for him in the beginning as he was only saying what he felt needed to be said in order to run game and take some money from Kree. The more time he spent with her, however, the deeper his feelings grew.

Alonzo was left doubting himself soon after realizing he had fallen for Kree and he'd turned to cocaine in order to be able to at least tolerate the situation. He knew what Kree was expecting of him on this day if he wanted to get back with her, but he couldn't let what the two of them had going on get out because it would damage his reputation and possibly prevent him from signing a major production deal.

Big Derrick and Torre`, the CEOs of the rap label, Dirty Deeds, LLC, was prepared to pay his label a six-figure contract upon completion of a twenty track compilation album for their very popular R&B singer named Narshea, and several other artists they had on their roster. Alonzo was on the verge of earning a half million dollars, the first major payout for his label. There was no way he going to risk the deal by putting Kree on his arms. She may have been high-caliber, she may have been true to herself, but Alonzo wasn't ready to travel that road just yet, if ever at all, regardless of his feelings for Kree.

Kree watched Alonzo staring down at the floor and she knew full-well he was not about to take an alternative stance concerning their rapport. The realization disappointed and angered her at the same time. She began wondering why she'd even entertained Alonzo by accepting his flowers and calling him, let alone visiting his studio, because much hadn't changed in her eyes. He still wanted to keep her tucked away, and he wasn't completely off drugs. She looked down at her daimond-trimmed Tag Heuer watch and saw that was a quarter past eight.

"Look," Kree sighed as she ran her hands through her hair, "I don't wanna be late for dinner with my girls so I have to go. I'm happy for you and all, Alonzo, but you and I? I think not."

"You happy with that nigga you with now, Kree?" Alonzo asked, a hint of frustration rising in his voice.

"I do okay with him because I know where I stand with him."

"But you know where you stand with me too. I was your first. What he better than me?" Alonzo asked as he grabbed Kree's arm.

"I know where I *stood* with you, Alonzo. Where I *stood*,"

Kree responded. "And it seems as if where I stood in the past is no different than where I stand today. Nothing significant has changed with you—with us. I'd rather not subject myself to the heartache."

"But he ain't me. That nigga not me, Kree." Alonzo asserted as he grew nearer to Kree and gripped her arm tighter.

"You're right. 'Cause see? He and I don't just 'kick it'. We have something real. We love one another," Kree replied as she eased out of Alonzo's grip.

"But you can have something real with me," Alonzo said as he held onto Kree.

"I'm not leaving him for you if that's what you're asking. Let me get my keys so I can go," Kree said as she pulled away from Alonzo completely and opened her handbag and jiggled her keys, but she was actually placing her hand on her faithful chrome .380 semi-automatic because she felt Alonzo was becoming a little too aggressive. He'd tried to fight her once before and she had to scramble to her gun. She was ready if he tried something this time, however; she continued to pretend to be searching for her keys and congratulated Alonzo on his studio before heading for the door.

Alonzo put his hand on Kree's stomach to pause her just before she reached the studio exit. "You right. I'm sorry for coming at you like that," he said softly as he gently nudged Kree over to the couch where eased past her and sat down and pulled her before him. The purple all-in-one silk dress she wore had a grip on her body and she smelled of raspberry. The sweet smell of her soft skin was driving Alonzo mad with lust.

Kree stood holding Alonzo's hands, watching him with an apprehensive look as he looked her over. "What do you want from me," she asked in wonderment as she looked down upon Alonzo, those old feelings reemerging once more.

"Another chance with you. Let me show you how much I really care for you," Alonzo responded, staring Kree in the eyes as his hands moved towards her rear end.

Kree's temperature began to rise feeling Alonzo's hands on

her body. She was beginning to feel herself sinking deeper into familiar territory and it was weakening her resolve. She had not only a connection, but a history with this man. She still loved his touch. And the way he was touching her on this night was exactly the same way he'd touched her on Christmas Day back 2004 when she knelt before him and pulled down her gym shorts to reveal her bare flesh. Remembering all the good times she and Alonzo had shared before they parted ways a year ago, Kree reached out and rubbed his shoulders gently and bit her lower lip. "How will you show me that you care for me," she asked softly while staring down into Alonzo's eyes.

Alonzo stood up and cupped Kree's lower jaw and pulled her in for a lingering French kiss, capturing her off guard. It was the first time he'd ever kissed her, but it was welcomed. She dropped her purse and wrapped her arms around Alonzo's neck and returned his gesture with passion as their bodies meshed together.

Alonzo soon backed away and sat back down before Kree and raised her dress above her waist, his actions causing her to get excited more than what she already was. She moaned in surprise and gasped when Alonzo moved her silk panties to the side and began licking her before he began sucking for all he was worth. She grabbed the back of his head and began gyrating back and forth, caught totally off guard, but aroused nonetheless. Alonzo nudged her around after licking her for several minutes and spread her cheeks and licked her from behind.

"Alonzo, yes," Kree moaned as she bent at the waist and reached back with one hand and pulled herself open. "Lick it, baby," she pleaded.

Alonzo kissed and licked Kree's backside while stroking her gently, savoring her taste as he lapped up her juices. Within a couple of minutes, she was thrusting back into Alonzo's face, working herself on his swirling tongue. His stroking hand was driving her crazy. "I'm gonna cum, Alonzo," she purred.

"I wanna taste it," Alonzo said through a muffled voice as he was too busy sucking on Kree.

Kree began thrusting backwards at that moment and grinding down onto Alonzo's face. She now had both hands planted firmly on the table before her and was squatting as her body began trembling. Alonzo's tongue and hand had her thinking of Curtis and she was driven over the edge. She shuddered and stood on the tip of her toes and cried out, her eyes closed and her mouth agape as she exploded, her juices spilling into Alonzo's waiting mouth. She eased down onto her knees seconds after her orgasm and leaned back, resting her body on her hands that were planted on the carpet and looked over to her purse, knowing she had a couple of condoms inside. She was caught off guard when Alonzo placed a hand under her armpit and pulled her up onto her feet and kissed her lips tenderly, allowing her to taste her own flavor as she moaned into his hungry mouth.

"You like that, shit?" Alonzo asked in between kisses as he tugged on Kree's panties.

"It was far more than I expected," Kree moaned as she slid her panties over her boots while licking Alonzo's lips clean. "What else do you wanna do to me," she asked through intoxicated eyes as she backed away from Alonzo and placed her hands on her hips and eased her dress up above her waist, spreading her legs slightly, thereby putting her half-naked body on full display.

Alonzo eyed Kree standing before him with her purple dress above her waist and her knee-length black boots hugging her calves and was lust-struck. He stood before her tempting body and unzipped his baggy white jeans and released his hardened tool. Kree's mouth watered as she stared at Alonzo's package throbbing before her. She remembered what it first felt like to take Alonzo into her mouth for the first time and hold sway over his psyche and there was no denying it—she wanted to experience that dominance again before allowing him to take her once more. She eyed Alonzo as she tucked her hands behind her back. "Wait a minute," she said lowly.

Alonzo watched as Kree walked over to her purse sitting in the middle of the floor and knelt down. She came up with a small, brown packet and tugged on it gently to release its contents.

Kree stared Alonzo in the eyes as she walked over and stood before him. She then looked down and reached out and placed the condom to the head of his phallus.

Kree's touch forced a sigh from Alonzo. He reached out and placed his hand over hers and the two simultaneously rolled the condom onto his rigid rod. Alonzo then placed a hand on the back of Kree's neck. She reached out and clutched his shaft at that moment and began stroking him slowly while raising his t-shirt with her freehand and began planting soft kisses all across his muscular chest while working her way down to his member. Just as she knelt before Alonzo, eye level with his stiff rod with her mouth ready to slide over his phallus, a bell buzzed outside in the hallway, snapping her from her trance.

"Shit!" Alonzo snapped as he pulled up his jeans.

Kree hopped up from her knees at that moment and trotted towards the bathroom across from the studio while pulling her dress down.

"Look," Alonzo whispered. "Let me get rid of whoever this is and we can finish what we started."

"I have to go anyway," Kree responded as she trotted back into the studio and picked her panties up from the floor. "That might be about business," she added as she exited the studio once more.

Once the two were straightened and headed towards the front door, Alonzo paused and kissed Kree for a second time. "You see what I offer now?"

"It was a first from you and I liked it."

"What I need is time. Let me get this money first and everything else gone fall into place."

"You know I'm involved with another man, Alonzo. What about that? How do you feel about it?"

"I know I can't stop you from seeing who you wanna see. I can't say I like the situation as it is, but I'm willing to deal with it if that's what it take to win you back."

"Win me back," Kree smiled. She was stunned to realize she had the affections of two men, but the feeling was indescribable. "Alonzo, I make no promises. But, I'm willing to give us another try," she said seriously.

"That's all I'm asking," Alonzo remarked just before he opened the doors leading from the hall to the main office.

"You know how to reach me," Kree said lowly as she tailed Alonzo towards the exit. Alonzo unlocked the door and just as he reached out to pull it open, the door was pushed in and three people stepped into the building.

"Nigga, we been calling your ass all day here. How long you been here?" Jason David, whom everybody called Jay-D, asked in an aggravated tone as he walked in with his younger brother Dooney, and his niece, Nancy Cottonwood trailing him.

"He better be tryna get my daddy his money back and then some," fifteen year-old Nancy Cottonwood snapped as she folded her arms and tapped her G-Nikes on the floor. She then shifted her weight and eyed Alonzo harshly. "Well?" she asked as she stretched her hands. Nancy followed Alonzo's eyes and soon caught sight of Kree standing over the by the exit. "I thought that was you, girl," she smiled. "For real?" she then laughed aloud as she pointed towards Alonzo.

Alonzo's heart began to palpate rapidly and his palms grew sweaty. At the same time, Kree knew Alonzo didn't want his business broadcast, nor did she, for that matter. She knew Nancy from *Bangin' Heads*, and knew exactly what the fifteen year-old was referring to when she laughed and pointed towards Alonzo.

"Girl, please," Kree retorted through laughter. "He had me over here to listen to some music and was trying to get me to sing on a song."

"Okay," Nancy said through a sly smile. "You was singin' for him. We gone, we gone roll with that," she laughed while shaking her head.

"Girl, you are too funny," Kree responded through a pretentious smile. "Forget you and all that. I'm sorry I couldn't help you, Alonzo. Talk to you later," she said before leaving the studio. Kree walked briskly to her car and got behind the wheel and lay back in the headrest with her hand over her forehead. She massaged her temples in frustration as she looked at the front door of the studio. She was hoping Nancy would say nothing about what she suspected was going on between her and Alonzo because she really didn't want what they were doing to ruin his business. She started her car and pulled away from the curb and went and met up with Jessie, Loopy and Sweet Pea, hoping everything would work out for Alonzo.

Meanwhile, back inside the studio, Jay-D had walked around the small office and sat down behind a cherry wood lacquered desk after hanging up his silk suit jacket. His shoulder holster was on full display as he sat down and turned on a laptop and began running a sales report for the past week. While the file was downloading, Jay-D loosened his light-grey silk suit tie. "You charging one hundred an hour for the studio time, right?" he asked as he looked over to Alonzo while rubbing his neatly-trimmed beard.

"Yeah, just like you said. Them niggas don't mind payin' that. Shit, they dope boys, they feel like they gettin' a deal."

"Well, I don't know about all that dope boy, shit. So long as they paying what I'm asking in here they can do whatever the fuck they wanna do outside them doors," Jay-D said matter-of-factly as he leaned back and crossed his legs. "What its looking like on that deal with them boys from Dirty Deeds?"

Jay-D was the money man behind *Alonzo Milton Productions*. AMP was his investment, and the twenty-four year-old, skinny, dark-skinned, braided-haired Chicago native was stopping by to make sure Alonzo was up on his job.

"I'm almost done." Alonzo responded to Jay-D's question.

"So I take it you tellin' me you don't have all twenty tracks," Jay- D said casually as he removed a .44 desert eagle from his shoulder holster and placed it in his lap. "We put a lotta money into this venture. And after only a year in the game we got a major deal on the line. We can't let this deal fall through, ya' feel? What's the delay on the tracks?"

"I'm working overtime, man," Alonzo reasoned. "We gettin' twenty-five stacks a track so all these instrumentals gotta be on point."

"Well, how long you need? 'Cause the deadline on this deal is three months from now. How many tracks you got so far?"

"I got four."

"Four," Jay-D said in disbelief as he stood up with the gun at his side. "Nigga, you been at this three months already and all you have is four mutherfuckin' tracks? We halfway through! You should have at least ten tracks," he scoffed.

"This nigga playin' games with my daddy money, man," Nancy sighed as she looked towards the ceiling. "We should body this dude just on the strength," the knot-kneed chocolate, slender female version of Jay-D exclaimed as she patted her neatly-styled hair.

"I concur," Dooney, a round-faced, light-skinned, medium-height, chubby nineteen year-old said matter-of-factly as he stood near the entrance.

Jay-D and his family were some real gangsters, none more than Jay-D himself. He had helped his organization trackdown a major drug dealer in Mexico in October of 2004 and was in on that hit south of the border. He moved cocaine by the kilogram and had been in the game for years. Alonzo had met them when he was passing out samples of his music and they took interest. By the time Jay-D had invested into Alonzo, who knew not his reputation at the outset, Alonzo was in too deep with him and his family. He didn't have a lawyer when Jay-D presented a contract for him to sign and was only looking at the $250,000 dollars Jay-D kept high-lighting in the contract.

Had he read the fine print, however, Alonzo would've understood that Jay-D had plans to not only take over his record label's name, but he would also own the rights to everything Alonzo had ever produced in the past and anything he produced in the future. Upon signing the contract, Alonzo had gone from a record label owner to an employee with the mere stroke of a pen. Now he was caught up in a $250,000 dollar racket that could possibly cost him his life if Jay-D, AMPs owner by law, didn't see a profit.

Alonzo knew he was messing up, but the few times Jay-D had come by, all was well. He talked a good game and had Jay-D under the impression that he was up on things. In all actuality, Alonzo had been flossing with the label's money as if he'd actually made it in the business. He bought two cars and some jewelry and began hitting the club scene with a mix tape he'd produced that was earning a few thousands on the streets. His name was ringing loud on the Saint Louis underground music scene. And the rumor surrounding his purported deal with Dirty Deeds, one of the biggest record labels in the Midwest and south, had given him some status on the streets. The truth behind the matter, however, was that Alonzo was blowing through his label's expense account while ignoring his responsibilities, and Jay-D knew it. It was only a matter of time before things came to a head between the two.

"I been on it, Jay," Alonzo bargained. "Let me show y'all the track that's gone set this Dirty Deed compilation off. It's a sample from Li'l Wayne song Lollipop I got working for Narshea. That's gone put us to five," he said as he led Jay D, Dooney and Nancy back down the hall towards the studio.

Midway down the hall, Nancy paused and turned to Dooney. "Yo," she whispered to her uncle as the two of them trailed Jay-D and Alonzo, "you recognize Kree?"

"From Bangin' Heads, huh?" Dooney whispered as he slowed his walk and extended his hand to stop Nancy in her tracks. "You think them two fuckin'?" he leaned in and whispered.

"He said they ain't, but I wouldn't put nothing pass these boys on the streets now-a-days," Nancy said under her breath as she and Dooney resumed walking.

CHAPTER SIX

THE GREAT PRETENDER

Curtis had just received Kree's text as he was pulling up to his three-car garage. He placed his Mercedes in park and read the message. *Having dinner with my girls. Miss you.* He smiled and deleted the text before placing his phone on vibrate. Kree was ready to apologize for earlier and he knew it. He grabbed his briefcase and exited the car and secured the garage and walked along the sidewalk under a short breezeway bordered by brick columns where he unlocked the front door to the home. He sat his briefcase down and removed his jacket and stepped out of the foyer and looked around in wonderment.

Curtis was expecting to see a guy in a white suit and hat with the smell of tomato sauce and stir fry emanating through the house; instead, he smelled the familiar aroma of roast duck and heard the melodic sounds of Atlantic Starr's song *Always* playing on the stereo. The chef was nowhere in sight, and more importantly, his oldest son, five year-old Curtis Junior, who would've usually greeted him by now with football in hand, was nowhere to be found. Puzzled over the change in routine, Curtis called out for his son. "Curtis where are you? Are you hiding from your father?" he chided.

"The boys are away, my love," Denobria said over the

music. "In here!"

Curtis walked down the stage stairs into the open area with his hands tucked into the front pockets of his brown silk slacks and stood in the center of the room under the large crystal chandelier and watched his wife as she danced slowly before the fireplace in a black negligee and high-heeled, black, fur slippers. Denobria's high-yellow, thick thighs were on full display and her eyes were closed as she sung with one hand in the air..."*Ooh you're like the sun...chasing all of the rain away...when you come around...you bring brighter days... you're the perfect one...for me...and you forever will be...and I will love you so...for always...*"

Denobria opened her eyes and smiled with a finger on her bottom lip. "I'm sorry about earlier, Curtis," she said as she walked over to her husband, kissed him on the lips and hugged him tightly. "I didn't mean to end the call so rudely."

"All is forgiven," Curtis said, a little perplexed over the scenario that lay before his eyes. "Where're the boys?"

"I had my sister pick them up from school and daycare and I came straight home after work," Denobria replied as she turned away from her husband and pranced over to the wine section. She grabbed a stem glass from the wet bar and poured up a glass of red wine and went and handed it to Curtis. "Here you go, love," she said as she headed towards the kitchen.

Curtis grabbed the glass and took an immediate sip, admiring his wife's curves as she walked past him and rounded the corner leading to the kitchen. "Your famous duck dinner," he remarked as he trailed his wife into the gourmet area and nuzzled his nose up against his wife's nose.

"Yes," Denobria cooed as she raised her head and licked the flavored wine from her husband's lips. "And I cancelled the catered chef because this is something your wife knows you and her both need? Some our time?" she pouted as she draped her arm over Curtis' shoulder and sulked.

"You feel guilty for hanging up on me," Curtis laughed as he leaned forward and gave Denobria a slow, sensual kiss.

"I do," Denobria chuckled as she ran her hands across Curtis' chest. "But tell me, am I on my way to earning a reprieve?" she asked as she sat her glass down on the marble countertop and loosened the silk rope on her negligee, putting her plump breasts and bald vagina on full display.

"My, my, my...my, my, my, my...you sure look good tonight," Curtis sang as he set his glass down and pressed up against Denobria, pinning her to the counter.

"I love you," Denobria whispered as she leaned back and stared up at Curtis.

Curtis ran his hands through his wife's hair and stared into her gorgeous brown eyes, eyes that were bright and emanating love and happiness. He thought briefly of the years he'd spent with Denobria, a beautiful woman who loved him more than life itself, and could only imagine the devastation he would cause her when he revealed to her that he wanted a divorce. He cupped his wife's lower jaw, brushing those thoughts aside for now and concentrating on the moment. With Denobria's face held tenderly in his hands, Curtis leaned down and kissed his wife deeply as he removed her negligee.

Denobria lay back against the counter and grabbed her husband's neck and pulled his head down to her breasts. She moaned when Curtis' lips suckled one of her nipples as he massaged the other. He rose slowly and led Denobria by the hand out of the kitchen. She walked behind him with her arms around his waist and the two of them began dancing, rocking slowly to Atlantic Starr's music.

Curtis turned around and eased Denobria back into a soft leather chair beside the fireplace and began removing his clothes. This man was gorgeous to Denobria. He still had some of those handsome, boyish features from the day they'd first met. She'd been adoring his sexy lips and pearl white teeth from the moment she'd first laid eyes him. And he'd always been in good shape. He had smooth, cocoa-colored skin and he kept himself well-groomed and smelling good at all times. He was successful; he was a good father and a sensitive man, caring and understanding. And those were just some of the things Denobria loved about her husband.

She eased up to the edge of the seat and spread herself open and watched as Curtis' head lowered towards her moistened slit. The feel of her husband's sexy lips sliding across her clitoris was pure joy for Denobria. She loved the way her husband made her feel, in and out of the bed. "Ohh, Curtis," Denobria moaned through closed eyes as she began rotating her hips, matching his motions.

Denobria's soft voice brought images of Kree to Curtis's mind. He couldn't help but to think about her as he pleased his wife. They sounded nearly identical at times.

Denobria had no clue where her husband's mind had drifted off to; all she knew was that he was taking her to a special place. She lay back with her eyes closed and her mouth agape, humping her husband's face and relishing in the smacking sounds and becoming ever-stimulated by his extensive oral skills. A wave of pleasure consumed her after several minutes. She threw her head back and let out a guttural moan, coating her husband's face with her secretions as she clasped her thick thighs around his head.

Curtis rested on his knees before the chair and removed his slacks and placed his phallus to his wife's opening. He thrust forward, impaling Denobria fully in one swift motion and was overcome with the warmth and snugness of his wife's vagina. The two were looking into one another's eyes, but Curtis had to close his eyes and pictured it was Kree that he was actually stroking—it was the mere thought of her that was exciting him —not Denobria. He leaned down and nuzzled his wife neck as he stroked her deeply.

"Give it to me, baby," Denobria whispered as she raised her legs and wrapped her arms around her husband's back. "Make love to me," she whispered through closed eyes while rotating her hips and clenching her vaginal muscles around Curtis' hard shaft.

The couple was just getting into the groove of things, the leather chair rocking back and forth, when the kitchen alarm suddenly went off, breaking the spell. Curtis jumped up and headed for the kitchen and Denobria followed. "Oh, noo," she said anxiously while grabbing a pair of oven mitts. "I've ruined dinner!"

"It's okay, baby." Curtis said as he headed for the circuit breaker at the end of the hall leading to the garage.

"No it's not," Denobria complained as she removed the scorched duck from the oven and set it inside the sink. "This is a disaster! A real disaster," she cried. "I'm sorry, baby. I knew you were upset about earlier and I felt bad about it and I wanted to make it up to you. This was a bad idea," she ended as she doused the bird with cold water.

"Baby, it's okay," Curtis reassured as he reentered the kitchen and hugged Denobria from behind, the two of them still naked.

"How many times does this make?" Denobria asked as she laughed slightly.

"Ohh, like a dozen—but who's counting," Curtis chided as he leaned to the side and looked into his wife's eyes and made a funny face, bringing about a smile. "I am enjoying everything about tonight," he then said lovingly while running his hands through his wife's short, brown hair. "Thank you for everything, baby. This is wonderful. Dinner's not ruined, and we're only just beginning," he ended before heading back towards the living room where he gathered his clothes.

"Things were going so well, in there, though," Denobria squealed in delight as she pulled out a Chinese takeout menu. "You want Chinese," she asked aloud to Curtis from the kitchen. "We can still have duck if we order Chinese."

"That's fine," Curtis replied. "What I'm going to do now is go upstairs and light some candles, draw you a bath and cater to you, baby."

"I can't wait," Denobria smiled. "I be up in minute so we can order. Love you."

"I love you too," Curtis said as he walked towards the stairs.

A vibrating of his phone inisde his silk slacks, one set to a special hum, alerted Curtis to the fact that he had a message just as he entered his and Denobria's spacious master bathroom. *I'm sorry about earlier. Didn't mean to be rude.*

Miss you, have a good night was all it said. Curtis smiled to himself, things were now okay with both of the people in his life. Denobria was fine. She hadn't a clue, he knew, about his affair. And since his wife had already declined his trip to Oregon, Curtis now saw an opportunity to do something very special with Kree. He began gathering towels and oils needed to draw his wife a bath while planning an upcoming get-a-way.

****

Kree was caught off guard by the offer. She scampered about her apartment grabbing every essential item she thought she'd need for the trip to Oregon as time ticked down. Curtis had never done anything like this the eight months or so she'd known him; but he'd promised her he was going to do something special with her and he was upholding his end of the deal. Kree was expecting Curtis to take her to dinner back in Saint Louis or maybe to a movie, something a little more laidback. A trip to the west coast where they could be open with one another was more than she'd ever even dreamed.

It was early April of 2007, two weeks after Kree had met up with Alonzo in his studio. She'd been anticipating this day ever since she'd gotten the news early the week before. She'd been planning and packing all week and had just stuffed another one of her makeup bags into her suitcase when she heard a knock on her door. She trotted out of her bedroom towards the living room and opened the door and in walked Jessie, Sweet Pea and Loopy, the three of them dressed extravagantly in tight-fitting all-in-one dresses and stilettoes with their hair and nails done up.

"Look at you," Sweet Pea snapped. "Them jeans and them boots is nice with that blouse. You looking fly. Who is this man that has your nose wide open?" she chided.

"You know about Curtis, Sweet Pea. Don't play," Kree laughed. "Now look, I'm gone leave y'all copies of my house keys so you can feed Riley. He likes his walk early in the morning and just before ten at night."

"That damn dog and me don't get along for nothing. Where he at?" Jessie asked as she walked around the living room searching for the remote control.

"In his bedroom sleeping."

"The dog has his own room," Loopy said as she walked into the kitchen searching for the liquor. "Kree, you ballin'. You doing more than hair. What else you got going on?"

"That's none of your business, Loopy." Kree sassed. "You know I don't discuss those things, but if you must know, I make pretty good money doing hair."

"Everybody got they own hustle, I suppose. You don't have to tell me, but I know you doing something other than hair. And then you got this man takin' you out of town. You getting cake."

"What are you hinting at, Loopy?" Kree asked as she filled up an ice tray with fresh water.

"You don't have a TV in your room. When you get back here, you can have a new TV mounted on your wall in your bedroom facing the foot of the bed the same day if you got three hundred dollars. We gone hit this furniture store over in Granite City again."

Kree just shook her head and smiled. The Cruz cousins were always looking for a hustle. She actually did want a TV on her wall, though; she'd mention it to Loopy the day they came through *Bangin' Heads* with the laptop. "Okay," she said happily as she placed dishes back into her cabinets. "But y'all are going to have to wait until I get back with the money."

"That's right," Sweet Pea chimed in as she mixed a margarita. "You go there to Oregon and put it down on Curtis and make him pay for the new television."

"I'm not going there for that, Donatella," Kree laughed.

"You only fooling yourself," Jessie chuckled as she sat in a chair in the living room rolling a blunt under the lamp light. "Y'all gone fuck like it ain't no tomorrow everyday y'all out there and you know it."

Kree blushed over her friend's remark. "This is going to be a romantic get-a-way, okay? Whatever form of lovemaking we do share I am all for it."

"I bet you are. What about Alonzo, though?" Jessie asked as she spread bud into her grape cigarillo.

"Me and Alonzo aren't serious. I haven't talked to him in over a week, and that was brief and about nothing. He knows about Curtis and how I feel about him."

"Better be careful with that shit," Jessie said seriously.

"Look who's talking," Kree replied, curling her lips while cutting her eyes at Jessie. "All the women you sleep with and bribe you gone sit there and give me lessons on how to deal with the men in my life?"

"I ain't giving no lesson," Jessie said before she lit up the blunt. "The streets'll teach you a lesson if you ain't careful is all I'm saying given the circumstances. You did get down with Alonzo a couple of weeks ago and now you bouncing with this dude."

"I appreciate the concern, Jessie, but I know how to handle myself around the men in my life. Enough of me and mines because this conversation between you and I is really beginning to dampen the mood. I'm giddy about this trip and I'm going enjoy myself." Kree stated as she went back into the kitchen and mixed herself a strawberry margarita.

Two hours hour later, Kree was dropped off by her friends at Lambert-Saint Louis International shortly after midnight. Jessie had driven Kree's car and parked it at the airport's garage so she wouldn't have to wait to be picked up on her return flight. After a brief farewell-for-now conversation and hugs all around for her friends, Kree went ahead and checked her luggage and went inside the terminal and headed for the lounge.

The entire main terminal was nearly vacant at this early Wednesday morning hour. Only a few flights were landing and taking off and there wasn't much activity on the main floor. Kree walked along the terminal with her purse and jacket draped over her arms in a dreamlike state, a wide smile planted on her face. She couldn't believe what she was about to experience. The thought was surreal to her and left her wanting to cry out in joy sometimes. She entered the near-empty lounge and saw Curtis out the corner of her right eye, but she didn't acknowledge him. She walked over the bar and presented her I.D. and ordered a strawberry margarita. Just as the bartender began mixing her drink, Kree received a text. *Glad you made it*

Wouldn't hav miss it for the world

Drink?

I got it thnx

The two sat and texted one another from across the room while awaiting their flight. Forty minutes later, their flight number came across the speakers. Curtis waited for Kree to leave and he walked out towards the gateway a few minutes afterwards. Kree was overjoyed. She was a few places ahead of Curtis, but couldn't help looking back just one time while smiling to no one in particular.

Curtis was secretly admiring Kree as he eyed her on occasion. She looked stunning to him in her light-beige jeans, brown, short leather jacket and brown and thick-heeled boots. Her hair was pinned up exposing her neck and a pair of tear drop pearl earrings trimmed in gold hung from her earlobes. Curtis loved everything about Kree. The way she carried herself, her zeal for life and the way she genuinely cared for him and their relationship, amongst many other things.

Once aboard the plane, the two sat side by side and talked lightly inside the sparsely-filled jet as if they were mere travelers who'd happen to be aboard the same flight. A brief layover and exchange in Sacramento had the two sitting separate from one another, taking a little joy out of the flight. And things got a little more tense inside the rental agency once the two had actually made it to the city of Portland shortly before six in the morning.

"What do you mean all you have is a compact car at this time?" Curtis asked the rental agent in disbelief.

"We had a few missed deadlines and some rentals are due for service, Mister Morrow," the agent replied, as if she was annoyed by Curtis' stance.

"I made these reservations over a *week ago*," Curtis emphasized. "Do you not know our destination?" he asked as he pointed to the map in his hands. "There's no way we're going to take a compact car into the mountains. There's still snow on the ground and we won't even have enough room after we pick up items along the way."

"Wait here," the agent said dryly before she walked off into an office directly behind the counter.

She came back a few minutes later and said, "You're in luck. Seems we had an eight 'o' clock cancel."

"You mean you were going to hold an SUV for someone coming in at a later time when I'm here almost two hours early and in need of the same vehicle?" Curtis asked in dismay.

"Those reservations were made this morning," the agent replied through a smile that obviously pained her. "I'm sorry for the confusion. Can I have your credit card to verify the information?"

After receiving what they'd both perceived as being biased service, Curtis filed a complaint against the agent and soon, he and Kree were presented with a black 2006 four door Ford Expedition. The bags were tossed into the back of the SUV and the two climbed inside just as the sun began to peek over the snowcapped mountains from the east. Kree closed her door and looked over to Curtis and smiled. He was staring back at her, his arm draped across the back of her seat as he pulled her in for a long, lingering kiss.

"What did I tell you? Didn't I tell you we were going to do something special," Curtis smiled as he ran the back of his hands down the side of Kree's face.

"You did. This is wonderful. Way more than what I expected."

"That's why I'm your man, because I do unexpected things in a big way," Curtis replied as he pulled away from the rental office.

"Where're we going again?" Kree asked as Curtis guided the

vehicle through the parking lot.

"You forgot already," Curtis asked while setting the GPS. "The town is called La Pine, and it is about three and a half hour's drive southeast of here. Now, we have a wonderful ride through the mountains ahead of us, we can stop and get breakfast after a while, and then stop down in Bend and pick up some things before we get into town."

"That sounds nice." Kree said as she eyed the rugged, picturesque terrain surrounding the city of Portland.

"Five days," Curtis smiled as he grabbed Kree's hand and kissed the back of it tenderly.

"Five days," Kree sighed as she intertwined her hand with Curtis's hand as she sat back to enjoy the ride.

CHAPTER SEVEN
PLAYING WITH PEOPLE

"Y'all trippin' not grabbing nothing. I'm bouta make this lady pay for all this stuff, watch." Jessie quipped as she walked through the women's section of Nordstrom's picking up items at random. Price was no object today for Jessie because the luxurious clothing she was selecting was going on someone else's tab. "This bitch here gone tell me the other day that she can't deal with me dealing with somebody else. I said, 'bitch you married so how the fuck you gone tell me not to fuck around with other people'?"

Sweet Pea and Loopy were getting their kicks out of Jessie as they followed her around the clothing section of the department store. "Does she even know she's paying today?" Sweet Pea asked with a smirk.

"I don't know. I don't think she saw me come in because she work over there in the young men's section." Jessie quipped. "I took off today because I just *knew* she was gone be here. She changed her schedule on me, but I got her ass today."

"She play with people a lot," Loopy remarked as she shook her head, her opaque eyes hidden by the ball cap she had pulled down tight over her skull.

"Look who talkin'. You two got some light hands. At least I ain't tryna walk out with shit like y'all did with them Adidas y'all swiped outta Footlocker and the rest of the stuff y'all boosted around the city today." Jessie said under her breath as she toted the clothes towards the young men's section.

"The stuff we hit was a special order," Sweet Pea remarked. "You doing what you're doing outta spite."

"Spite my ass! She gone play with me and upset my nerves? I'm gone do it right back to her," Jessie said as she paused in front a rack containing Calvin Klein jeans. "Look, throw, I need a young men's twenty-six width and a thirty-six length," she said as she nodded towards the rack.

"I bet Pepper would like these too. You think Chastity gone pay for these, too?" Loopy asked. "We need like four pair."

"That's what I been tryna tell y'all," Jessie said under her breath as she eyed the register where she'd seen Chastity standing when she first walked into the young men's section. "That chick? She got money. She married to a dude that owns his own electric repair company. Get what y'all want." Loopy and Sweet Pea each grabbed two pairs of jeans and piled them into Jessie's already-full arms. "Grab four for me," Jessie remarked as she started for the counter.

The sales lady, a thirty-two year-old married Caucasian woman named Chastity Hubbert, had spotted Jessie the moment she'd entered her department and she'd kept an eye on her the whole time. This was where she'd met Jessie a little over a month ago when she came in to buy some gym shorts. The two had a conversation, exchanged numbers and went out a week later after messaging one another back and forth in secret. Two daughters, and a son, all under the age of ten, a sick mother and an alcoholic electrician for a husband had forced the freckled faced, brown-eyed brunette into the arms of another woman. Jessie saw something in Chastity right away. She was real talkative, as if she were looking for someone to just listen to her problems. All it took was one question the day she and Chastity had encountered one another a month earlier, back in March of 2007.

"*How you think these shorts will look on me if they hang low?*" *Jessie asked as she held the nylon shorts up to her waist.*

"*Whatever way you wear them it'll fit you nicely. I wish I could wear those.*" *Chastity replied through a wide smile as she stood beside the clothing rack, subtly eyeing Jessie, who'd purposely put her physique on display in order to feel the woman out.*

"*Step over to women's section and grab some for yourself.*"

"*I don't have the body for shorts at all,*" *Chastity sighed.* "*Look at these pillars.*"

Jessie looked down at Chastity's jean-covered legs and her eyes quickly shot up to her ass. Chastity was one of those women who had a thick, voluptuous body, but viewed herself as being fat, and that's what Jessie played on. "Girl, you bangin'," *she remarked as he tapped Chastity's leg. "A body like yours'll set some shit on fire,*" *she added, feeling Chastity tremble slightly having touched her once.*

"*You think?*" *Chastity questioned as she looked down at her figure.*

"*I don't think, I know, baby. Who you with?*"

"*Somebody. But he's not all he's cracked up to be. I'm married actually.*" *Chastity remarked as she looked down to the floor.*

"*You ever been with a woman before,*" *Jessie asked as she smiled and leaned over and looked Chastity in the eyes.*

Chastity blushed at that moment and shifted her weight. "That was like in high-school. Me and my best friend used to kiss all the time, but we were never serious."

"*That's all y'all did was kiss?*"

"*Well, you know, she, she used to—I don't even know you and I'm sharing all of this with you,*" *Chastity laughed nervously, covering her lower face.*

"That's because we vibing," Jessie said as she tapped Chastity's elbow. "Let me get your number and we text? I wanna take you back to high school. Can I be your new best friend?"

"Maybe. What's your name?" Chastity asked as she tilted her head up and eyed Jessie.

"I'm Jessica, but everybody calls me Jessie."

A week and a day later, Jessie was in her bedroom inside her apartment on Armand Place laying flat on her stomach with her face in between Chastity's thick, creamy, pale-white thighs giving her mind-blowing cunninglingus. "Umm, hmm. You like that shit don't you, bitch?" Jessie asked in between laps of Chastity's bald vagina.

"You know I do. You do it just like you said, too. Feels so fuckin' good. Eat me."

The bedroom was filling with aroma of marijuana and sex as Jessie licked and sucked on Chastity, who was biting down on a pair of nylon gym shorts, one of nearly a dozen pair she had stolen to give away to Jessie for her agreeing to please her in secret and solace. Chastity spread her legs wide and gripped the back Jessie's head and held it in place, commanding her to suck harder, to stick her tongue inside. After several minutes of grinding against Jessie's face, Chastity shuddered and climaxed, screaming into the shorts inside her clasped jaws.

Once Chastity had calmed down, Jessie sat up and leaned over her and grabbed a half-smoked blunt off her night stand and sat back on her heels and relit it and took a deep toke. She then straddled Chastity and turned the blunt around and covered it with her entire mouth.

"I haven't smoked in years." Chastity said as she rose up from the mattress, resting on her elbows.

"You gone like this here. You ready?" Jessie asked in a low, sexy voice over The Gap Band's song Yearning for Your Love.

Chastity leaned in and exhaled a cloud of marijuana and coughed hard. "My, my mother would die if she knew what I was doing," she said as she leaned back into the silk pillows and blew the smoke out through her nostrils.

"Why? Your people don't like my people or something?"
Jessie asked she continued straddling Chastity.

Chastity laughed and said, "Don't take it the wrong way,
Jessie. We all get along fine with any and everybody."

"Your husband look like he would kill you if he knew what
you was doing."

"He probably would kill you and me both," Chastity
laughed. "He would never think to look for me here though.
I'm at P-T-A.! I'm leaving church! Picking the kids up from
practice! He believes it all and leaves me alone to do as I
please so long as he can have his liquor!"

"Yeah?" Jessie remarked as she leaned over and plucked the
ashes from the tip of the blunt. She then lay beside Chastity.
"You a fine mutherfucka and you know it," she said as she
reached down and tweaked Chastity's nipples. "You been
doing this shit for a minute, huh? Hooking up with women."

"I got tired of being taken for granted by my husband. I do
everything around that house. Sometimes I just need a break
from it all."

"Why not just find a man? What makes you want to be with
somebody like me?" Jessie asked seriously.

"I don't really feel as if this is cheating," Chastity said as
she lay on her back staring at the ceiling.

"How could it not be? You sleeping with somebody else
besides your husband. If that ain't cheating then what is?"

"Oh no," Chastity sighed. "You're not gonna stalk me are
you?"

"You a conceited ass," Jessie laughed as she toked on her
blunt.

"Noo," Chastity pouted as she bumped her forehead against
Jessie's arm. "I was seeing one of the teachers at my son's
school two years ago and she wanted to leave her husband for
me. It was like she was obsessed or something. Kept sending
me messages, threatening to tell my husband and her husband

what we were doing."

"How you handled that?" Jessie asked.

"We moved. I transferred the children to another school and we moved, changed our number and everything. My husband didn't find out."

"He didn't find out that time."

"And he want this time," Chastity said as she turned onto her stomach and placed her chin on Jessie's stomach while rubbing her thighs.

Jessie eased her leg up and opened it slightly as Chastity began kissing her navel. She then leaned over and sat her blunt down and flipped her hair over the silk pillows atop her king-sized mattress and pushed Chastity's head down towards her soaking wet vagina.

Reminiscing on the many sexual escapades she and Chastity had shared over the past month or so after that first night had Jessie smiling to herself as she walked up to the counter dressed in a pair of tight-fitting light-blue Capri pants, white open-toed heeled sandals and a white, tight-fitting blouse with a pair of Gucci shades over her eyes. She wasn't smiling over the good times, though, she was smiling because she knew she had Chastity's ass dead right.

"Yo," Loopy said as she checked her phone notification. "Check out this picture Kree just sent me."

"My girl done made it to Lapina," Jessie quipped as she looked back at the picture. "Aww," she smiled. "They really look good together."

"They really do. And it's La Pine where they're staying, Jessie." Sweet Pea corrected.

"Wherever she at she really looks as if she's enjoying herself." Jessie replied. "I'm happy for her."

"What if Curtis is like a serial killer or something," Sweet Pea said as she paused, as if she'd had a premonition. "What if he tie Kree up and torture her until he get tired and bury her alive? Dig a grave in the woods and dump her body."

"I'm tired just thinking about having to do all that," Loopy chuckled.

"But who really would know? It's a good thing we know where's she's at." Sweet Pea said seriously. "There's a lot of crazy people out here."

"Curtis ain't gone trip out like that, Donatella," Loopy laughed. "I think he really loves Kree. You right about the world being full of crazy people, though. I wanna see what's gone happen with this crazy person right here," she said in reference to Jessie.

Jessie threw a huge pile of clothes, eight pairs of Calvin Klein jeans, several silk designer suits, and six pairs of nylon gym shorts onto the counter. Chastity was standing by with a puzzled look on her face, not knowing what to expect because Jessie was acting as if she weren't even present the whole time she walked around the young men's section shopping. She hadn't seen Jessie in a week and a half, ever since the day she rode over to her apartment to surprise her and eyed her entering her apartment with another woman on her arms. Not wanting to confront her at that moment, Chastity rode off and called Jessie when she got to her home and asked her about the female. Jessie went on and told Chastity the deal—she and the female were going to get intimate. Her revelation had unknowingly set Chastity off, however; she went to calling her all kinds of sluts and whores and said she'd regretted ever coming to the 'ghetto' just to get her pussy licked by somebody who wasn't a good fuck anyway.

Jessie was in her kitchen fixing drinks at the moment Chastity went into her rant. She was left in total shock over the things she was being told. She'd talked to Chastity their first night being intimate and thought they'd had an understanding. Now she knew otherwise; who really was the stalker in times past, she began to wonder. She walked into her living room and handed her partner a drink and walked into her bedroom where she let Chastity go on and on as she sipped on Paul Masson. While Chasity was rambling on about how she wished she'd never met her, Jessie was going through several videos on her cell phone, searching for the most raunchiest and clearest film she could find of her and Chastity.

Jessie really didn't set out to bribe people per say; but if someone she was dealing with got on her nerves and she had a way to get back at them, however, she would do it. The only problem was that Jessie got into it with everybody she became involved with and it would always end the same way—with her blackmailing her lovers to keep quiet. She didn't view it as betraying one's trust, because if they'd all stayed in their lane and not caught any feelings, she would've kept the videos secret for all times. At least that's what she told herself each and every time she set out to blackmail someone. Chastity realized Jessie wasn't paying her any mind as she ranted and raved over the phone so she hung up, ending the call by calling her a 'trifling bitch'.

Jessie had all of those things on her mind as she stood before the counter removing hair from her face and looking around. She was as calm as the day is long.

"How you been?" Chastity asked lowly as she began ringing up Jessie's clothes.

"Chillin," Jessie quickly snapped, never making eye contact with Chastity.

"I was meaning to call you and apologize about the things I said. I'm not that type of a person, Jessie. Can you forgive me?"

Chastity may have been sincerely apologetic, but Jessie had already reached her own resolve. "I forgive you, Chastity," she said nonchalantly while looking around.

"Thanks, Jessie. You and your new friend are doing okay I take it?"

"No. I dropped her," Jessie replied as she scratched the back of her neck. "I'm solo right now, baby."

Chastity said nothing else while ringing the items up. She didn't miss anything about Jessie. For her it was just sex, but she couldn't tolerate knowing Jessie was sleeping with another woman. She wanted Jessie all to herself or not at all. She rung the last item up and bagged it with the rest of the clothes.

"Seven hundred and seventy one dollars and forty-six cents," she told Jessie.

"Why don't you go on and handle that for me okay, honey?" Jessie said in a polite manner.

"Excuse me," Chastity asked as she tucked in her chin and stared over at Jessie from behind the counter.

"Let me make myself clear," Jessie remarked calmly as she took off her sunshades, removed her hair from the corners of her eyes and stared at Chastity. "If you refuse to do what I ask? Which is to pay for every single item you've rung up for me today? You're going to have more problems than just a seven or eight hundred dollar deficit on your husband's credit card."

"Nothing you can say will ever make me take me husband's credit card and pay for these clothes. Not even if we still had a future." Chastity said matter-of-factly as she stared back at Jessie.

Jessie stepped forth and scratched one of her eyebrows. "I see...I see you really don't know much about me, miss," she said calmly while pulling out her cell phone.

"Are you going to pay for this?" Chastity asked in an agitated manner.

"Wait a minute," Jessie said lowly as she ran her finger across her screen. "No one's in line so just give me a minute. The items will be paid for in a minute."

"I have other things I need to be doing, Jessie. If you don't have any money, I don't see how these clothes are ever going to be bought."

"Will you just," Jessie stomped her foot and looked up at Chastity. "Just give me a minute, okay," she asked in frustration as she held up her hand. "God! I'm trying to get these clothes purchased like you asked!"

"I'm going call security." Chastity said as she turned away from the counter.

"Wait!" Jessie responded ecstatically as she jumped up and down in place, pausing Chastity in her tracks. "I found it! I found it!" she laughed as she leaned forward with a big smile on her face and tapped the screen. She then stepped closer to Chastity and held the phone up.

"You like talking dirty and shit, huh?"

"I like everything you do and say to me."

"What if I say I want you to eat my pussy until I come in your mouth?"

"I love doing that to you. Talk to me like the slut I am while I'm doing it."

"Recognize that voice and those people," Jessie asked, unable to contain her joy as she watched the shocked expression developing on Chastity's face.

"Jessie, how could you?" Chastity whispered as she backed away from the counter and covered her lower face while staring at the video playing on the phone.

"How could *you*?" Jessie scoffed under her breath as she leaned into the counter. "You wanna criticize me? Call me a trifling bitch? I don't like how you played me. Now, you can try me, but I know where you stay. See if a copy of this video don't pop up in your mailbox one day. Like *today* if I don't get my items paid for," she ended as she pounded the counter lightly with her balled fist.

"What guarantee I have that no one will ever see this?" Chastity whispered as she stood upright.

"You don't have a guarantee with that, but what's certain is if you don't do it..." Jessie went silent and looked to her feet at that moment. A man, woman and a teenage boy had walked up to the register and stood behind the group, waiting to check out. "You don't want your house to get fucked up, girl. You better go on and pay for this," Jessie said under her breath. "Don't make me cause a scene up in here. Start yelling how much I love you and all that shit," she added.

Chastity understood that Jessie was going to act like a heartbroken lover and say aloud that the two were having an affair if she didn't pay for the items. She was a respected manager in the store and always praised God and family. If her coworkers were to witness her arguing with a young woman nearly ten years her junior, with whom she was having an affair, she would never be able face them again. She would have to quit her job and then explain the reasons why to her husband. And there was no telling if word wouldn't get back to her spouse. She grabbed her purse and swiped her husband's credit card and handed Jessie the bags and the receipt without saying a word, only smiling pretentiously.

The three friends left the mall without giving a second thought to what had transpired and hopped into the Durango. "I need my own car," Jessie said as Loopy pulled out of the slot. "What y'all wanna do now?"

"Let's go get some lunch before we dip over to Fox Park. We need to feed Kree's dog too."

"Y'all didn't go and feed the dog this morning?"

"We woke up late." Loopy responded.

"So the dog ain't been walked or nothing?" Jessie asked she held out her hands.

"He be all right, he don't never doo-doo in the house." Loopy stated.

"Y'all two just can't keep a schedule. We can get something to eat," Jessie said from the back seat while looking over some of her new clothes. "But I wanna go home before y'all head out to Saint Charles after we eat. I'm gone go in and put this stuff up."

"That'll work," Sweet Pea remarked. "We gotta go drop some stuff off to Pepper anyway before we head out there to Kree's house."

"Poor li'l dog gone bust waiting on y'all," Jessie laughed as Loopy merged in with the traffic.

CHAPTER EIGHT
A DREAM FULFILLED

"...I know it's not the first time...that you've ever felt this way before...but those memories are still lasting...of the pain you got for your trusting...so when love comes you walk out the door...but this time, boy...don't be afraid of the way you feel...(don't be afraid now)...open your heart and you'll see it's real...it's real love..."

Thirty miles southwest of Bend, Oregon lay the city of La Pine. A small town with a population of only 1,700 or so residents, the community is more of a recreational destination for outdoor types who love to hike, camp and/or fish. The outdoors may have been the destination for most visitors, but a cozy suite on the top floor of the town's three story wooden lodge was the perfect escape for two lovers who'd arrived in town only several hours earlier looking to enjoy one another's company in secret and serenity.

The sweet sounds of Skyy's song *Real Love* play on the stereo above the fireplace inside the luxurious two story suite's grandiose master bathroom. Lights were dim, and candles were lit all around the large Jacuzzi and the fireplace mantle, giving off an orange hue inside the bathroom. The Clementine Cupcake pillar candles' flames produced clear reflections on the glossy, brown marble floor and stairs leading up to the tub. Kree and Curtis sipped champagne while relaxing in the steamy, hot water that bubbled just a tad.

Kree lay back in Curtis's chest, kissing him on occasion as the two listened to the smooth sounds playing on the stereo. This was all she had ever asked for and was now in heavenly bliss. Being with Curtis alone in this antiquated town, and the atmosphere therein only enhanced her joyful experience. It was early April 2007, spring around the country, but this high up in the mountains of Oregon, snow still covered the ground. It was still a little cool out during the day as well, which made it seem more winter than spring in Kree's mind and she loved that about the place.

There was a gourmet kitchen on the first floor of the suite, with low hanging lights over an island counter that featured all the appliances guests would need to prepare whatever meal their hearts desired. Before they'd arrived at the lodge, Kree and Curtis stopped at a Safeway grocery store in Bend, Oregon and bought a load of groceries. They'd also stopped at a mall there in Bend where Kree purchased some sexy underwear and a couple of negligees and heeled slippers. She was planning on dressing in her sexy attire and fix baked salmon, vegetable medley, and pecan rice for herself and Curtis later on, but the moment at hand was all that mattered as she sat inside the Jacuzzi beside her lover.

Curtis's cocoa brown skin contrasted perfectly with Kree's high-yellow skin. She was petite, and Curtis loved the feel of her body next to his. The mere sight of her made him throb, and being this close to her for an extended period of time was too much for the man to resist. The bath had been nice, but Curtis wanted to do more than just cleanse his lover's skin.

Kree had had her back pressed against Curtis' erection for some time. She knew she was driving him mad with lust moving against his pole, sliding her back across his member as the two drank and listened to the music. With the passion building, Kree reached for the bottle of champagne, gliding gently across the Jacuzzi. She was reaching for the champagne bottle when she felt Curtis's hands kneading her behind.

The ass massage was welcomed, but a gasp spilled forth from her mouth when she was suddenly lifted up out of the water. Moans of delight seeped from her lips the instant she felt Curtis's tongue servicing her crevice. Kree loved the way Curtis handled her body, treating it like a delicate rose, but able to handle it just rough enough without knocking off any petals. The way Curtis licked and sucked on her was indescribable. He made her feel like the most worshiped woman on Earth with his tongue love. He placed her back into the water gently and continued lapping at her hole.

"Curtis, yes," Kree purred as she held her one of her cheeks open, allowing her man's tongue complete access.

Curtis rested on his knees behind Kree and the two slowly rose and stood in the center of the Jacuzzi. She began kissing her way down Curtis's chest while holding onto his thick biceps. Both their bodies glistened under the lit candles, the music no longer mattering as both were focused on one another completely. The look in Kree's alluring, brown eyes as she sunk to her knees while staring up at him had given Curtis a diamond-cutter of an erection.

Kree knelt down and grabbed hold. Curtis' was a pretty one, long, veiny and thick. She could barely wrap her hands around it. She began rubbing the back of Curtis legs as she slowly eased forward, her breath now blowing across the tip of Curtis's plum-shaped head. She took her right hand and stroked his shaft and slid her lips down the left side, occasionally rubbing his member across her face and forehead. She leaned down and tickled Curtis' sack with the tip of her tongue before taking him into her mouth. This was the first time Kree had ever given oral sex without a condom. Curtis made her feel as if she really mattered to him. Ever since the day he'd told her about this trip, her love for him had deepened even more, right along with her resolve and commitment. She moved her head back and forth over Curtis' pole slowly, sucking gently.

"Suck it just like that," Curtis moaned as he grabbed a handful of Kree's hair and placed one hand on the wall beside the Jacuzzi to balance himself.

"Mmm," Kree moaned as her head began moving back and forth rapidly. She went all the way down to the base of Curtis' tool and slid her head back slowly, letting it pop from her mouth as she gasped for air. She then clutched his stiff member with both hands and kissed the tip of Curtis' dick and began alternating between quick pecks and flicking her tongue over the tip in a swift motion as she rotated her head in a rapid motion.

Curtis was nearing completion, but he didn't want to arrive in Kree's mouth. He pulled her up and kissed her passionately. "You're going to let me make love to you without a condom also?" he asked as he took her into his arms and began slow dancing with her inside the Jacuzzi.

"Do you love me more than you love your wife?" Kree asked as she hugged Curtis tightly.

Curtis looked down at the top Kree's head. He then tilted her chin up, looked into her brown eyes and said, "Yes I do. That's what my heart has been telling me for some time now."

"Then yes. But I want you to call me your wife. The whole while we're here, can I be your wife?" Kree asked while staring deep into Curtis' eyes. He leaned down and kissed her and she rested her face in his chest.

"Is that want you want, baby?" Curtis asked as he rubbed Kree's body.

"Yes," Kree whispered to Curtis as she brought her gaze back up to meet his. "And I want you to make love to me like I'm your wife every time we're together," she requested.

Curtis sat down on the edge of the tub and pulled Kree into him. He reached up and wiped her tears and had her straddle his legs. "You want me to treat you like you're my wife, baby?" he asked as he pulled Kree down into his lap and began kissing her neck and breasts. "You want me to make love to you like you're like my wife?" he asked in a passionate tone.

"Please," Kree moaned as she sat atop Curtis and place his pole at her opening and eased down slowly. "This is my dream come true."

Both lovers moaned and closed their eyes when the pleasure took over their bodies just as Skyy's song replayed on the stereo.

"Oh my God, this is wonderful," Kree whispered over the song's saxophone intro as she leaned forward and kissed Curtis deeply while rocking back and forth on his thick, rigid pole.

Curtis grabbed Kree's waist and began driving into her a little deeper and harder. "I love you," he moaned as he ran his hands over her body.

"I love you, too, baby," Kree responded through closed eyes as the pleasure between her and Curtis increased in intensity.

"Baby," Curtis moaned as he ground up into Kree. "Damn, baby," he whispered.

"Feels good?" Kree asked softly as she ran her hands over Curtis' wavy hair.

"Yes it does. I don't know how long I'm gonna last you keep doing that," Curtis sighed as he nuzzled Kree's neck while stroking her at slow, intense pace.

"I want you to come inside me," Kree whispered as she leaned down and kissed Curtis.

"Mmm," Curtis moaned as he began to stroke Kree at a faster pace.

"*El bebe,*" (Baby,) Kree moaned as Curtis tightened his grip on her and began convulsing while letting out a deep, guttural groan of pleasure. "*¡Y Dios, que está haciendo que me sienta tan bien que voy a entrar ahora mismo!*" (Oh my God, you are making me feel so good I'm going to come right now!) Kree screamed aloud as her body shuddered with delight, she herself climaxing with the succor of Curtis' hands. She lay atop him with a smile of contentment while running her hands down the sides of his face. "That felt amazing," she said lowly.

"It really did," Curtis sighed as he eased Kree up and pulled her down into the water.

"I'm ready for more if you are," Kree responded as she eased into Curtis' arms.

"Let's have another drink first before we do," Curtis responded. "No need to rush," he said as he began kissing

Kree's neck while reaching for the champagne bottle.

"This is so much fun. You sexed the Spanish out of me, Curtis," Kree chuckled as she reached for the glasses. The trip was going far better than expected and she couldn't wait to see what else would transpire on her trip to La Pine, Oregon with Curtis.

CHAPTER NINE
PLAYING POSSUM

"Esto no es ni siquiera el color correcto y todo eso." (This ain't even the right color and shit.) sixteen year-old Pepper told Loopy and Sweet Pea as she and her best friend, Simone Cortez, eyed a pair of white and yellow shell toe Adidas with disdain in their eyes.

Loopy and Sweet Pea had dropped Jessie off at her apartment on Armand Place a few minutes earlier and the two cousins were now over on Kree's old block on Saint Louis Street sitting inside Pepper's apartment toking blunts while showing her the rest of the clothes and jewelry they'd stolen from different malls throughout the day.

Pepper was one of the neighborhood drug dealers in Fox Park. She and her best friend, eighteen year-old Simone Cortez, had been in the game for several years selling cocaine. Pepper, whose real name was Peppi Vargas, was a yellow-skinned, black haired Mexican who'd lost her mother at the tender age of ten down in Valle Hermoso, Mexico. The go-getting teenager, barely standing five foot tall, was taken in by a drug kingpin and brought to America the day after her mother was killed.

Pepper's benefactor was killed down in Mexico in October of 2004. Soon after, she and Simone Cortez, a tan-skinned, voluptuous Uruguayan with short, bald-faded hair, started hustling the streets together. Getting money was Pepper and Simone's expertise. They sometimes robbed other drug dealers around town when they had no product of their own. They were a deadly combination by all measures.

Pepper sat on her sofa toking a blunt with her feet up on the edge of the table before her. Shawty Lo's song *Dunn Dunn* was bumping on her stereo and a fully-loaded MP-5 Heckler and Koch submachine Uzi lay at her side.

Pepper considered Loopy, Sweet Pea and Jessie to be her friends; Kree also, because she used to hang with her when she lived on the block. She never forgot the party Kree had thrown for her the day she introduced her to Sweet Pea and Loopy. It was the nicest thing anybody had done for her in a long time. She hadn't been to a party since the day her mother was killed, and was actually scared of parties after witnessing her mother's murder; but Kree had unknowingly helped her overcome that fear and she never forgot her for that.

Pepper was the tightest with Loopy and Sweet Pea, though because they were street; she had in mind to recruit the two as they could be more muscle for her on the streets.

Simone was across the way sitting on the love seat toking on a blunt of her own, a semi-automatic twelve gauge shotgun nestled in between her feet as she eyed a couple of cuff-link bracelets and a diamond princess cut ring. "These some nice pieces right *here*," she emphasized as she bobbed her head to the music.

The drug business was going good for Pepper, but she was caught up in some drama that'd gone down last year and was in a little bit of danger in and around Fox Park and she knew it. Her former supplier, Malik Gomez's boss, had been killed by an associate of hers; Pepper's associate, a young woman named Toodie Perez, wanted her back on her team after everything had gone down so she could continue warring with the people she'd wanted dead.

Pepper refused, however; Toodie was way in over her head warring with the mob in her eyes. She either didn't see death coming or didn't know it was coming; either way, the people Toodie was trying to go up against weren't to be fucked with and Pepper understood that fact very well.

Toodie was going to lose that war and the sixteen year-old wasn't trying to die alongside her, not to mention she now hated the mere sight of Toodie. The two were now at odds because of the stance Pepper had taken, although neither would admit that fact. She and Toodie were actually beefing in silence while keeping an eye on one another while anticipating a spark that would kick off the blood-letting.

In the meantime, Pepper was on her hustle and rebuilding her wardrobe. She'd put in an order for five pairs of Seven For All Mankind jeans, four pairs of baggy fit, black, Calvin Klein jeans, twenty solid polo shirts, four pairs of white Airforce One's, and a pair of blue and white shell toe Adidas. The order was on point; the only thing not up to par was the fact that Loopy and Sweet Pea had stolen the wrong color Adidas.

"*¿Sabes cómo es cuando te abofetear mierda, Peppi*" (You know how it is when you cuffing shit, Peppi.) Loopy said as she sat beside Pepper as she looked over the stolen goods.

"Okay, Loopy," Pepper said as she blew smoke from her nostrils, "Me and Simone gone cop all this shit, but I ain't paying for them Adidas. You can take that shit up the street. I can't fuck with yellow."

"*Su amarillo trasero.*" (Your ass yellow.) Sweet Pea joked as Simone passed her the blunt.

"*Supongo que por eso que no puedo joder con mi maldito auto.*" (I guess that mean I can't fuck with my damn self.) Pepper said through laughter as she counted out twelve hundred dollars for the jeans, Nike's and Polo shirts.

Just then there was a loud knock on the back door and all four females went silent. Pepper grabbed her MP-5 and Simone grabbed her twelve gauge and racked it as she went over and turned the stereo off.

Loopy and Sweet Pea had left their burners in their Durango out in front the apartment. They both began looking around under the sofa cushions and came up with two .9mm Berettas. Simone pulled the front door open at that moment and the girls eased out in the darkness. Pepper walked briskly towards her right with Simone on her heels.

Pepper's apartment was located on the right end of a four unit complex if you were facing the building. She never used her back door for any reason. The knocking had spooked her and Simone both and they were going to investigate. They reached the far side of the apartment and trotted down the side of the building towards a wooded area bordered by a chain-link fence where they looked down the back alley at their apartment situated on the opposite end.

Loopy and Sweet Pea, meanwhile, were standing out on the sidewalk in front of the apartment watching the right side of the building when Jessie ran out from the right side of the home with her clothes in disarray and her heels in her right hand. "Y'all seen a...y'all seen like a white Cadillac CTS riding through here?" she asked as she looked around nervously.

"We just came out. What's up?" Loopy asked.

Jessie saw a pair of headlights traveling down the oak-tree-lined street approaching from *Kirk's Coner Store* just up the long block and she ducked inside Pepper's apartment, leaving the door open. Loopy and Sweet Pea had their guns cocked as they back up towards the apartment, ready to open fire. "That's not them," Jessie said as she stepped out the apartment and watched the car cruise by. "That's not them. Where Pep at?"

Pepper and Simone were furious. They'd seen Jessie banging on their back door under the bright lights before she took off down the alleyway and ran up to the front. They knew she knew better than to even be back there; especially after dark. The back of Pepper's building was off limits because a kick door was her worse fear. She'd done her own fair share of home invasions and that wasn't to be her fate was her reasoning. She and Simone walked briskly back to their apartment with their guns draping their sides. "We gone have to get some big ass dogs to put back there," Pepper said as she jogged beside Simone. "Them searchlights not enough."

"Si," Simone replied as she and Pepper neared their apartment.

Once everyone had reentered the apartment, Pepper turned to Jessie. "The fuck is your problem knocking on my back door, bitch," she scoffed as she slammed her door shut.

"This lady is trippin' hard," Jessie responded as she turned out the living room light and opened the blinds.

"Who you talking about? Who you ducking?" Pepper asked as she locked and chained her door and went and stood beside Jessie and looked out the blinds.

"I showed this woman I was dealing with a video of me and her having sex and made her buy me a bunch of clothes earlier today." Jessie explained. "Loopy and Sweet dropped me off at home after we ate and I was just chilling. I'm taking the trash out and this white Caddy pull up and this trick Chastity jump out from behind the wheel. I know she 'bouta trip so I start walking back to my apartment tryna ignore the bitch. But her car in between me and my shit," she said as she trotted to the back door in the kitchen and checked to make sure the that door was locked.

"The doors are locked. What happened? What she did?" Pepper inquired.

"She wasn't by herself," Jessie said as she returned to the blinds, watching to see if Chastity's car passed down the street. "I coulda fought that bitch, but she had some guy and two ladies with her. I don't know if they were her family or what. But they looked like a bunch of angry white folks that wanted to kill my black ass. One of 'em had a gun too. So you know I ain't stick around. I took off runnin'. My apartment is locked up and everything and I ain't going back there until I'm sure they gone."

"So you done got chased by a scorned woman you done tried to bribe and some of her friends," Pepper told Jessie as she walked off from her while shaking her head. "You gone learn to stop playing with people like that."

"Shit, I ain't have nothing on me. My heater was *in* the

house. I knew I wasn't gone make it to that mutherfucka in time," Jessie laughed as she closed the blinds and turned on the living room light. "Okay, this bitch tryna get real serious now," she said lowly. "I got something for that ass."

"You wanna go body that bitch," Simone asked from across the room.

"That would be nice. But I'm gone send ole girl a message," Jessie said as she went into the bathroom and turned on the water.

"What you got in mind like that," Simone asked aloud.

Jessie came back into living room and sat in a chair inside the kitchen. "Y'all know if Dibble still rent his car out?" she asked as she wiped the bottom of her feet clean and then checked the straps on her heels.

"Hell yeah," Pepper said as she laid a pair of Calvin Klein jeans over her legs to size them up. "We used that car a couple of days ago to go down to Cape Girardeau and score."

"Yo, we out. Those guns are back under the sofa cushions," Sweet Pea chimed in. "Let us know what you're going to do about what happened with you and that lady," she told Jessie as she headed for the front door.

"Where y'all going?" Jessie asked as she placed her shoes back onto her feet.

"We going check on Kree dog right now." Loopy replied as she counted three thousand dollars, the total amount she and Loopy were paid for stealing Pepper's clothes and tennis and Simone's jewelry. She then gave half to Sweet Pea before she opened the door.

"Cool," Jessie said as she hopped up from the chair. "I'm gone take that ride with y'all."

"If you change your mind about killing your mad ass ex-lover come back and see us," Simone said seriously.

Jessie only laughed as she eased out the door. What Simone said sounded funny, but she knew her homegirl was dead serious. If she wanted Chastity dead she could have gotten it done on this very night. Killing the woman was a little extreme in her eyes, however; but Jessie couldn't stand not having the last say so in any matter. She had an idea on how she would get back at Chastity; but she had no idea just how much trouble she would eventually find herself involved in.

****

Sweet Pea, Loopy and Jessie arrived over to Kree's home an hour after leaving Pepper and Simone's place. As they pulled up to the home, Jessie immediately announced that she was staying inside the car. "Riley don't like my ass and I can't stand him. I'm not going nowhere near that dog," she snapped.

"Whatever," Sweet Pea sighed as she and her cousin exited the ride.

"Peso muerto a veces." (She dead weight sometimes.) Loopy remarked, shaking her head from side to side as she and Sweet Pea walked up the sidewalk to Kree's home.

"Watch your mouth, Loopy!" Jessie snapped from the backseat. "I know when y'all talking about me and don't you forget it," she laughed.

Sweet Pea had just unlocked the door. The whole time the cousins were walking up the sidewalk, they could hear Riley, a white Boston Terrier, barking uncontrollably. The moment Sweet Pea opened the door, Riley jetted out into the front yard. Loopy and Sweet Pea merely thought the dog was going to use the grass so they both went in and headed for Kree's kitchen where they knew the liquor was stashed away.

Jessie, meanwhile, was sitting in the Durango bobbing her head to the music while checking her phone for messages. She heard Riley barking and looked down and saw the dog right outside the window peeing in the grass while barking at her.

"That's why I didn't go in the house! And you find your way over here to fuck with me? Hold on," Jessie snapped as she looked around for something to throw at the animal.

Jessie came up with an old Jordan belonging to Loopy. She let the window all the way down and threw the shoe and Riley took off running. He paused a few feet away from the jeep and turned and started barking again. Jessie hated Kree's dog. He was a real pest in her eyes. Always barking for nothing, growling at people whenever they were in Kree's house and walking around as if he owned the joint. She was trying her best to ignore the animal, but his continued barking had reached its apex. She picked up another shoe and jumped out the back of the jeep and flung it towards Riley, who took off running again, this time headed towards the street.

Headlights just down the block and the running dog created a scenario in Jessie's mind that she just knew would not end well. "Riley," she called out lowly as she picked up Loopy's Jordans and jogged behind the dog, clapping the backs of the tennis together in order to try and lure the dog back from the street. "Riley, come here," she yelled again just as the dog ran out into the street from the backside of Loopy and Sweet Pea's Durango.

The car traveling up the road couldn't see Riley because he'd run out from the back of the jeep. Jessie tried to stop the car, but she was too late. Traveling at about forty miles an hour, the car rolled over Riley and kept going, leaving the dog crushed in the road. A couple of lights went out inside of Kree's home at that moment, alerting Jessie to the fact that Sweet Pea and Loopy were on their way out. She ran and hopped into the jeep, threw the shoes onto the floorboard, closed her eyes and lay back against the head rest as if she were asleep.

"Riley," Loopy called out, whistling on occasion to summon the dog. "Riley! Come on, boy!"

Sweet Pea and Loopy were both looking for the dog now. They walked around the front yard, the side of the home and checked the backyard. They went back over to the jeep where they saw Jessie was asleep. It was at that moment that Loopy spotted Riley lying dead in the road.

"*¿Qué pasó con el perro?*" (What the fuck happened to the dog?) Loopy yelled aloud while staring down at the dead animal.

Sweet Pea had shoved Jessie awake from her slumber. "Jessie, what happened to Riley," she asked anxiously.

"How I'm supposed to know what happened to Riley," Jessie asked, letting out a pretend yawn while rubbing her eyes. "I been sleep for a minute. Y'all ready to go?"

Sweet Pea and Loopy eyed one another as they stood at the back of their Durango trying to figure out what to do.

Jessie, meanwhile, was saying nothing. Riley was dead and she knew she'd contributed to the Cause. In her mind, though, everything was Loopy and Sweet Pea's fault. They should've stayed outside with the pesky mammal to make sure he was okay. Jessie had said she wasn't going near the dog and had stayed outside. Riley came fucking with her was her reasoning as she waited on Loopy and Sweet Pea to figure out what they were going to do about the matter.

"What's up with Riley?" Jessie asked, breaking the silence.

"He's dead. A car must have hit him. We have to get Kree a new dog. One just like it. How long before she get back?" Loopy asked as she climbed behind the steering wheel.

"About four days," Jessie answered as the three left the neighborhood. "I'll help out y'all," she added, now feeling a little guilty Kree had lost her pet, yet unwilling to admit what part she'd played in the animal's demise.

CHAPTER TEN

THEIR LITTLE GAME

"So the program director says to me, 'You're gonna be hated when the rest of the staff finds out you're able to work from home on a daily basis'," Denobria laughed over the phone.

"But he's going to back you on this, right?" Curtis asked as he sat at the dining room table on the first floor inside the suite he and Kree were renting.

It was a few hours after Kree had unknowingly lost her pet. She and Curtis were enthralled in a game of chess, listening to music and sipping glasses of wine when Denobria called, unknowingly interrupting their quality time. Curtis had started not to answer, but he didn't want his wife to grow suspicious so he told Kree to remain calm and quiet while he took the call.

"Of course he is, baby," Denobria said happily. "I swear, Curtis, I never thought he would give me an opportunity to work from home! I can go out and actually find my own stories! I get to spend more time with the kids, I can cook every night—for whatever that's worth," the joyful wife laughed. "This is huge. There's no telling what other possibilities may unfold. I just may be on my way to becoming a news anchor if I do a good job," Denobria said proudly as she moved about in the kitchen inside her home.

"Well, it was a career goal of yours. Now you're one step closer." Curtis said proudly.

"That I am. We must celebrate when you get back from Oregon. How's the trip going by the way?" Denobria asked as she pulled a tray of sliced apples and caramel sauce out of the refrigerator.

"It's going terrific, baby," Curtis replied as he eyed Kree walking around the kitchen quietly in her black, silk negligee and black heeled slippers with the fur on the top. "I miss being next to you already," he added, the words spoken meant more for Kree as he smiled and blew her a kiss.

"I miss you too, as do your sons." Denobria said lovingly as she grabbed the tray with the apple slices and exited the kitchen, steadily talking about her promotion. She was beside herself with a strong feeling of accomplishment that left her unable to cease talking about the events that had unfolded on her job.

"How my boys," Curtis asked as Kree slid another glass of wine before him, rubbed his face and eased away. Curtis patted her on the rear as she walked off, making her blush.

"Your sons are driving me up the wall here, Curtis." Denobria responded through light laughter as she entered the den and placed the apples and caramel sauce before her sons, who were sitting at a small table playing electronic educational games. "They're playing their little games and waiting on dinner."

"Playing their little game are they," Curtis smirked as eyed Kree, who was cheesing herself. "Give them a kiss for me will you?"

"Okay. Now, how will we celebrate," Denobria asked as she headed back towards the kitchen. "I would like for us to do something before the month ends because I'll be doing a lot of reading and editing. And if I get to make anchor I'll be away from the house for extended periods of time. My hours may vary in the beginning, if that ever happens, but the station manager says…"

Denobria's voice faded into the background as Curtis sipped his wine and shook his head, a hint of disgust planted on his face. Kree picked up on his agitation and she was in full agreement. Denobria was interrupting *their* time, and she felt herself growing jealous. She turned and faced Curtis, one hand resting on the counter, and the other on her hip, and rolled her neck and grew wide-eyed, wanting him to end the call so they could get back to doing their own thing. Deciding to be naughty, she walked over to the double door steel refrigerator and pulled a door open and leaned inside, her gesture raising her negligee over her hips exposing her cheeks and center as she removed a bowl of uncooked broccoli, carrots and cauliflower from the top shelf.

"…either the six 'o' clock news or the ten 'o' clock news. What do you think, Curtis? What hour should I chose if I were to become an anchor?" Denobria waited a few seconds, but got no response. "Curtis, are you listening to me?" she laughed.

"Yeah, baby. Six or ten would be perfect."

"You're not listening to me, baby." Denobria said a little dejected as she grabbed an oven mitt. "I'm sharing my dream with you and you aren't listening to me."

"I am listening to your dream, baby. You'll get more viewers with the six 'o' clock news. And can't they run a shorter version of your report in the ten 'o' clock hour so you won't have to do it live? That way you'll be home around what? Eight at the latest?"

"Hmm," Denobria perked up as she walked over to the wall-mounted oven. "I never even considered asking the station manager that particular question. Thanks, baby, I'm going to— oh no," Denobria sighed.

"What happened," Curtis asked as he sat up in his seat. "Baby, what's wrong?"

"The meatloaf is overcooked! The boys will not eat overcooked meatloaf!"

"Won't be the first time," Curtis chuckled, relieved that nothing too dramatic was taking place inside his home.

"What are you saying, Mister Morrow?" Denobria sassed as she ran water into the pan and covered it with aluminum foil to tenderize it.

"Your meatloaf, your meatloaf could hold up a building."

"Is it that bad?"

"I'm just kidding with you. The boys will love it. Kiss them for me, okay? I have to go."

"Okay, love. Muah!"

Curtis blew his wife a kiss and hung up the phone and leaned back in the chair and was immediately greeted by Kree. "Now we can get back to us," she said as she straddled Curtis' lap, grabbed his glass of wine and took a sip.

"Yes. Where were we?"

"I was about to do this," Kree said as she stood up and turned around and made her cheeks clap before Curtis while looking back at him.

"Ohh, what a bad, bad, bad little girl you are," Curtis said lowly as he slapped Kree's cheeks repeatedly.

Kree was laughing aloud as Curtis stood up and removed his silk robe, wearing nothing but his boxer shorts as he grabbed her from behind and ground against her rear end. "I am loving everything about you, baby. You are such a temptation."

"Shit!" Kree yelled suddenly as she trotted towards the kitchen.

"What did I say?" Curtis asked confusedly.

"Nothing, love," Kree replied as she hastily pulled the oven door open. "Ohh no," she sighed as she stomped her feet. "The baked salmon is going to be dry and flaky! I should have taken it out ten minutes ago!"

Curtis sipped his wine and laughed as he walked over to Kree. "Just like home," he said as he wrapped his arms around her and trailed her to the sink while she was holding onto the baking pan.

"Better than home," Kree retorted. "How long are we going to do this?" she then asked, turning to face her lover head on.

"Once I file for the divorce in the next month or so, I will tell her. Not before, baby. We just can't risk it." Curtis said as he picked up a seasoned piece of broccoli and eased it into Kree's mouth and handed the uneaten portion to her.

Kree savored the taste of her seasoned medley. "I understand," she responded as she fed the uneaten portion of broccoli to her lover. "Just promise me that Denobria is all I will have to contend with the whole time."

"I promise, Kree," Curtis remarked tenderly after swallowing the broccoli and pecking her lips while hugging her waist. "I want you in my life, baby. And I don't ever wanna have to hide you from no one and nothing. I love what we have."

Just then Kree's phone rung. She reached over to the counter and checked and saw that it was Loopy calling. She was about to answer, but the call ended abruptly. "That was my girl," she told Curtis while eyeing the number. "I guess it wasn't important because she hung up. Now, where were we?"

"Burning our dinner and playing chess," Curtis joked as he and Kree continued on with the rest of their evening.

****

The following afternoon, back in Saint Louis, Sweet Pea, Loopy and Jessie had just pulled up to PetSmart and were exiting the vehicle.

"Y'all two got a lotta gumption," Jessie quipped as she righted her platinum chain. "I said I was willing to help and this the plan y'all two come up with? I mean this is the best y'all can do?"

"That dog cost five hundred dollars. Kree lost her mind paying that much for an animal," Loopy snapped. "She shoulda came to us early on and got a deal."

"If we pull this off, we got us a new hustle. Everybody want those li'l small dogs now." Sweet Pea said happily as the three entered the store and separated.

The store had just opened and only had three other customers besides Sweet Pea, Loopy and Jessie. Jessie went and looked at the fish inside the store while Loopy entered to the toy aisle, both of them watching for any witnesses.

Sweet Pea, meanwhile, was walking down an aisle that had a bunch of cats inside kennels. She soon began sneezing uncontrollably, catching the eye of one of the salesclerks. "Ma'am, are, are you okay?" the young woman asked curiously.

Sweet Pea was laying it on thick in the middle of the aisle, sneezing hysterically while bending at the waist. "¡ *Hombre! No sabía que era alérgica a los gatos!*" (Man! I never knew I was allergic to cats!) she said as she took to one knee and started gagging.

The salesclerk called for her manager, and a couple of customers who'd heard the commotion, ran over onto the aisle as well. While most of the people in the store were tending to the fallen customer, Loopy was over by the dogs where she pulled out a pair of wire cutters and snapped the small padlock off a cage that held a dog identical to Riley. She scooped the dog up and tucked it under her armpit and eased out the door and disappeared from sight, Jessie soon following.

Sweet Pea was sitting down on her rear end in the aisle now. Her auburn hair was frayed and she'd even mustered up a few tears that had spilled forth from her green eyes. The manager had brought her a bottle of water and some Benadryl and had offered a discount on anything she wanted out the store. "Ma'am, are, are you okay? Do you need me to call you an ambulance," the manager asked in a compassionate tone.

"*Mi abogado fue saber de eso! Yo voy a demandar a los pantalones de este lugar.*" (My lawyer gone hear about this shit! I'm suing the pants off this place!) Sweet Pea snapped as she grabbed her cell phone and dialed a number.

"What is she saying? Is she calling the police or an ambulance?" the manager asked the salesclerk.

"Have you ever heard me speak Spanish since I've been working here?" the Asian salesclerk sassed.

"*¿Tienes el perro?*" (You got the dog?) Sweet Pea asked Loopy over the phone.

"Come on! We ready to roll," Loopy said as she pulled out

of the parking slot. "Come to the door."

"I speak Spanish," a female customer responded. "She said she is going to sue you guys. And she's asking about a dog."

"A dog," the manager asked just as another salesclerk ran onto the aisle and told him that one of the store's dogs had been stolen.

"¡ *Oh Dios!*" (Oh shit!) Sweet Pea snapped as she closed her phone and hopped up off the floor, realizing someone in the group had understood her conversation. She broke through the people surrounding her at that moment and the manager quickly gave chase, chasing her out the store just as Loopy and Jessie pulled up in the Durango. The manager accosted Sweet Pea around the shoulder just outside the entrance, but she turned and punched the husky middle-aged man in the throat, gagging him before she broke free and jumped in the backseat of the Durango where Loopy peeled out.

"I ain't never seen nothing like that in my life," Jessie laughed as Sweet Pea sped out the parking lot. "Y'all better hope that shit was worth it!" she ended.

CHAPTER ELEVEN
CAN'T HIDE THE FACTS

It was the day before Kree and Curtis's scheduled departure. Their blissful trip was coming to an end soon, but it was an experience both wanted to repeat again and again. They were already making plans for a summer get-a-way in the upcoming months to celebrate Curtis' divorce. Their relationship was budding tremendously, and Kree was overjoyed on this day as she and Curtis had walked around the entire downtown area hand in hand. If ever Kree felt like she and Curtis belonged together, today was undoubtedly the day.

Dressed in a pair of tight fitting blue jeans, white Ugg boots with fur around the tops, and a matching white hooded, leather bubble jacket, Kree ran ahead of Curtis towards the entrance leading to the trail that led up the side of a mountain. The dirt trail was bordered on both sides by lush evergreens and its pathway was covered in snow. She stepped off the trail and dipped her glove-clad hands into the snow amongst the trees and patted a snow ball. She then eyed Curtis, who was busy checking a compass, and smiled mischievously as he neared.

The thick grove of evergreen pine trees was her cover as she waited for her lover to walk pass her. The moment Curtis strode by, Kree jumped out from behind the pine tree she was hiding behind and slammed the snow ball into the back of his head, knocking his leather b-bop cap to the ground and leaving his wool scarf slight twisted. It was a big wallop that left Curtis stunned. "You're gonna get it now," he laughed as he picked up his hat and ran towards Kree.

Kree took off running back down the trail, but Curtis caught up with her at the trail's foot and grabbed her around the waist. The joy on Kree's face was undeniable. Being far away from her real world with the man she loved was in a word, exhilarating. The picturesque mountains, the quaint town with its antique shoppes and the snow-covered ground, not to mention the wonderful lodge the two were staying in, it was all magical to her. This was the happiest time of her life, and it had been delivered by the one man she'd wanted to spend the rest of her years with; even with his flaws, his marriage and an unwillingness to see her outside of a hotel room back in Saint Louis, Kree felt as if she had seen the real Curtis on this trip. She loved everything about her man—yes—her man—because Curtis had all but assured her on this trip that Denobria would be a mere afterthought in the very near future.

Curtis grabbed Kree, spun her around and lay her down in the snow and fell down beside her; the two were in a world of their own, laughing loudly, kissing sporadically and gazing into one another's eyes with that all-too-familiar look of love on full display. This twenty-three year-old really had a hold on Curtis; but it was a hold he readily welcomed. To him, she was vibrant and full of life with a spirit of adventure, much like his wife, only younger and a little less conservative. Kree had age and time on her side, and their lovemaking was beyond compare in his eyes. She was more than he could ask for was his thinking as he gazed into her brown eyes.

"Look, here," Curtis said as he sat up in the snow and went into his tan wool coat and pulled out a small, white velvet box.

Kree sat back on her heels and covered her lower face. She knew what those boxes contained. "Curtis, you didn't have to do that," she said lowly as her heart pounded with anticipation.

"It's okay, baby," Curtis responded tenderly before he pecked Kree's lips. "A couple of days ago you wanted to know if you were the only one outside of my obligations at home.

You are, Kree," he said as he opened the box and put a half karat princess cut diamond on display.

"This is such a beautiful piece of jewelry, baby," Kree responded as she removed the ring from the box. "When did you sneak off and get this?" she smiled.

"I been had it," Curtis replied as he touched the side of Kree's face. "I bought it the day before I told you about the trip."

"What does this mean exactly," Kree asked as Curtis slid the ring onto her wedding finger.

"What it means is that you are mines, and mines only now, Kree. Whatever you had in mind to do, whatever outside interests you had besides me? It's over now. I'm, I so much want to be with you, baby. We've talked. This is what I want to do, okay? Let's make it all official. Let's make life happen for us."

"I would love that, Curtis." Kree said as she sat beside him in the snow and slid the ring onto her index finger while smiling proudly.

"I don't blame you," a middle-aged white man said as he approached Curtis and Kree, interrupting their conversation and flow. "She's gorgeous, young man."

"Thank you," Curtis said as he stood up and helped Kree up from the snow-covered ground.

"I saw that move," the man smiled as he tucked his hands inside of his thick flannel jacket. "You two have just become engaged. Am I right?"

Curtis and Kree were both laughing on the inside, but it felt good to be admired in such a way by a total stranger. "We sure have, mister," Curtis responded as he handed the old man a digital camera and pulled Kree in to him.

"Ahh! A photograph to capture the moment," the man said joyously.

****

The following morning, Kree woke from her slumber feeling

drained. She lay naked next to Curtis, his muscular body spooning her as she grabbed his hand and kissed it gently. Their final night in La Pine was fairylike. Music, more wine and the two had made love before the fireplace where Kree shuddered and had one of the most intense orgasms ever as Curtis took her in the missionary position with her legs over his shoulders. The trip had been everything she'd dreamed of and more in her eyes. Five glorious days that had given her deep insight into a life she'd only been dreaming of for years, yet had always thought of as being conceivable between her and Curtis. Now, it was nearing.

Kree eased out of Curtis's grip and placed a robe over her naked body and headed for the bathroom where she turned on the hot water and brushed her pearly whites. A quick shower had awakened her completely and she emerged from the bathroom naked and brushing her hair when she was greeted by a groggy Curtis, who said nothing as he pulled her into his biceps and kissed her forehead before disappearing into the bathroom himself.

Kree hated the fact that the time she'd spent with Curtis was coming to an end because she knew she would have to return back to her reality. The make-believe would be over. She would no longer be Curtis' wife. She and her lover would become mere strangers back in their home state of Missouri and return to their life of secrecy. Not wanting to dampen her mood, Kree grabbed her phone and texted Loopy and told her she would be back in the late evening and reminded her to check on Riley as she began packing her clothes for the return trip.

The three hour ride back to Portland was a quiet one. Both lovers were reminiscing over the trip and having the least bit of regret, save for it all having to come to an end. They held hands most of the way, eyeing one another and smiling on occasion, blushing over the intimate moments they'd shared. No words need be spoken. Kree had been ravaged, and she loved the entire process.

Curtis was blown away. His resolve solidified. Kree was the one for him, the unmitigated love of his life.

"So," Curtis said as the two neared the city of Portland, Oregon, "I'm thinking the first weekend after the divorce, I schedule a trip to Vermont and we travel there for our time alone to make this thing official?"

"Vermont sounds nice. I've never been there." Kree smiled as she rested her head in her hand, her elbow situated on the SUV's window.

"It's marvelous during the summer, baby. If you loved the snow back in that little town, you'll love the forested peaks of Vermont in the spring and summer."

"I'm looking forward to it."

"Yeah, it'll be nice. I'm hoping to have a special surprise gift for you, too, when we go."

"What is it?" Kree smiled.

"If I were to tell you it wouldn't be a surprise now would it? It's bigger than that ring is all I'll say."

Kree laughed lowly as she turned her head away from Curtis. "You can't blame a woman for trying," she said as she turned back towards him and eyed him like he was the most precious thing in the world. "Thank you for the wonderful time. You really made my dreams come true on this trip."

Curtis pulled Kree into his arms as he drove with one hand. She was all smiles as she lay nuzzled in his chest, running her hands across his flat stomach. "Umm, umm," Curtis said. "You know what that touch does to me."

"Here, right now," Kree whispered as she eased up and kissed Curtis' neck. "I wanna taste you one last time," she cooed into his ear as she unzipped his silk slacks.

There was no protest from Curtis when he felt Kree's hand engulf his member and release his erection as he flicked the blinker on to move over into the right lane. The coolness surrounding his exposed member inside the SUV was quickly replaced with a warm sensation and for a brief second, he closed his eyes and let his head drift off slightly as he released a low moan. He quickly regained his composure and guided the Expedition down the four-lane highway with both hands on the steering wheel with Kree's face planted firmly in his lap.

Cars whizzed by the slow-moving SUV cruising in the right lane, unable to see the black head of hair rotating wildly in the driver's lap. Curtis was checking the mirrors and watching the road ahead with a distressed look on his face. He wanted Kree to stop as he was losing control of the vehicle, but the sensation was too irresistible. Through blurred vision he guided the car for several miles as his rod stiffened and Kree's sucking intensified. "I'm there," Curtis groaned as he gripped the steering wheel, stretching the skin around his knuckles as he exploded.

"Yes, daddy," Kree moaned as she pulled back and let Curtis' fluid splash across her face. She then placed the tip of his shaft in between her lips and sucked him hard, sending tantalizing streaks of pleasure coursing throughout his body to the point that his legs began to tremble. The SUV sped up and slowed down, and then sped up again as Kree wiped her face clean with the her lover's shaft and then took him back into her mouth once more to suck him clean and dry.

"How was that?" Kree smiled as she sat upright and opened the glove compartment to grab a few napkins and a bottle of water from her handbag.

"Unbelievable. I've never experienced anything like that. Wow," Curtis remarked in stunned appreciation.

"That was wonderful. We could have so much fun together if I was your wife, Curtis," Kree said in a seductive manner as she wet her napkins with the bottled water and wiped her face clean. She then wet another stack of napkins and wiped Curtis clean and zipped him up gently before resting back in her seat. "I don't ever want to lose you," she said somberly as she gazed out upon the mountainous terrain lining the highway.

"What we did on this trip was only a prelude of a life on the horizon," Curtis said as he pulled Kree back close. "The love we made, the shopping, going out in public? That ring? That's the real me, Kree. This is the real us, okay, baby? Remember this time and look forward to it being our life pretty soon."

"Promise?"

"Cross my heart," Curtis replied as he continued down the highway.

The couple reached the rental agency near the airport about an hour later. They climbed out of the SUV and stretched their legs as three employees came over and greeted them right away. They were handed surveys and offered complimentary coffee and bagels while they waited for the airport shuttle.

"They're being extra nice this go around," Kree said as she had her luggage gently removed from her grasp by one of the service technicians.

"They have some men in suits watching things," Curtis said as he pointed towards a couple of elderly men in expensive-looking business suits walking around with a couple of managers from the car rental agency. "Maybe that complaint I filed raised eyebrows around here for a change."

The two rode over to the airport and boarded their flight an hour later. During their traveling to Oregon, Curtis and Kree grew closer and closer the nearer they got to their destination. Upon their return trip to Missouri, the further away they got from Oregon, the further they drew apart. But it was only temporary in both of their minds.

Curtis had been won over by Kree. He was completely in love and willing to put everything he owned on the line for love's sake. The return flight to Saint Louis from their exchange in Sacramento had split the lovers apart for good. When they stepped off the flight and left the gangway, no words were spoken, only loving gazes and smiles that had them both reflecting on what a wonderful moment in time they'd shared, and dreams of a life to come.

****

It was just after five in the evening when Kree turned onto her block. Her body was aching in a good way, and her head was up in the clouds as she cruised up to the front of her cozy three bedroom home. She was planning on going in, shower and relax the remainder of the day, but Loopy and Sweet Pea's Durango parked at the foot of her driveway had changed her plans. She left her luggage in the trunk of her car and entered her apartment where she saw Jessie sitting on her couch with the TV remote control in her hand flipping through channels while toking a blunt. Loopy and Sweet Pea were sitting at the kitchen counter with her bottle of Ace of Spades nearly empty. Shop was wide open inside Kree's home.

"Hola!" Loopy snapped as she poured another glass of cognac. "Your new flat screen TV is on the wall in your bedroom, homegirl."

"Damn," Kree snapped. "I forgot about that!"

"Yo," Loopy said to Sweet Pea as she eased up from her bar stool and dusted her hands. "Help me take this TV down off Kree's wall."

"Don't touch my TV!" Kree laughed. "I'll have your money tomorrow. What y'all doing here this early?"

"You texted and said to make sure Riley was okay," Sweet Pea answered as she sipped a margarita.

"That didn't mean for y'all to come and turn my place into a lounge. Where's Riley? I'm surprised he let you sit in here, Jessie," Kree remarked as she knocked her feet down off the coffee table and began straightening the pillows on her sofa.

"Nahh. That one there, I mean, Riley, Riley done jumped cool with a bitch all of a sudden," Jessie said as she sat up on the sofa. "Watch this here," she added as she whistled for the dog.

Riley came wobbling from the back of the home and sat at Jessie's feet. She leaned down and picked the dog up and placed it in her lap and the dog sat quietly while being petted.

"Aww," Kree sighed. "Y'all did an excellent job taking care of my child."

Loopy and Sweet Pea said nothing as they watched Kree pet the dog in Jessie's lap. They were hoping the switch went smooth, and by all accounts, things were going along quite well.

"I missed you, Riley," Kree said lovingly as she picked the dog up from Jessie's lap. "Did they walk you today, boy," she asked as she nuzzled the dog's nose with hers. "Did they walk you today. Did they—oh my God!" Kree suddenly screamed as she threw the dog down onto her couch.

"What happened?" Jessie asked as she watched the dog yelp as it jumped down from the couch and run to the back of the house.

Kree took off running after the dog. Jessie, Loopy and Sweet Pea all stood at the foot of the hall and watched as she went from room to room searching for the animal. "Where is it? Where is it?" Kree yelled repeatedly.

"What's wrong? It's the same kind of dog," Loopy whispered to Jessie and Sweet Pea as she scratched her head.

"People know they kinfolk, I guess," Jessie reasoned just as Kree emerged from her third bedroom with the dog in her arms.

"What—is—this?" Kree asked she held out the dog before her friends.

"What?" Jessie, Loopy and Sweet Pea said in unison.

"This is not Riley!" Kree yelled. "This isn't my dog! What have you three done with Riley?"

"That is Riley," Loopy retorted. "It's the same dog you left here!"

"Well, unless he went and had a sex change while I was away this isn't my dog!"

"Huh?" Loopy asked dumbfounded.

"This isn't Riley!" Kree yelled as she held the dog up, putting its privates on display. "The balls are missing on this dog! Riley was a male! This isn't a male dog because he doesn't have a set of balls or a dick!"

Loopy, Sweet Pea and Jessie all leaned in for a closer look. "Eh, yo," Jessie laughed. "Y'all mutherfuckas? How in the fuck could y'all two miss that significant detail?"

"What happened to Riley? Where's my dog?" Kree asked as she sat the dog down onto the carpet.

Jessie looked over to Loopy and Sweet Pea and copped a seat on the sofa. "Hey," she laughed as she picked up the remote control, "I was around, but I ain't have shit to do with what happened to Riley's ass."

Kree eyed her friends with a heartbroken look as tears filled her eyes.

"Aww, man. You, you're gonna cry now? She's fixing to cry behind Riley, man. She ain't even had that dog that long," Loopy remarked as she tapped her cousin's elbow.

"We came over and let Riley out a couple of days ago and he was hit by a car," Sweet Pea admitted as she went and stood before Kree. "He's, Riley is a little bit dead," she said somberly.

Kree covered her heart in surprise and gasped. "A little bit dead?" she exclaimed as she began to cry. "How could, how could he be a little bit dead? You couldn't take him to a vet after he was hit?" she asked through tears.

"Your li'l buddy was crushed beyond repair. We came back the next day to move his dead ass, but the city or somebody had already shoveled everything up. Take New Riley and be happy," Jessie said nonchalantly as she flipped through the channels and chomped down on a Snickers bar. "Damn, they ain't got shit on TV tonight."

"You wanna go bowling then?" Loopy asked Jessie.

"Nahh. It's, well, yeah, that's cool. Kree, you feel like going bowling?" Jessie asked as she propped her feet up on Kree's table once more.

Kree eyed her friends in disbelief. They'd told her that her pet had been hit by a car and killed and seemed not to care that she was feeling a sense of loss at this moment. She eyed them harshly for a minute, growing ever angrier as the seconds ticked by before she stormed off, mumbling to herself. "*Ellos quieren matar a mi perro que tengo algo para ellos.*" (They want to kill my dog I got something for them.)

Loopy and Sweet Pea heard a portion of Kree's remark as she passed by the kitchen. They walked from behind the island counter and peeked down the hall just in time to witness Kree trotting into her bedroom.

"Eh, Jessie, you know what Kree said that time?" Sweet Pea asked anxiously.

"Something about her dog," Jessie shrugged as she reclined on the sofa.

"Yeah," Sweet Pea said as she tip toed over to the hallway's threshold. "That was part of it—but I think—yep—she got her gun!" she yelped the moment she saw Kree reenter the hallway with her pistol.

Loopy saw what was up as well. She and Sweet Pea both scurried through the living room. Jessie heard the word 'gun' and she hopped up and followed the Cruz cousins' out to the Durango.

Kree emerged from her hall with her gun in hand, yelling aloud at her friends. "Y'all ain't shit!" she cried. "Thanks for nothing! Thanks for nothing!"

"Sorry about Riley! You don't owe us anything for the TV or the New Riley!" Loopy yelled from behind the steering wheel as she peeled out from in front of Kree's home.

After slamming the door, Kree turned and was headed to her kitchen to fix herself a drink to calm her frayed nerves. She accidently tripped over the new dog and stumbled a bit, but she quickly caught her balance and righted herself. She turned around and eyed the dog with rage. When she saw the animal lying on his back, seemingly begging for a belly rub, however, she couldn't help but to grow warm-hearted. "Aww," she purred as she sat her gun on the coffee table and kneeled before the creature and eyed him with appreciation.

Kree loved pets. She'd had a catering instinct from birth. Some days, like this day, and at this very moment, she would look back on her life and wonder if that inherent nurturing instinct was why she found it so hard to leave Alonzo alone. She'd had several pets back in Brazil, all were canines, and they were all strays. From the first day she'd encountered the wandering puppies, she had never stopped caring for them, until they left on their own. They'd always leave, and each time, she would always be saddened; but there was one particular dog that would always return and Kree would always take him back in and care for him again, knowing he had no place else to go—just as she'd done with Alonzo in times past.

The irony of it all was that Kree had met Alonzo and Riley under similar circumstances. It was cold and cloudy and both were hungry. Kree had found Riley just six months ago digging through her trash in search of food; but had it even been longer since she'd began catering to the helpless soul, she felt as if she wouldn't really miss him being dead, Riley that is.

The feeling was far more different with Alonzo, however; although he'd dogged her out at times, she still had feelings for him and would never wish anything bad on the guy, no matter how many times he'd disappointed her and broken her heart and shattered her dreams of the future she saw with him at the outset. Letting Alonzo go wasn't going to be easy, but it was a decision she knew she had to make if ever her dream of being with Curtis were to come true. She reached out to rub the dog's belly with a contented heart and it was at that moment that she noticed the ring Curtis had given her the day before they left Oregon was not on her finger.

Kree's heart sunk to her stomach as she jumped up and ran to her bedroom to search for the missing piece of jewelry. She searched her closet, her dresser drawers and bathrooms and all the bedrooms. She'd even looked in places where she knew she'd never even set foot upon inside her home as of yet. She then remembered the luggage in the trunk of her car and started for the door. She exited her home leaving the door wide open, walking anxiously and in a frantic state, fumbling her hands and breathing hard. She was halfway to her car when she remembered she'd left her keys inside the house so she turned and grabbed her head and walked slowly back towards her home. Tears filled her eyes and she paused under the overhang. "I can't believe I lost that ring," she cried as she leaned against her threshold with weak knees.

Kree's mind was going in a thousand different places. Deep down inside, she knew she wasn't going to find that ring in her luggage because she'd never taken it off. She didn't believe it had fallen off her finger in her car, which would be the best case scenario at this point. The only other possible places the ring could have been lost outside of her losing it in her car, she knew, was the airport parking lot, the airport itself, or on one of the planes during the return trip, all possibilities that had left her with little hope that she would ever see that ring again.

She walked into her home and grabbed her keys off the night stand as tears began to drip from her eyes. Losing that ring hurt her heart deeply. How could she let Curtis down was her reasoning. She walked out the front door and unlocked her car and turned on the interior light and grabbed a small flashlight from her glove compartment and began searching, all-the-while knowing she was wasting her time. The ring was not in the car and she knew it. She climbed behind the steering wheel and covered her mouth to suppress her anguish, screaming into her hands as tears ran over her fingers.

After calming down several minutes later, Kree started her car and backed out of her driveway and drove back to Saint Louis International. She paid to get into the parking lot where she had her car parked and pulled up to the slot and looked around to no avail. The walk through the terminal had made her dizzy. The ring was not in the airport and it wasn't in the parking lot, she'd simply misplaced it, and didn't know where. She left the airport and headed back home in a trance. That ring meant the world to her and she was mad at herself for being so careless. *I can't tell him. He's going to think I took everything in Oregon for granted.* Kree said to herself as she pulled back into her driveway.

She turned the car off and eased out of the seat in a daze and went and opened her trunk. She grabbed her two suitcases and began wheeling them to the bedroom where she unpacked her luggage slowly, running her hands over every item of clothing before shaking it out to make sure the ring wasn't lodged into the fabric.

When her luggage was unpacked, Kree lay amongst her clothes atop her comforter and just cried. A perfect trip had been ruined. She hadn't the heart to tell Curtis she'd lost that ring, and she was even madder at herself for doing so, disappointed in fact. She decided that she would keep what had happened a secret from Curtis and replace the ring as soon as possible. All she had to do was get her lover to tell her where he'd purchased the ring; which may require her to have to lie. She squinted her eyes and her lips trembled, hurt over what she would have to do to replace the ring, but she feared Curtis getting upset at her above all else. She didn't want to let him down by telling him she'd lost the ring he'd given to her after she'd had it for only one day. Distraught over the loss of her cherished item, Kree rolled over onto her stomach and cried herself to sleep as New Riley lay at her side.

CHAPTER TWELVE
BREAKING A HABIT

It was now early May of 2007, a couple of weeks after Kree's trip to Oregon and the events that had transpired with her pet dog and the lost ring. She was waiting on Kantrell to close up shop as the sun began to set on the city of the Saint Louis on a Thursday evening. The spunky owner of *Bangin' Heads* was going about her business with a smile on her face as she sang along with Deborah Cox's song *Stranger in My House*. Kantrell had gotten some good-loving last night, and she was looking forward to another rendezvous with Malik Gomez, her friend with benefits, once she closed shop.

"Ain't no stranger in my house right about now, Kree," Kantrell said aloud inside the empty shop while straightening aerosol cans along the counter at different stations, her way of starting a conversation. "Oooh oui! Can't wait to leave here tonight and get back to it! Malik blew my back out last night and damn near got me sprung, but he'll never know that shit with his good-cooking ass!"

"I can't wait until I'm able to go home to my man every night," Kree said as she bobbed her head to the music. "And it won't be long."

"Yeah? How soon before that happens?" Kantrell asked as she sprayed glass cleaner on the mirror that spanned the entire length of the marble counter behind the stations. "Why you sittin' there, how 'bout grabbing some napkins and helping me clean this mirror so we can get outta here."

Kree slid from her chair and unrolled a few paper towels and began polishing the mirror. Kantrell looked over to her friend, watching her as she wiped the glass in obvious deep thought. Ever since Kree had returned from her trip to Oregon she'd been behaving differently in Kantrell's eyes. She'd seemed to mature a little and had become more focused. Whenever she talked about the trip her eyes would light up. She talked of Curtis often, more than she'd ever had in her life. Kantrell knew Kree's excitement wasn't just because of the trip she'd taken with Curtis, however; there was more, much more—and she wanted to know everything.

"What's on your mind?" Kantrell asked as she placed the glass cleaner underneath one of the cabinets. "How're things going with you and Curtis?"

"Curtis and I are fine," Kree smiled as she pulled a trash bag out of a small bin and tied the top into a knot. "I've met up with him over to Embassy Suites once since we've returned from Oregon, but I was so nervous, girl, hoping he didn't ask me where that ring was. I was going to tell him the next time we got together, which was supposed to be a week ago, but he cancelled because he told me he's in the process of talking to his lawyer to see what kind of settlement would come from his divorce so we're only texting now."

"Kree!" Kantrell said in a high-pitched voice as she shuffled her feet across the floor and gave her a tight hug. "He's really going to go all the way with you, girl!"

"Yes he is!" Kree screamed happily as she ran and hopped into a salon chair and twirled around in a circle with her arms in the air. "It's like a dream come true, Kantrell!"

"Now if it was me, you know I would kill your ass dead, right?" Kantrell said as she placed a hand on her hip and pointed at Kree. "Not because it's you, or somebody like you," she said matter-of-factly as she eyed Kree. "But I'd be like, 'I put all these years into this marriage and you gone leave me for somebody else?' I wonder how his wife gone take that news. He gone tell her about you? Y'all gone ever meet?"

"He said he didn't want for me and his wife to meet, but he's going to take me to meet his family down in Thayer, Missouri after the divorce. I don't think his wife would want to meet me," Kree said as the chair she was spinning in slowed to a halt. "I wouldn't wanna do anything like that. Kantrell, if you were married and your husband were to leave you for someone else, would you want to meet the person he left you for?"

"After hearing what I'm hearing today? And witnessing the entire thing go down over the past nine months with you and Curtis? Yes!" Kantrell replied as she walked into the lobby area and turned off the TVs and dimmed the lights.

"Why?" Kree asked as she spun around in the chair. "Why would you want to meet the one person responsible for ruining your marriage?"

"I would wanna know what was so mutherfuckin' good that he decided to up and leave my ass," Kantrell responded aggressively as she stepped back into the work area. "I know good and well I can compete with just about anybody. I own my own business, got my own house, got two cars *and* money. What man wouldn't want me? So if he was to leave? Yes! I would wanna know who the cow is because she'd better be a bad somebody. She better be up there with Mariah Carey or Alicia Keys or some other bitch along those lines because it ain't too many women out here that can keep up with Kantrell, baby, trust me."

"I guess I just can't imagine Curtis doing that to me. I can't picture him leaving me ever after his divorce." Kree said as she crossed he legs and stared up into the ceiling.

"You done shed some light on a whole lotta shit when it comes to certain men, Kree," Kantrell said as she grabbed her purse and the keys to her 2007 Cadillac Escalade off the counter. "I'm happy for you, though. I don't like how it's going down really, but you found what I know you've been looking for ever since I've known you. You found your true love. And seeing you happy, makes me happy for you."

"Thank you, Kantrell," Kree said as she hopped up from the chair went to hug her.

"Go on with all that mushy stuff, now," Kantrell said as she fanned Kree off. "I'm still pissed at your ass for stealing somebody's husband. I told you your ass was shysty."

"I'm not shysty nor did I steal Curtis," Kree retorted as she trotted over to the counter and turned off the vanity lights. "I told you how the two of us met and what happened afterwards."

"Umm, hmm, but what didn't happen the day y'all two ran into one another was you leaving that man alone when you found out he was married, Kree Devereaux." Kantrell said as she approached the wall opposite the work stations. "Stand by the door so I can set the alarm."

"Curtis looked at me first. And he said he would ask me out. That was an open door."

"An open door you didn't have to walk through, though, Kree," Kantrell said while activating the alarm. "But fuck that. He made that decision to step out on his wife. And if you working it like that, sister girl, then by all means go and get your man," Kantrell said as she scampered towards the front door.

"That's what I'm going to do," Kree said as she unlocked the door and held it open for Kantrell. "I understand all you're saying, too. Am I wrong really?"

"It's not about right or wrong anymore, Kree," Kantrell said, staring her in the eyes with a smile on her face as she locked up her salon. "Right now? It's about real love. You two have something special in this world. We can't control who we fall in love with. Some loves are worth letting go. Alonzo," she said as she tapped the side of Kree's temple in hopes of tapping some sense into her skull.

"Trust me," Kree replied through laughter as she raised her hands, "I know exactly what you mean, Kantrell. But it's not so easy."

"Whether it's easy or not, Kree," Kantrell stated as she eyed her friend sternly. "What you're up against, baby girl? In order for you to move forward in your life and achieve what it is that you've been yearning for? You must say good-bye to old love, in order to gain that new and lasting love. Curtis really loves you. If he's actually doing what he says? He truly loves you, Kree. And knowing you? That's a dream worth holding to. I really do hope and pray that y'all live happily ever after."

"That means a lot to me," Kree said sincerely as she stared Kantrell in the eyes. "Coming from you? That really means a lot to me. Thank you."

Kantrell smiled and closed her eyes briefly. "You wanna go have a drink to celebrate?" she then asked.

"No, thanks. I think, well, I still have one thing that's troubling me," Kree said as she and Kantrell walked under the parking lot lights towards their vehicles.

"Is this about that ring you lost?"

"Yeah." Kree replied shamefully.

"Look at that there," Kantrell said as she paused and placed her hands on her hips and shook her head from side to side while staring Kree down. "You're standing there bowing your head because you know you wrong, Kree. I told you to tell that man that you lost his ring before he finds out on his own and he really be upset. Why you didn't take my advice on that matter?"

"I was scared. I think I'm going to just replace it. I just have to get him to tell me where he bought the ring from," Kree responded as she and Kantrell resumed walking.

"Don't be scared, Kree. From what you tell me, that man loves you. If you're thinking he gone leave you over that ring you're wrong. And if he does, well I guess he wouldn't have loved you as much as you thought he did."

"You speak the truth," Kree replied as she and Kantrell neared their vehicles, which were parked side by side. "But I think I'll just ask him where he got the ring from and tell him I want the ring cleaned and the diamond polished. Then I'll buy another one. I'll tell him the truth some time later."

"I think you should tell him upfront. You don't wanna go into a full commitment with Curtis hiding anything. If you don't take any more advice from me, take this advice and tell Curtis as soon as possible that you lost that ring." Kantrell said as she unlocked her doors to her Escalade with the remote.

Kree did the same to her car and she and Kantrell left the near empty parking lot and went their separate ways. A couple of things were troubling Kree on this night. For one, she had to get Curtis to tell her where he'd gotten the ring. Kantrell may have had a good point about telling him upfront, but Curtis was in the process of divorcing his wife and she didn't want to put anything outside of that delicate procedure in front of him. Second, she wanted to end things with Alonzo and Sean. The dream of her and Curtis having an open relationship was within reach and she didn't want anything to stop it from becoming a reality.

Kree perked up after reflecting on her future as she drove home. She grabbed her cell phone and was dialing Jessie's number when her phone suddenly rang. She eyed Alonzo's number on the screen and answered. "Mister Milton," she said matter-of-factly.

"Stop by the studio," Alonzo replied seriously.

"For what?" Kree asked as wheeled her ride through the city streets.

"I wanna discuss something with you tonight. Some plans for you and I."

"I have some things I have to tell you, too, Alonzo. Give me a few minutes and I'll be there and we can talk." Kree said as she began making her way over to Soulard, where Alonzo's studio was located.

Alonzo licked his lips and smiled as he hung up the phone. He was feeling Kree to the fullest and had good news to share about his future dealings with her. He went about straightening the studio as he toked on a blunt while gathering his thoughts.

It took Kree just over twenty minutes to reach Alonzo's studio. She pulled over to the curb on the darkened block, just down from the building and sat in the car texting Alonzo to let him know she'd arrived, paying no attention to the white cargo van cruising past her car and continuing on up the street. Alonzo opened the single glass door a few seconds later and Kree exited her ride and walked towards the entrance.

Once Kree entered, Alonzo locked the door and turned to face her with a warm smile on his face. "We meet again," he said softly.

"Yes we do," Kree responded in kind as her eyes focused in on double doors where light was emanating from the hall.

The lights in the front of the studio were all off; and only a few hall lights leading to the studio were operating, creating two silhouettes in the front office. Kree eyed Alonzo as she walked past him, headed towards the lighted hall, but Alonzo had ceased her movements by reaching out and grabbing her left arm.

Kree slowed her stroll when Alonzo tugged on her arm and she looked back at him. He, in turn, looked down upon her in admiration as she turned to face him, her pearly whites clearly visible, even in the dim light. She was dressed in a black, silk all-in-one knee-length dress and wore a pair of knee-length black-heeled boots. Her wavy, black hair was pinned up, exposing her neck and earlobes, which were adorned with diamond-drop earrings that twinkled in the sparsely-lit studio office. She began walking backwards as Alonzo pressed his body to hers, pinning her against the wall just before the lighted hallway.

Kree wrapped her arms around Alonzo's waist and tilted her head, knowing what was to come. This was only the third time, but she couldn't deny the fact that kissing Alonzo excited her and left her craving more of him. With his body pressed firmly against hers, Alonzo grabbed Kree's hands and raised them above her head and pinned her hands to the wall as he drove his tongue down her throat. Kree couldn't resist. She raised her left leg and clamped it around Alonzo's back. She then raised her right leg and did the same, wrapping it around Alonzo as she forced her arms forward in order to wrap them around his neck.

Alonzo gripped Kree's rear end, raising her dress above her waist in the process as he moved away from the wall, carrying her in his arms down the dimly lit hall leading to his studio. A wave of guilt hit Kree at that moment. She opened her eyes and looked around, having been hit a dose of reality. The last time she had entered Alonzo's studio she'd succumbed to temptation. She knew if she were to continue on, she and Alonzo would repeat the experience once again and go even further. What was she doing? She had a man that loved her in Curtis and she was determined not cheat on him.

"Alonzo wait," Kree said as she began squirming in his arms.

"What's the matter?" Alonzo asked as he lowered her back onto her feet.

"I can't do this. This isn't what I've come here for. I really had something I wanted to say to you," Kree said as she hurried back into the main office. "Where's the lights?" she asked anxiously as she ran her hands along the walls inside the room.

Alonzo walked into the office and turned on the lights. "Calm down, baby. Calm down," he comforted. "What you wanted to tell me then?" he asked as he walked past Kree and leaned back on the desk.

"I'm in love with someone else. You and I, we were good, I almost considered giving us second try, but I don't think you and I getting back together is a good idea." Kree said as she removed hanging curls from her face.

"You come way over here to tell me that? That's your news?" Alonzo asked disappointedly as he stood up from the desk. "That's nothing close to what I was gonna say, Kree."

"What were you going to say to me?" Kree asked as she walked over and stood before Alonzo.

"I was gone ask you if you wanted to go the movies or something. You and I go out together. I'm ready now. "

Kree was far beyond 'movies or something' at this point in her life. Curtis had shown her an entirely different world and had given her a new outlook on her life. She'd sampled real love now; and it was a love she did not want to loose herself from. Alonzo was too little, too late in her eyes. "That's a sweet offer," she placated. "But I want more in a relationship now—and with him I have want I want with who I want."

"I guess I lost you forever, huh?" Alonzo asked in a defeated tone as he looked to the floor. "I fucked up."

"We just weren't ready," Kree said as she stepped closer to Alonzo and touched his hands. "We tried to make it work, but someone else's love got in the way and I don't wanna let it go now."

"You really come a long way, Kree," Alonzo said seriously as he stared into her eyes while tenderly rubbing his thumbs across the back of her hands. "You not that naïve person I met back in two thousand four any more, you grown now. You a woman. A woman who knows what she wants and ain't afraid to go after it. I respect that to the fullest."

"Thank you for understanding. You've grown into a man that would make any woman happy," Kree said as she leaned in and hugged Alonzo tightly. She then leaned back and ran her hands over his shoulders before backing away and looking over towards the front door.

Alonzo sensed Kree was ready to leave so he walked over and unlocked the door to let her out. "I love you," he admitted as he ran his hands through Kree's hair. "I been fighting it for so long, but, I, I just have to admit it. I love you, girl."

Kree turned back to Alonzo and looked deep into his eyes and realized he was telling the truth. She'd always cared for him, and had indeed loved him once upon a time; but she'd be lying if she were to say she loved Alonzo at this point in time. Her heart and soul wanted to be with Curtis. Had been since the day she'd met the man. No one could replace him now. Not even her first love. What she had with Alonzo early on had been more lust than love she now understood. The real love was with Curtis and it was where she wanted to be. She ran her hand across Alonzo's heart as tears began to flow down her cheeks. "I'm sorry," she cried as she turned and pushed the door open.

"Kree," Alonzo said lowly. "Don't leave yet. At least, at least stay for a little while longer and kick it with me one more time."

"What we had will never be forgotten," Kree said softly as tears streamed down her face. "This is something I have to do. Understand that, please."

"Kree," Alonzo pleaded. "You know I would never hurt you. Just stay for a while."

"I can't," Kree responded as she stepped out onto the sidewalk. "You are true to yourself now, Alonzo, and that is what matters here," she said through heart-felt conviction.

"Fuck it then," Alonzo said with a hint of anger. "Do what you do."

Kree was saddened at that moment. She'd wanted things to end amicably with her and Alonzo. His last remark was brushed off and chalked up to his coming out on the losing end of the battle for her heart. She pressed her hand to her lips and kissed her fingers and touched Alonzo's lips.

Alonzo swatted her hand away from his face and pulled the studio door closed without saying a word. Kree stared at the tinted window on the door as she wiped tears from her eyes. It was not the ending she had hoped for. "Good-bye love," she said aloud before she turned and walked away, never looking back, but all-the-while hoping and praying that everything in Alonzo's life would work out for the better.

CHAPTER THIRTEEN
IT CAME TO A HEAD

"Bitch gone pull a gun on me? I'm a show her ass," Jessie said as she rode with Loopy and Sweet Pea through Union Square Plaza Shopping Center's parking lot, just minutes after Kree had left Alonzo's studio.

It had been just over a month since Chastity had entered Fox Park and rode up on Jessie after she let it be known that she had video footage of the two having sex. Jessie had learned that the people riding with Chastity were her brother and her two aunts via texts with Chastity. They were looking to jump Jessie, she knew, that night, but she'd gotten away. Now it was the month of May and she was looking for payback. She and the Cruz cousins were riding in the 2001 four door Buick Skylark that they'd rented from Dibble back in Fox Park and they were on the prowl. Jessie had called the store where Chastity worked from a payphone earlier and learned that she had come in early, and that meant she would be getting off about an hour before the mall closed.

The three circled the parking lot while toking on blunts and sipping tequila. "How you wanna handle this?" Loopy asked from the front passenger seat as she blew smoke from her lungs, a chrome .9mm Beretta resting in her lap.

"Eh, put that gun up," Jessie said. "It ain't that serious."

Loopy looked over to Sweet Pea and both cousins shook their heads somberly.

"You can't be serious," Sweet Pea said as she looked back at Jessie. "Either Chastity or someone with her pulled a gun on you. How could it not be that serious?"

"I don't wanna kill the girl, Donatella," Jessie snapped from the backseat. "I just wanna knock her white ass the fuck out one good time for disrespecting me."

"You might wanna rethink this," Sweet Pea said as she wheeled the car down a long aisle that was sparsely-filled with parked cars. "She hasn't been back in Fox Park since then and you said you haven't texted her in three weeks now."

"You can't sleep on hoes like that, though." Jessie said as she scanned the parking lot. "See, people like Chastity? You gotta let 'em know you ain't afraid of they shit. She gone learn I ain't the one and to stay the fuck away from me forever. There go her ride right there. Park down from that li'l purple minivan."

Sweet Pea went on and parked the next row over and the three females now had a clear view of Chastity's minivan. Forty-five minutes before the mall closed, Chastity exited one of the entrances and made her way over to her ride where she climbed inside and started the engine.

Sweet Pea had Chastity in her sights the whole time. When she back out of her parking slot, she pulled forward and tailed Chastity towards and exits. Being that the mall was close to its closing time, there weren't many cars or shoppers around. It was also dark at the entrance Chastity was pulling up to. She paused at the red light and was waiting to make a left turn when she felt a bump from the rear of her minivan. She turned around and saw a car right up on her bumper. "Oh my God," she sighed. "How could they not see me?" she questioned as she placed her vehicle into park and opened the door.

The moment Jessie saw Chastity exiting her minivan, she slid over to the driver's side and hopped out the back of the Skylark and ran up on her. It didn't take Chastity long to realize she'd been set up. She ran back to her minivan and came up from under the driver's seat with a black .22 semi-automatic. She aimed it and squeezed the trigger just as Jessie ran up her.

The gun didn't fire, however; and Jessie was able to run up on Chastity and knock her down with a balled up fist to the face. Chastity was so panicked she'd forgotten to take the gun off safety before she pulled the trigger. She lay on the asphalt beside her car screaming to the top of her lungs while covering her face.

"Shut up, bitch!" Jessie hissed as she began kicking and stomping Chastity.

Sweet Pea and Loopy were standing by watching for a few seconds until they noticed several people exiting their cars with cell phones. Loopy ran over and picked up Chastity's gun. "Yo, let's be out. They got witnesses now," she said calmly as she tugged on Jessie's t-shirt.

"I ain't done with this hoe! I'm a whip that ass tonight!" Jessie yelled as she leaned over and punched Chastity in the face with her bare knuckles.

"People watching!" Loopy said under her breath, steadily pulling Jessie away from the scene.

"Jessie! Jessie no!" Chastity screamed as she kicked her legs up into the air while flailing about on the ground.

"Shit was good a month ago, huh, bitch? Fuck you!" Jessie yelled angrily as she pulled away from Loopy's grip and ran up and kicked Chastity in the face. A muffled, cracking sound was heard by Jessie and Chastity's body began twitching uncontrollably as she lay on the asphalt.

"Ohh, fuck," Jessie gasped as she backed away from Chastity while staring down at her trembling body.

Loopy stepped forth and knelt down beside Chastity for a closer look. Blood was leaking from her ears and she was vomiting uncontrollably. It was at that moment that Jessie, Loopy and Sweet Pea realized that what was only meant to be a beat down for get-back had morphed into something far more serious. The three ran back to the Skylark and fled the scene, leaving behind several onlookers who'd witnessed the melee to help the woman who'd been assaulted.

****

Meanwhile, back inside AMP Studios, Alonzo was in the front office on the phone talking to Jay-D, telling him about his upcoming trip to Atlanta where he was scheduled to close the deal with Dirty Deeds.

"We gone be there for that contract signing, ya' feel me?" Jay-D told Alonzo.

"Jay, I was thinking I could do this solo, you know? I mean, I got everything under control, my nig." Alonzo said as he went and peeked out the tinted window on the front door. "Where you at," he asked as he scanned the block. "You comin' through tonight?"

"Nahh, I'm not coming through there tonight because I'm outta town handlin' some other business right now. I be back the day after tomorrow," Jay-D replied. "What's the reason you don't wanna us to make that trip, though? The check going to my label anyway."

"Yeah, but that label was once mines," Alonzo retorted. "Dirty Deeds is dealing with *me*, son. Deal don't happen without me."

Jay-D was parked at the end of Alonzo's street in a white cargo van, although he'd told him he was out of town. A chrome .44 automatic was resting in his lap as he sat behind the steering wheel. His niece Nancy was beside him and his brother Dooney was in the cargo bay with an AR-15 assault rifle resting in his lap and an AK-47 on his side.

Jay-D had had enough of Alonzo. Word had gotten back to him that Alonzo was back on cocaine. More than that, he had an engineer from the college near his home come into the studio and pull up the music Alonzo claimed he was producing, and the only thing the student could ever pull up were the same five tracks Alonzo had been playing for him for weeks. And the last one he did, which was a sample of Li'l Wayne's song *Lollipop* , was the wackest thing Jay-D had ever heard in his life.

The deadline with Dirty Deeds was near and Jay-D knew Alonzo wasn't going to have the album ready so he'd washed his hands with the situation. He was preparing to close AMP Studios, take the quarter million dollar hit, and relocate the business to a night club in Saint Charles that his bosses were preparing to open in a year or so. He could put the studio inside the club when it opened up, and by then, the heat of his immediate actions concerning AMP would've been blown over.

"Look," Jay-D said, going along with Alonzo's lie. "When you, what day you going to Atlanta?"

"It's like three or four weeks from now. The first part of June." Alonzo answered. Alonzo knew he and Jay-D were at odds and things would possibly come to a head. He wasn't going to take any chances with his life because he knew Jay-D was the type to kill over his money. He tucked a .45 semi-automatic into his waistband and then set about locking up the studio with the phone pressed to his ear.

"Okay. Let me know the official date." Jay-D remarked casually as he eyed the studio entrance.

"Aite," Alonzo said and then ended the call.

"You seen that shit earlier?" Jay-D's niece, fifteen year-old Nancy Cottonwood, snapped from the passenger seat of the van the moment her uncle hung up the phone. "Kree kissed her hand and put her hand to Alonzo lips! They fucking! I told y'all that shit the day she was in there but y'all didn't believe me," she dragged. "Y'all gone learn to trust what I say—trust me, baby!" she sassed through closed eyes as she rolled her neck.

"Okay, you called that," nineteen year-old Dooney said from the cargo bay as he loaded bullet shells into an extra banana clip, a smile planted across his chubby, light-skinned face as he chewed on a wallop of Big League Chew bubble gum. "That nigga Alonzo wild as the fuck," he laughed.

"That's how it be happenin', though," Nancy quipped. "It be

the ones who you least expect. Everybody know about Kree. But Alonzo? He *should* get popped up for that shit he was doing."

"Hold up," Jay-D said as he looked over to his niece and laughed. "You think we after Alonzo because of who he fucking with? I don't give a fuck what that nigga do or who he do it with. That boy going to the morgue because he done laid up there and fucked up—"

"My daddy two hundred and fifty thousand dollars and ain't got Narshea 'nem shit ready for they compilation album plus he been lying and stealing from our record label boom there it is!" Nancy said in one breath.

"Yep that 'bout sum it up," Dooney chuckled as he blew gun powder from the top of the cartridge and loaded it into an AK-47. "Yo, Jay you want this chopper?" he asked.

"Nah," Jay-D said as he saw the lights in the office go dark. "I got this four-four up here in my lap—but I ain't gone need it if you let loose with that A-R like you supposed to. Check it, the lights just went out so he should be comin' out soon."

"Good, I'm ready to pop this punk so I can finish whippin' Nancy ass on the PlayStation back at the crib." Dooney said nonchalantly as he racked the AR-15.

"This your first mark, li'l brother. I got the go 'head from Dawk and Eddie, and daddy said don't let him down. When we done we gone take this van over to Malik shop in Maplewood and pick up his Benz and hold it for a couple of days."

"Cool. And on the real? That boy done, Jay dog," Dooney sighed nonchalantly.

"We gone see. When Nancy pull that door open handle your biz like a real nigga should."

"Let me shoot his ass, too!" Nancy exclaimed as she bounced in her seat. She then broke out into song. "*'Bouta to pop Alonnnzooo…'bouta pop Alonnnzooo,*" she sang as she snapped her fingers. "*'Bouta pop Alonnnzooo…'cause he be bussin' people bootyy hole.*"

Jay-D and Dooney laughed at Nancy's song as the two took

their respective weapons off safety. "I told you it's not about that," Jay-D chuckled as he turned down the radio.

"Whatever," Nancy said as she focused in on the studio's front door. "I hope he come on so we can get this over with. 'Cause Dooney back there talking shit. I been kickin' his all day on NBA 2K. Can we get some fried fish from Malik's Grill after we murk this dude, Jay-D?" she then asked.

Jay-D didn't answer Nancy. He sat watching the front door of the studio with a cold, dead stare. He could smell a murder coming on. Minutes after Nancy had finished speaking, the studio door opened, and Jay-D spied Alonzo as he exited the building and walked over to his BMW. He eyed Alonzo like a hungry preying wolf as he unlocked the doors and climbed inside his BMW.

Alonzo had no clue he was being stalked. He reached down into his console and popped two ecstasy pills into his mouth and snorted a line of cocaine before pulling off. He reached the end of the block and was preparing to make a left turn when a white van pulled up with the side door open.

Alonzo didn't know what was going down, but he smelled death in the air all of a sudden when he eyed a ski-masked bandit pointing a large rifle at him. He pressed the gas and turned the steering to his right. The car lurched forward just as whomever it was kneeling in the open bay of the van opened fire with a semi-automatic rifle. The windows and tires on Alonzo's car shattered and burst. Bullets penetrated the driver's side door and flew through the shattered windows.

Alonzo was struck multiple times in the face and on his left side. He slumped over into the passenger seat as the car sped out of control through the intersection and slammed into a parked car as the white van sped off the scene into the darkness of the city as faint sirens began to be heard off in the distance under the city lights.

****

Kree had left Alonzo's studio just minutes earlier. She was wondering where all the police cars were headed to as she left the neighborhood of Soulard. Her phone vibrated and she looked down and saw that she had a text from Curtis. A simple one saying he loved her, which made her smile outwardly. Kree then had a thought. Given the text, she decided to text Curtis back immediately as she drove. *I love and miss you too baby. Where did you get this ring? I want to take it back to the jeweler and have it cleaned and polished. It's dirty.*

Elleard Heffern in Clayton.

Thnx love. I will show it to you next time.

TTYL

K

Kree's plan to replace the ring had been resolved with seeming ease. She knew from observation that the ring was worth at least three-thousand dollars, but it was money she was willing to spend if only to keep Curtis from finding out that she'd ever lost the ring in the first place. She made her way home and was exiting her car when her phone rung. She knew exactly who was calling because she had a special ring tone set up for this particular person and she knew what he wanted.

"I've been holding out so long...I've been sleeping all alone...lord I miss you..." Kree let the lyrics to the Rolling Stones' song *I Miss You* play out for a few seconds, snapping her fingers and dancing to the tune while doing an updated version of the Cabbage Patch before she picked up. "Hello?" she said with a smile as she opened her door and let New Riley out to use the grass.

"Hey, beautiful!" Sean said jubilantly with the same Rolling Stones song blaring in the background.

"Good evening, Mister Bradsworth," Kree responded as she placed a finger to her ear in order to hear the man speaking.

"I am having a party all by myself and you're, you're invited to come and, shmuck me—excuse me," Sean laughed over the music. "Not shmuck me, fuck me!"

"You are a shmuck," Kree sassed.

"Don't you be so cruel, now, young lady! Save it for when you get here!"

Kree had been aiming to talk to Sean for some time now in order to end their business relationship and she now saw the perfect opportunity. "I'm going to come there now. There's something I have to tell you."

"Oooh, a confession." Sean remarked. "I'll be waiting, dear."

****

"Police are said to be looking for three suspects in the brutal beating that left a woman with two fractured ribs and a *broken neck* of all things," the news reporter emphasized as she gave details on an attack that had taken place at an entrance leading to Union Square Plaza Shopping Center. "Video footage shows three suspects fleeing the scene in what witnesses said was an older model Chrysler or Buick. Details are scant, but the victim will survive and make a complete recovery."

"This has got to be some of the dumbest shit you three could have ever done in your lives," sixteen year-old Peppi Vargas told Jessie, Sweet Pea and Loopy as the four of them, along with Peppi's friend, Simone Cortez, stood in a semi-circle around the TV inside Peppi's apartment staring at the flat screen TV.

Simone shook her head somberly. "And the bitch gone live, too. I put everything on the fact that she gone tell on your ass, Jessie," she said as she pointed at the TV screen.

"Shit, she probably done already told the law who did it," Peppi remarked as she shook her head in disbelief while eyeing her three friends. "And if they identify that car? You best believe that crack head mutherfucka Dibble gone tell it all."

Jessie, Sweet Pea and Loopy had nothing to say. A woman's neck had been broken. Although Sweet Pea and Loopy hadn't touched Chastity, they were on the scene, Loopy had even stolen her gun. She knew she had to get rid of it immediately now. The bigger problem, however, was the fact that she and Sweet Pea was accessory to the fact and could be charged with anything from attempted murder to simple assault. Whatever charges Jessie was hit with, Sweet Pea and Loopy would be charged with the same thing. Loopy and Sweet Pea had no intention on rolling over on Jessie, however; whatever the outcome, the three were all in it together now.

"How y'all gone play this out?" Pepper asked the three. "Because one way or the other? Somebody gettin' charged for this here."

"Fuck it, man," Jessie said, throwing up her arms. "I'm just gone deal with it as it comes. I ain't turning myself in, though. And Sweet Pea and Loopy ain't have nothing to do with this here. It's all on me," she snapped as she flopped down on the couch.

"That's why you gotta be silencing them hoes," Simone said as she bumped her fists together while staring at Jessie. "We asked you if you wanted us to handle that for ya', but nooo," she sang. "You wanna go and beat a bitch damn near to death," she ended through laughter.

"I swear on everything I love I never meant to hurt that woman that bad," Jessie said as she wrung her hands anxiously.

"The judge not gone won't hear that, though." Sweet Pea remarked. "We done fucked up big time, y'all."

"Pshh! Ya' think?" Simone sassed. "I feel for y'all, but I'm glad I'm not in none of y'all shoes tonight. Might as well get high and..." Simone's voice trailed off at that moment as she had no more to say. Her friends were caught up in a serious situation that could put them behind bars for a long time over something stupid and she felt for them.

"They had a dude back here, he got major time on a plea bargain for attempted murder," Pepper said as she walked into the kitchen and poured herself a glass of cognac. "Now, on the low end, simple assault might get ya' two years, but this here serious. Y'all could be looking at a forty year sentence."

"Forty years?" Jessie, Loopy and Sweet Pea exclaimed in unison.

"Don't scare 'em, Pepper," Simone laughed.

"I'm for real though, Simone. Jessie? Y'all three gone have to lay low if y'all don't wanna go to jail for a long time."

"How laying low gone keep us from being charged with attempted murder? Dammit, man!" Jessie yelled as she leaned forward and ran her hands through her hair in frustration.

"Because the more time pass, the more this gone cool off," Pepper stated. "The judge might just look at it like y'all got into a lover's spat or something and it was a accident and hit you with simple assault. That's like two years at the most. We all know Loopy and Sweet Pea ain't gone say nothing if they get questioned so that's not even a factor. It'll be your word against hers. As long as Loopy and Sweet Pea don't say nothing about what happened, a good lawyer can beat that attempted murder charge for you, for real."

Jessie was shocked over the whole ordeal. It was no doubt in her mind that Chastity would rat her out the moment she was able to do so, if she hadn't already, and she would soon be facing serious charges. What those charges were remained to be seen, but in the time she had remaining, Jessie was going to take Pepper's advice and lay low and try and gather as much money as she could in order to be able make bail and fight the charges in court.

In the immediate future, though, Jessie knew she needed a place to hide out. She knew Loopy and Sweet Pea would duck off over to their aunt's house in East Saint Louis, but she didn't want to crowd them; and if she were caught there by the law, her friends would be thrust into the situation as well. As of now, Sweet Pea and Loopy could deny that they were ever on the scene and Jessie wanted to keep them in the clear. The crew sat and drank and smoked for a while and after a couple of hours, Jessie asked Sweet Pea and Loopy to take her to a place she felt she could hide out for a while.

****

"Ooohh! You big dick mutherfucka! Beat it up, esse! Beat it up!" Kantrell screamed, her face planted down into her mattress and her ass high in the air.

That good-good was back in Kantrell's life in the early morning hours of Friday morning. Her sex partner, twenty-two year-old Malik Gomez, a bona fide hustler from Fox Park who ran with Jay-D, was laying it down right, gripping her hips and pulling her back onto his rigid pole while pounding her pussy relentlessly. Kantrell was thrusting back hard and squeezing Malik's dick with her vaginal muscles, meeting his every stroke while trying her best to milk all the juice from his shaft. The two had perfect rhythm going atop Kantrell's king-sized mattress and silk sheets. They'd smoked a blunt and downed a half fifth of Grey Goose and were lost in lust.

"*¡ Maldita sea, esto un apretado coño! ¡Me encanta, Kantrell!*" (Damn, this a tight pussy! I love it, Kantrell!) Malik said as he began slapping Kantrell's ass while stroking her deeply.

"Yes, Jesus," Kantrell moaned in a raspy voice as she rose up and leaned back and kissed Malik passionately.

Malik pushed Kantrell flat onto her stomach and lay on her back and it felt as if his dick was touching her spine as he pistoned in and out of her vagina as if he were doing push-ups.

"Un-fuckin—oh my god! Maliiikkk," Kantrell sang.

"Come on!" Malik demanded as he slapped Kantrell's cheeks with his free hand. "You know you want to, mami! Come for me, huh? You're gonna come for me?"

"Yes!"

Kantrell was in the middle of one the most intense orgasms ever when loud knocking and door bell ringing began filling her home.

Malik jumped up immediately and grabbed his Mac-10 laying beside the bed.

Kantrell rolled over and grabbed her Glock .40 off the night stand.

The two stood opposite one another on either side of the bed breathing hard and staring at the bedroom door, ready for whatever.

"Who the fuck is that," Malik asked under his breath.

"Fuck I'm supposed to know? Some, somebody followed you over here or something?" Kantrell whispered.

"Nobody knows about us. If this was a kick door they would not come knocking. Let's go and check it out together," Malik whispered back.

Kantrell waved her gun and nodded her head towards her bedroom door, signaling for Malik to go first as she donned a silk robe and racked her pistol.

Malik eased out of the bedroom butt-naked and stood beside the door. "Who?"

"This Jessie!"

Kantrell rolled her eyes and waved Malik off. "No this bitch didn't," she said under her breath as she cracked the chained door, Malik standing just out of sight with his Mac-10 ready to let loose.

The look in Jessie's eyes let Kantrell know something fucked up had gone down. "Bitch, have you lost your mind coming to my shit this time of morning?"

"Yo, I need a place to hide out for a minute."

Kantrell reared back and eyed Jessie like she was stupid. "You is interrupting my dick time, bitch," she hissed.

"I'm sorry," Jessie pleaded. "I almost killed somebody tonight and the law might be looking for me. Just give me a couple of days to sort everything out."

Kantrell closed her eyes and shook her head in disbelief. Jessie stayed in some bullshit, and now she was at her door with the foolishness. She slammed the door shut and removed the chain. "What the fuck happened?" she asked as she stepped aside and let Jessie into her home.

"This lady I made pay for my—" Jessie stopped talking when she saw Malik standing in the foyer butt-naked. "What's up, big homie? You be in Fox Park and shit! Put that big mutherfucka up before you kill a bitch," she said, pointing to Malik's semi-hard member.

"Malik, let me and this girl talk for a minute," Kantrell requested.

When Malik cleared out, Kantrell and Jessie sat in the living room where Jessie ran everything down after she had waved Sweet Pea and Loopy off. Kantrell was angry Jessie had brought her bullshit into her home, but she couldn't, or wouldn't deny her friend a place to hide out. "Two days, hoe," she said before she got up. "Wait here."

Kantrell returned a few minutes later with a robe and fresh towels. "Use the bathroom in the den," she requested in a low tone as she handed Jessie the items. "I put some weed in there for you to roll a blunt, and they got liquor on the counter in the dining room and some leftover meatloaf in the refrigerator. Now, I'm going finish getting my spine tore out? And I don't wanna here a peep outta your ass. We'll talk in the morning," she ended before walking out of the room.

****

"When I was a child I had a fever...my hands felt just like... two balloons......now I've got that feeling once again...I can't explain...you would not understand...this is not how I am...I... have become...comfortably numb..."

"You've found that man you've been dreaming about all your years. Congratulations, Kree," Sean said as he sat at his bar sipping champagne as Pink Floyd's song *Comfortably Numb* played on his surround sound system inside his well-lit master suite.

Kree had been over to Sean's condominium in O'Fallon for nearly three hours conversing. Unlike with Alonzo, this good-bye was very casual and inspirational. Sean was genuinely supportive of her plans for the future, and he was elated she'd found true love.

"He's everything I've been dreaming about, Sean," Kree said through happy eyes as she sat beside the man at his bar sipping a glass of champagne and enjoying his old rock and roll CDs. "A couple of months from now? We'll be together always."

"You know? You have had a romantic outlook on life from the day I first met you," Sean smiled. "I bet your whole world is one big love song isn't it?"

Kree blushed at that moment. "I don't know," she giggled. "I just know I love the man I'm with now and forever."

"Well, that's all that matters, sweet heart." Sean remarked. "What fun we had, though. I'm going to miss you, dearly. But I'm happy you're happy. Remember the night we first met?"

"When you almost fell out of your chair," Kree laughed.

Sean laughed right along with Kree. He then dropped his smile and reached out and patted the back of her hand tenderly. "When you caught me, you touched my heart that night you know?"

"I had to hold my hand on your chest to keep you up, man." Kree responded as she placed her hand atop Sean's and smiled.

"No, Kree," Sean said as he grabbed the champagne and topped off their glasses. "You really touched my heart. I enjoyed watching your transformation," he continued as he stood up from the bar stool with his glass, wearing a silk robe. "You were a flat-chested, wandering soul when you visited my home the first night we met, but you were full of life and adventure. I saw a lot of potential in you at the time—and my oh my, how right my assumptions were."

"I was actually trying to get over my first love that night," Kree admitted. "I was finally able to do that tonight. We've parted ways for good."

"You're closing chapters aren't you? You're going to go all the way with this guy aren't you," Sean asked as he stepped closer to Kree and rubbed her shoulder with a calming smile on his face.

"I am going to go all the way," Kree said happily. "I want to be his woman forever."

"Seems to me as if you've been that man's woman for some time now. You've earned his love forever, Kree, as if you don't recognize the fact that you've stolen his heart already you she-devil of a woman!" Sean snapped.

Kree laughed before she sipped her champagne. "We may never do what we've done in the past ever again, but this is one chapter of my life that I'll never forget," she said as she leaned back into Sean.

"The year or so we've been doing business? I've watched you grow. I've tasted the best you had to offer, literally speaking," Sean laughed. "Look at you," he chuckled as he touched the bottom of Kree's chin. "Brains, beauty, compassion and loyalty—major assets that epitomize woman —and I've seen you grow into all those things and then some. I'm proud of you, Kree. My work paid off," he chided.

"Your work?" Kree laughed as she reared her head back. "What was I? An experiment?"

"Experiment or not, was I not helpful?" Sean chuckled as he sat back beside Kree.

"You were," Kree confessed. "I learned a lot about myself from you. Especially how to treat a man. I thank you for that."

"This is the first time I've ever been used as a launching pad," Sean laughed aloud as he threw his hands up.

"No, Sean. That's not what I meant." Kree sighed.

"No, no," Sean laughed, leaning over into the bar. "I'm glad your experimenting with me was successful for you," he added as he slapped the bar counter.

"I was not experimenting with you, Sean," Kree smiled before sipping her champagne.

"Are you serious, Kree? You and I both were using one another to get our own individual goals accomplished from the beginning and I enjoyed every minute of it!" Sean laughed aloud as he stood up from his seat. "Ohh, Kree! What an interesting life you live, girlfriend. An *interesting* life because you *dare* to go after what it is that you want and make it happen, baby! More power to you, sister!"

"Ut, oh," Kree chuckled. "Is Shawna coming out tonight?"

"Not tonight. Tonight? This is Sean celebrating Kree's arrival!"

Just then, Kree's phone rang. She looked down and saw Jessie's number. "Excuse me, Sean. Hello?"

"Yo," Jessie said lowly. "I don't know if you heard—don't even know if I even care telling you this so I'm just gone say it

—Alonzo dead."

"What?" Kree gasped as she set her glass of champagne down. "When? Where?"

"Over to his studio like four hours ago. Kantrell ole man told her and she just told me. Niggas popped him up like twelve times in his car when he was headed out. He crashed into some other people shit and was dead by the time the police and ambulances got there."

"Oh no," Kree said as her eyes began to fill with tears. "I was just with him! I saw the police cars headed that way!"

"You was just with him?"

"Yeah. I went, I went to break things off with him. He wanted me to stay, but I couldn't. I was so over him, Jessie. I didn't want him to be dead, though. Oh my, God," Kree cried.

"Well, look at it this way—if you would've been there? Or in his car when it went down? You probably woulda got it too. So be happy for that. I know that's your first and all so I'm not gone speak what's on my mind. Not to mention I got my own shit to deal with. Just thought you'd like to know." Jessie said before she hung up the phone and lay back on Kantrell's couch and closed her eyes.

Kree was shocked and hurt. She never saw this coming with Alonzo and she wondered what he'd gotten himself into that led up to him being killed. She was also grateful that she didn't take Alonzo up on his offer to 'kick it' with him or else she would've probably ended up dead herself. She didn't know anyone in Alonzo's family and he'd moved from his old apartment near his studio. *"I really didn't know much about him, yet I loved him. I'll watch the obituaries and ask around so I can visit his grave."* Kree said to herself as the good times she'd shared with Alonzo ran through her mind.

"Everything okay?" Sean asked, shaking Kree from her thoughts.

"My first boyfriend," Kree said as she stared at Sean with a face full of tears. "The guy I was telling you about earlier, he was killed tonight."

"I'm sorry to hear that. Are you going to be okay? Are you in any danger?" Sean asked anxiously as he sat his glass down.

"I don't think so, but, can I, can I stay here tonight? I don't wanna role play or nothing. I just, I just," Kree broke down at that moment. "Alonzo!" she screamed as she covered her face. As many times as Alonzo had hurt her heart, she was saddened he'd been murdered. "Everybody was supposed to be okay!" she screamed as she covered her face. "Everybody was supposed to be okay!"

"Shh, shh," Sean said as he got up and hugged Kree and led her over to his bed. "Everybody doesn't get a happily ever after, Kree," he whispered as he lay her down.

"Everybody deserves one," Kree cried as she turned away from Sean and hid her face in the pillows. Sean then removed his robe, leaving his silk pajamas on, and removed Kree's heels. He went and turned the music off, dimmed the lights, and walked back over and slid into the bed behind her and cradled her in his arms the remainder of the night and then saw her off the following morning with his best wishes.

CHAPTER FOURTEEN
DON'T SCORN ME

Denobria Morrow stood on the sidewalk before her home in utter confusion. It was the morning after Jessie's encounter with Chastity and Alonzo's homicide. Curtis was at work at this early hour, but Denobria was home doing edits on upcoming newscasts. She was sitting in her and Curtis' adjoining home offices when she spotted the mail carrier placing mail inside the mailbox at the foot of the driveway and had decided to take a break. She took a sip of her coffee and exited her home in a pair of jogging shorts, a loose-fitting-shirt and canvas sneakers and retrieved the mail.

It was just a regular day inside the Morrow household as far as Denobria was concerned as she walked back towards the family home while scanning the envelopes, looking at the incoming bills and several credit card offers. She'd seen the small, white box earlier and had assumed it was another order of business cards for her husband. When she saw the title Mr. and Mrs. Morrow on the box, however, she opened it; and when she saw what was inside, her heart sunk to the pit of her stomach. She stood frozen halfway up the sidewalk, shocked over what she'd pulled out of the box while reading the small handwritten letter as she thought back to Curtis' trip to Oregon. She soon began to wonder what was going on with her husband, repeatedly asking herself why, all-the-while praying that what she now suspected was not a reality.

She went about the remainder of the morning in a daze, unable to comprehend the facts that lay before her eyes as she scanned the contents of the envelope repeatedly through downcast eyes. Curtis had called and left a message inviting her out to lunch, but she never bothered returning his call as she was lost, lost in a world of confusion, betrayal and sorrow. From the moment she'd opened that envelope and read the letter, Denobria had merely been going through the motions of the day. She sat at her desk for hours staring at nothing as tears poured down her face until a ringing phone stirred her from her trance. Without looking at the number, she took the call.

"Baby, I been trying to get in touch with you for lunch. Where are you?" Curtis smiled.

"Home," Denobria answered glumly. "Are you at work?"

"Of course I am," Curtis responded, picking up on his wife's sullenness. "Is everything okay with you?"

"Is it Curtis?"

"I'm going to have to ask what you're referring to, Denobria."

"Are you seeing someone else?" Denobria asked matter-of-factly as she stared at the items removed from the box.

"Whatever would give you that impression?" Curtis laughed, yet wondering what prompted his wife to ask that particular question. *"Does she know about Kree?"* he asked himself.

"You've barely touched me since you've come back from Oregon. I haven't been feeling any love lately, that's all." Denobria said as she picked up the item that she'd removed from the box and held it out flat in her hands.

"That's the problem here?" Curtis asked relieved. "You know I have the home going up in Arkansas and a new client coming on board. You're into your edits, the kids—we've both been real busy as of late."

"Come home and make love to me right now," Denobria

stated bluntly. "At this moment," she added, wanting to believe that the package she'd received was meant to be a gift from Curtis and all was well within her marriage.

Curtis was not in harmony with Denobria in the least bit. He'd thought about Kree the second he'd heard his wife proposition. He was so emotionally invested into his lover, he actually felt as if he would be cheating on her if he were to leave his job and travel home to sleep with his wife. "I have a couple of runs I have to make, Denobria. I can't come at this moment. Can I take a rain check?"

Tears flooded Denobria's eyes again. She squinted her eyes briefly and her lips began to tremble as she pressed the phone tighter to her ear. She felt as if she was on the verge of losing her husband and had no control over the situation. "Do you remember the day you asked me to marry you, Curtis?" she asked as her tears collected on her chin and dripped down onto the small handwritten letter resting on her desk.

"I remember," Curtis said as he leaned back in his chair and smiled, reflecting on happier times. The love he'd had for his wife in the beginning had been diminished soon after he'd begun his affair, but there was still enough affection left in his heart to allow him to reflect on the good times he'd shared with his wife over the years. "You couldn't stop screaming yes," he said.

"Yes," Denobria said as she wiped her tears. "And the same way I felt on that day is how I feel today. Don't take that away from me, Curtis. You hear me?" Denobria said through heartfelt conviction. "Don't, don't scorn me."

"Where is all this coming from?" Curtis asked as he leaned forward in his chair and looked to the floor.

Denobria thought about telling Curtis about the package, but on the other hand, maybe she was overreacting. Maybe it was a big misunderstanding. She just didn't know—but she was determined to find out. "I told you," she said anxiously, "you haven't been attentive to my needs. I've asked you to come home, and look where we are now. You haven't even answered. Clients can wait. Your wife needs you."

"My not being intimate with you has nothing to do with another woman if that's what's bothering you, Denobria." Curtis remarked.

"It doesn't?" Denobria asked in an unsure tone. "Are, are you sure, baby?"

"Trust me," Curtis responded calmly as his eyes watered, knowing that soon, he would have to break his wife's heart by telling her he wanted a divorce. "There's, there's not another woman in my life. That's the truth."

"What's going on with us then? Why aren't we as close as we once were?"

"Denobria," Curtis said as he eased up from his chair and donned his silk suit jacket. "Marriages are measured in years, not weeks. Remember shortly after Curtis Junior was born and the things that transpired between you and I?"

"We were both contemplating a separation." Denobria responded as she crossed her legs and rested her hand in her head. "I had even suggested it."

"We were so stressed we couldn't stand the sight of one another some days. That's not the problem here," Curtis remarked as he grabbed the keys to his Mercedes. "Sometimes, baby, sometimes life just gets in the way of what's normal. Routines change, and when that happens, everything else gets thrown into disarray. I understand how you feel."

"Do you really?" Denobria asked with a hint of uncertainty in her voice.

"I do," Curtis said lowly. "I have to go, Denobria."

"Okay, baby," Denobria said as she ended the call.

Denobria watched as lighted screen grew dark; her hands were trembling as she sat the phone down. She covered her heart with one hand and her mouth with the other, knowing full-well Curtis had been lying to her the entire time. She hadn't been with the man for twenty years and not learned his ways. Her husband's answers were vague at best, uniform and preplanned it seemed. He'd also stopped calling her 'baby' the moment she'd asked his whereabouts.

Curtis was the only man Denobria had ever been with in her life. She didn't need to know the behaviors of men in general because that wasn't her M.O. All she cared about was one man, a man she knew inside and out and could easily discern when he was distracted. The package she'd opened just a few hours earlier had burst upon the surface of the calm waters the family had been sailing and it was only the tip of the iceberg she believed. The tip of an iceberg that was in the path of her family's ship of life and was threatening to sink what was once a happy existence.

"Who is she?" Denobria asked herself as she eased up from her desk and began walking around the room while running her hands through her short, brown hair, her eyes steadily leaking tears of despair.

****

Curtis, meanwhile, had left his office and had driven over to his lawyer's office. He entered the small building just outside of downtown Saint Louis and waited in the lobby. While doing so, he booked a room over to Embassy Suites, planning to meet up with Kree as it was a Friday and he was wanting to be with her for a couple of hours before he returned home later on in the night.

"Mister Morrow," the attorney said as she stood in her threshold while extending her hand, inviting him into her office.

Curtis entered and the lawyer locked her door. "I have everything drawn up," she said as she rounded her desk and took a seat.

"How much damage will this decision inflict upon my finances?" Curtis asked as he sat before the mid-forties lawyer.

"If Denobria goes after the business you stand to lose half your interest. Missouri isn't a common law state, but being that you formed your company after the two of you were married? Misses Morrow is entitled to half a stake in your venture and your entire net worth overall."

"Can I dissolve the business and start anew?"

"You can," the lawyer replied as she scooted up closer to her marble desk. "But that action would not free you of your obligations to settle things with your wife on behalf of Morrow Construction in the eyes of the court. She's going to get half of the business if she asks for it."

"And the house? Joint custody of the kids? The cars?"

"Off the record," the lawyer said as she removed her glasses and rested her elbows on her desktop. "You have a net worth of nearly four hundred thousand dollars, not including the house you two share. You could be looking at a five thousand dollar a month settlement with child support and alimony— unless you were to remarry."

"Would an out-of-state marriage have some impact on the court's consideration for a reduction in the settlement?"

"This is where it gets tricky," the lawyer replied as she leaned back and crossed her legs. "Here in conservative Missouri? I think not, but it is a battle worth fighting if you wanna put you and Kree's business out on the front lines."

"I just want what's fair in order for the two of us to be able to build a life for ourselves after my marriage is dissolved. I can start another business, so long as I'm not left penniless."

"If you were to relocate to the state where you two are married that will have a definite impact on the court's decision. I could get a severe reduction in the settlement and child support payments if that were to occur."

"I don't wanna uproot Kree's life or be away from my sons," Curtis said as he looked to the floor.

"Denobria will gain joint custody of the children at worse, but you will be granted summers and holidays and that will lower your child support payments. Should you marry? That would reduce your alimony."

"If you can do that, that would be perfect. I have contacts in Vermont, too. I'm thinking I can open a granite tile company there, buy a new home and maybe rent here in Missouri? You know, be based in Vermont, but still operate here? Rent a home here in Saint Louis and handle things in New England from the rental property?"

"If you feel you and your significant other can work that out it's a good move. Just know any future earnings here in the state of Missouri would be included as a part of your income when Denobria goes up for recertification on the child support —which is every three years."

"By then we'll be okay," Curtis said as he eyed his lawyer. He then rubbed his hands over his eyes. "You know," he said as he eased up from his chair, "in situations like this, a man has a certain vision of how things will play out—and it's always a happy ending. Everything is wrapped up into one neat little bow and all parties are happy with the decisions being made, along with the settlements."

"Divorce is a messy thing, Mister Morrow—especially if you're ending a marriage abruptly and without solid grounds. Falling out of love doesn't earn you any points in the court room either. Does your wife know of your affair?"

"No," Curtis replied as he paced the floor. "She recognizes the changes. She even acknowledged them earlier today, but I chalked it up to our hectic lives and careers."

"Be careful, Mister Morrow," the lawyer admonished. "A woman scorned can be more than you bargained for. We have a certain intuition, you know?"

"I know about the sixth sense, but we have been totally discreet. Kree and I. I won't make any moves until after the divorce is final."

"You must really love this person to go out on a limb and put everything at risk," the lawyer said as she placed her glasses back onto her face and picked up the documents covering Curtis' divorce. "I can't say I admire it, but I respect the fact that you are facing the situation head on. And it is for that reason that I will do all I can to help you keep as much money in your pocket as possible while maintaining joint custody of your kids."

"That's all I ask."

"Okay, Mister Morrow. Now understand me clearly, if you

sign these papers today? Your wife will receive a copy of these documents, informing her of your intent. Are you certain this is what you want to do?"

"The door's been opened," Curtis replied as he stood before the lawyer's desk. "Might as well walk through it."

"Final counsel," the lawyer said as she eyed Curtis seriously. "Given the talks we've had, it's obvious you love who you love, but I must ask that you refrain from seeing your significant other lest you jeopardize the entire process. I'm acquainted with the judge and I could have this case done in thirty one days—which is the earliest that the state of Missouri will allow a divorce. Barring settlement, child support and alimony disagreements, all of which I know will be more than fair for your wife, five weeks from now? You'll be free to start your life all over again."

"You've been grade-A professional," Curtis smiled as he stepped forth and shook the counselor's hand.

"It's my job, sir," the lawyer responded as she slid the divorce documents before Curtis. "Sign here, here and here on this page," she said as she went to pour herself a cup of coffee. "Crack your knuckles and have a seat," she added, "because you have plenty more to sign."

After spending another thirty minutes signing documents and receiving further counsel from his attorney, Curtis left the lawyer's office and returned to his place of business and spent the rest of the day going over specs on granite tile for a new client that was scheduled to come on board soon in order to have their summer home down in Lake Ozark, Missouri remodeled. Just before sunset, he gathered his belongings and left his business and headed back to Saint Louis, against his lawyer's wishes.

CHAPTER FIFTEEN
SIMPLY IRRESISTIBLE

Kree lay on her side with her hand rubbing the back of Curtis' head as he lay behind her stoking her, the suite filled with an erotic energy that hadn't been accomplished since their trip to Oregon. For twenty minutes straight she lay on her side in complete awe as Curtis held her tightly, rubbing her breasts and kissing her furiously with his shaft planted deep inside, sending newfound waves of pleasure through her body that had forced her toes to curl as her bantu knots began to fail over the sweat pouring from her skull inside the passion-filled suite. She was in a constant orgasmic state the whole time, moaning uncontrollably and calling his name alongside of God's as she'd never experienced this form of lovemaking ever.

It was always a new discovery with Curtis for Kree. She'd only been with him one time since their trip, and he was always telling her how much he missed her and wanted to be near her, to be inside her. Kree could sense the need in her lover through his many texts. She knew of the impending divorce and how much stress it was bringing down on her man. Whatever pinned up frustration Curtis had with him on this night was definitely welcomed as she had never anticipated that the love they would share on this night would be so stimulating.

There wasn't much talking when Kree first walked through the door. Curtis had greeted her in the nude with a hard-on that was warm to the touch and demanded she take him into her mouth. She dropped her purse, and did the same with her knees just inside the locked room, moaning lustfully as her lips slowly slid back and forth over her lover's rod. Curtis' hands running through her hair, and his moans of delight were uplifting to Kree, who was only aiming to please.

Unable to withstand his lover's tongue any longer and wanting to feel her body next to his, Curtis eased Kree up from her knees and scooped her up into his arms. She squealed with delight as he toted her over to bed and laid her down and nudged her onto her stomach.

Kree was wearing a knee-length skirt and heels with a silk blouse, but her blouse was ripped off completely, its buttons scattering across the mattress. She'd slid her panties off at the door while fellating her man, and all was left was for him to do was raise her skirt and penetrate her opening from behind. No showering, no foreplay, this was an uninhibited fuck that was craved by both individuals. Curtis was sucking in air as he stroked Kree, smacking her ass and gripping her hair as he long-dicked her like a man possessed.

"*Me encanta tu polla! Me encanta tu polla!*"(I love your dick! I love your dick!) Kree cried aloud as Curtis pushed her over onto her stomach and began surfboarding her, dominating her body, owning it, in fact. "*Quiero dentro de mí para siempre! ¡Para siempre!*"(I want you inside of me forever! Forever!)

Curtis knew not what Kree was saying, but he knew when she began talking in what he called 'tongues', it was with the understanding he was taking her there. "Fuck!" Curtis yelled. "Oohh, good pussy!"

"*Mierda como yo soy tu esposa!* (Fuck me like I am your wife!) Kree cried aloud. "Fuck me like I'm your wife!"

Their time in Oregon came flooding back on Curtis. Again, he was taking Kree without a condom and she was begging for it. Her cries, their pleasure, his love, her love, and their wanting to be together without any restrictions, had driven him over the edge. He pressed his body to Kree's and hugged her tightly and groaned deeply as he took quick stabs, releasing his fluid into the depths of her insides.

Kree was shuddering herself as she came uncontrollably, coating the mattress between her legs with her juices as she turned her head to the side and stuck out her tongue, intertwining it with her man's as the two rode a wave of ecstasy that had sent them both off into a peaceful slumber while cradling one another; Curtis spooning Kree as he lay naked, and she herself resting half-clothed with her skirt above her waist and still wearing her heels.

An hour or so later, the two gathered themselves, called up for room service, and then showered. Kree was still in the bathroom when the food arrived and was stepping out into the living room naked when she eyed Curtis talking to the room attendant. The service attendant had her back to Kree and hadn't seen her standing behind her naked. She eased back into the bathroom and Curtis went and knocked once the lady had set up their grilled chicken and steak dinners and salad and left the suite.

"You didn't hear me unlock the door to let room service in?" Curtis asked as he sat in a robe at the table in the nook area of the suite, which had a panoramic view of the Saint Louis skyline.

"Everything is air tight in this place," Kree responded as she walked back into the master suite and grabbed a robe from the walk-in closet. She reentered the living area brushing her hair and took a seat opposite Curtis.

"That ring looks good on your finger," Curtis said while removing the steel lid from his steak dinner.

"Yeah. I picked it up," Kree paused at that moment, realizing she was about to reveal to Curtis that she'd bought another ring identical to one he'd given her in Oregon before she met him in the suite. "I picked it up and looked at it when I took it off to do the dishes the other day and saw it was blemished so I took back to the place you got it from and had cleaned today during lunch. You like?" she asked as she held the ring out before Curtis.

"It wouldn't be on your finger if I didn't think it would look stunning on your hand, baby." Curtis smiled.

Kree said nothing as she unwrapped her silverware. Deep inside, she felt bad for deceiving Curtis, but it was now a non-issue in her mind because he hadn't a clue she'd replaced the original ring only a few hours earlier.

"I, umm, I signed the divorce papers today." Curtis said as he eyed Kree seriously.

"Really? Does Denobria know?"

"Not yet, but she will in another week or so. I'm going to lose a lot on this deal."

"I figured as much. We'll get through it, baby." Kree responded as she removed her lid and began cutting into her grilled chicken.

"We most certainly will. The bigger picture is the fact that we're moving forward. No sense in hiding anymore. I don't even wanna do that. Now, things may get messy in court because she may try and go after the business, but that doesn't even matter now. Can you deal with me being worth half than what I am today?"

"Curtis," Kree said as she reached out placed her hand inside of his palm. "I was never with you for your money. You know that. Together? We can make it. We can do anything together, baby."

"I can't say I feel good about the way Denobria will be informed, though," Curtis remarked somberly as he leaned back in his chair. "I have a lot of maneuvering to do the next few weeks to get things in order. Things may get hectic and I may not be around, but I don't want you to ever think that I don't love you. Understand?"

"We've talked already. I know what you have to do and I'm not worried at all."

"Good. I'm thinking once things are settled, say in six weeks or so? We take that trip to Vermont?"

"I would love that, Curtis," Kree said happily.

"I love you, Kree Devereaux."

"I love you, Curtis Morrow." Kree responded lowly. The joyful twenty-three year-old couldn't help but to jump up from her seat. She ran around the table and sat in Curtis' lap, straddling his legs as she placed her hands to his cheeks and pulled him in for a tender kiss.

"You're going to start something here," Curtis smirked as he eased Kree's robe down over her shoulders and ran his hands through her damp hair.

"Let's hope so," Kree responded softly, staring deep into Curtis' eyes while biting her bottom lip. "No more condoms," she whispered as she eased up and placed Curtis' tool at her opening. "I'm all yours now, Curtis. All yours, baby."

The two made love once more at the table with the city skyline off in the distance before showering together. Curtis left earlier than normal on this night, wanting not to arouse suspicion with his wife in order to have his divorce go as smoothly as possible. Kree lounged around the suite the remainder of the night, eating her dinner and having a drink before she turned in around midnight to rest for the following morning.

CHAPTER SIXTEEN
THAT DAY BY PEPPER

Kree's phone had shaken her from her slumber. Her alarm was also vibrating as it slid across the night stand and it seemed as if she'd just gone to sleep only minutes ago. She stretched her arm out from under the covers and shut off her alarm. "Jessie? You are really going to make me fight you over tampering with my phone every weekend," she sighed through closed eyes.

"Because your ass always late on Saturdays when you get up with ole boy."

"He left early last night," Kree responded as she turned over in the bed and pulled the covers down. "He's taking me to Vermont in six weeks once he gets his divorce you know?"

"Oh yeah?" Jessie smiled. "Shiit, I gotta see this here! He really leaving his wife for you?"

"Signed the papers yesterday." Kree said happily as she jumped up from the bed.

"Damnnnn," Jessie laughed as she placed a balled up fist to her mouth. "You a bad bitch!"

"I just know what men want. What my man wants," Kree sassed. "Let me get dress. I'll be over in Fox Park in an hour at the latest so we don't have to deal with Kantrell's mouth."

"Look," Jessie said, "I'm over to Kantrell's house. Pick me up from here."

"Why you didn't just leave with her?"

"She left way early. She had to follow Malik over to Maplewood and take him back over to his grill this morning. I told her you was gone get me."

"Okay, then." Kree said before ending the call.

An hour and a half later, Kree and Jessie were pulling up to *Bangin' Heads,* late as usual. Kree was going on and on about her and Curtis' talk the night before; Jessie was listening attentively at first, but a crowd outside of *Bangin' Heads* had caught her attention. She then noticed three patrol cars and an unmarked car parked before Kantrell's salon.

"Kree, keep going! Keep going!" Jessie snapped as she shoved Kree's shoulder.

"What's the mat—oh my god!" Kree gasped. "What's going on at our job?"

Jessie looked over to Kree and shook her head as she went on and told her what'd happened between her and Chastity the night before as she continued up Fourteenth Avenue.

"You broke the woman's neck, Jessie? Didn't I tell you about them videos?" Kree said as she began making her way back to Fox Park.

"Hey, it was an accident alright? And that shit up to Bangin' Heads might be over something else. Look, just drop me back off in Fox Park by Pepper crib," Jessie said as she grabbed her phone to call Loopy and Sweet Pea and have them stay away from *Bangin' Heads.*

"You heard anything else about Alonzo?" Kree asked as she drove.

"Word on the street he messed up some money that was put into his studio after he got hooked back on that powder."

"Wow," Kree sighed. "I thought he was over that habit. He

was always bad with money, too."

"Blew six thousand of your dollars fuckin' with that music and ain't nothin' come of it. He got the right one this time, though," Jessie said as she looked to the floorboard somberly. "Fucked up how it happened."

"It is. I'm going to visit his grave after he's buried."

"I can respect that," Jessie responded as she leaned back in the seat. "That boy wasn't right, though. I'm just glad you wasn't around when it went down."

"I know. I missed it by like minutes. I was lucky."

"You know," Jessie remarked as she leaned back in the seat. "I do a lot of fucked up shit, Kree. I done played with people's emotions to the point that I done damn near killed somebody. I, I look at your life and see how everything falling into place and I want that for myself. I wonder if somebody would ever love me the way Curtis loves you."

"There's somebody for everybody, Jessie. You're a good person." Kree said as she pulled up to a red-light.

"But?" Jessie asked as she eyed Kree while wiping her tears.

"You're vindictive. I'm not judging or anything, but maybe, maybe if you were to stop with the videos, or at least have the person consent to it, you'll fair better. I would say get someone single, but look at me—I'm involved with a married man—so that's advice I can't even give."

"But your shit turnin' out all right. Maybe I should get serious and find that one. But ain't none of that gonna happen if my ass locked up."

"You would definitely have options behind bars. We both would," Kree joked as she eased through the changed light.

"Girl, your ass would have to fight every day!" Jessie laughed. "Kree, you would have the tier on lock!"

"Girl, I would lose my mind! Um, um. Can't do it," Kree said as she headed towards the neighborhood.

The two made it over to Fox Park and were happy to see

Loopy and Sweet Pea's Durango parked out front. They exited Kree's Maxima and walked up the sidewalk and knocked on the door. Pepper opened a few seconds later and smiled. "Girl," she said as she stood before Kree, "why you being a stranger with me? You know you know me!"

"My life has been really busy as of late, Pepper," Kree replied as she hugged the youngster.

"Y'all come on in! We was just about to blaze up and cook breakfast."

"What y'all making?" Kree asked as she stepped inside Pepper's apartment.

"Jenas. Y'all like jenas?"

"You ever tried it with steak?" Kree asked as she walked into the kitchen. Kree paused when she eyed the kitchen table. Pepper had rows of powdered cocaine and small packets of crack stuffed into small plastic bags laid out on the table with a large machine gun.

"Excuse my shit," Pepper said as she joined Kree in the kitchen. "If you wanna leave I understand."

"I'm, I'm okay for now. Do you have some steak? I can show you how to make those jenas with steak before I leave."

"I sure do," Pepper snapped as she went into her freezer and grabbed a pack of sirloin steak and sat it in the sink. "It'll be thawed in like thirty minutes, Kree," she said as she opened the pack of meat and turned on the hot water, she and Kree moving about in the kitchen gathering the rest of the ingredients to make jenas, which were stuffed jalapeno peppers filled with onions, meat, bell peppers and mozzarella cheese and baked inside the oven.

Jessie, meanwhile, was sitting on the sofa beside Simone, the two of them sharing a blunt as Loopy and Sweet Pea toked on a blunt of their own, the two cousins sitting side by side on a love seat opposite the sofa.

"Yo," Simone said as she sucked in smoke and passed the blunt back to Jessie, "one time was over to that boy Dibble house this morning. You know what that shit was about, right?"

"What's the word?" Jessie asked as she toked on the blunt.

"Nobody don't know what he said," Simone said as she sipped a glass of gin on the rocks, "but when they left, he went and hollared at Toodie and her peeps on Ann Avenue. Me and Pep think he looking for her to help him out because he rattin' on y'all three."

"He's runnin' his mouth," Loopy said from across the room. "But if we touch him now, that may kick off beef with Toodie."

"Y'all know what, though," Simone said nonchalantly as she took the blunt from Jessie and took a toke, "fuck that bitch Toodie and everything she stand for. If Dibble done ratted y'all out? He gotta go for that one," she said as she blew smoke from her nostrils.

"That's right!" Pepper snapped from behind the kitchen counter while holding a butcher's knife. "We gone back y'all on that one! He ain't got no business speakin' on nothin'! I hate a snitch! And Toodie wrong for even supportin' that bullshit! Be something if he turn around and rat on her stupid ass!"

Kree was silent the whole time her friends discussed the situation with Dibble. It was none of her business, but she couldn't help but to worry about her friends. In her eyes, they were headed for real danger. She knew Toodie through name and reputation. The woman was a drug-dealing murderer, had been for as long as Kree could remember. She wanted to speak out in protest, but she knew the caliber of people she were dealing with in Simone and Pepper. It was a given that they were gangsters. Jessie, Sweet Pea and Loopy, however, weren't like the two in her eyes, but she saw the two headed down that road and she was scared for her friends—all of them. They could die going up against Toodie.

"Kree, I'm gone have to get you to do my hair," Pepper said, shaking Kree from her thoughts. "This lady back here I deal with run a shop out her house and she don't never give me what I ask for. How much you charge?"

"Depends on what you want," Kree responded as she began cutting large jalapenos into halves. "Anywhere from seventy to two hundred dollars."

"That's all? Put your number in my phone. I'm gone get at you. And Jessie, you can line Simone raggedly head up when we come!" Pepper joked as she handed Kree her cell phone.

Jessie was toking on the blunt passed back to her by Simone when her phone rung. "Chea?"

"Who this?"

"You know who it is." Jessie responded.

"Okay, this is Miss Attempted Murder!" Kantrell snapped.

"What?" Jessie asked she passed the blunt back to Simone and stood up. "What happened?"

"John Law came through here and ran checks on everybody! They got a warrant out for twenty-two year-old Jessica-ass-Suede and they said they gone run through my spot anytime they get good and ready! Don't you bring your ass back up here until you get that shit sorted out! They done took two mutherfuckas to jail and now my shop is bone dry on a early Saturday morning over your bullshit!"

"Damn," Jessie said lowly. "I ain't think it was gone spread out like that."

"Well, it did! Where Kree at because I know she with you! Tell that red bitch I say she got the day off! Everybody got the day off because shop is closed over here! I told y'all! You fucks with my money shit get real real quick-like in rapid succession!"

"You firing me, Kantrell?"

"Ain't nobody fired! But your ass is hot! You already know to stay away so they won't be up here questioning and harassing folks! My whole day shot to shit!"

"Oh, okay, then. I'm sorry, Kantrell," Jessie responded somberly.

"Don't be sorry, be informed! You wanted for attempted

murder, girl! Whoop there it is!"

"I owe you for today," Jessie said as she rubbed her forehead. "I'll reimburse you when I can."

"Don't worry about me. I'm pissed over what happened, but take whatever money you were going to give to me and get yourself a lawyer, okay?" Kantrell stated as she flopped down into her seat and removed her heels.

Tears formed in Kantrell's eyes at that moment. As hard as she was trying to be with Jessie, she couldn't help but to worry about her friend. She'd seen things go from glam to glum with a friend of hers back in New Orleans, and everything had started at her shop when the guy received a visit from one his supposed friends from Memphis, Tennessee. Things had gotten so deep, Kantrell found herself having to testify on behalf of her friend. She lied under oath and had placed her entire life on the line. She couldn't do it again. Nor did she want to. She'd given Jessie fair warning and sound advice and had left it in Jessie's hands to rectify the matter, but deep down inside, she knew if her friend needed help, she would be there. "Where're you going tonight?" she asked Jessie calmly.

"I was coming back to your place, but I may just lay low by Kree."

"Well, you're welcome to come, but if the law show up? You gotta come on up outta there. I'll do what I can until this plays out, but you can't get back in the salon until you get everything straight."

"Thanks, Kantrell. I'll hollar later. I owe you."

"You don't owe me nothing but a promise that if and when you get out of this here? You will come your ass to work on time and do your job. Leave people alone, Jessie."

"I promise," Jessie said before she hung up the phone. Jessie relayed the news to Kree that she had the day off and she was surprised, yet happy.

"I'm gone go home and check on New Riley, hit the shower and go shopping. You girls wanna join me?" Kree asked happily.

"You see all that product on the table?" Simone asked. "We trappin' all day."

"Yeah," Pepper chimed in. "Look, though, when I come through, make me your last client and we'll hang out that day."

"Okay," Kree responded. "The steaks just have to be cut up and grilled. Stuff the peppers with all the ingredients we sliced up and bake them for thirty minutes on high and you're all set to go." Kree grabbed her purse and left Pepper's apartment, but not before hugging her friends and saying good-bye. She returned home and tended to her pet and rested for a few hours before heading back out to the mall.

****

"Be sure to catch the ball with both hands, CJ," Curtis told his son as he prepared to throw a football in his direction.

The Morrow family was out enjoying a day at the park on this late, sunny, Saturday afternoon. The night before, Curtis had returned home shortly before ten 'o' clock and he and Denobria had spoken all but a few words to one another. The woman was doing well hiding her angst towards her husband while putting on a good show before the public. Beneath her calm demeanor, however, lay a seething desire to find out who was the woman that had her husband's undivided attention. When the football Curtis was tossing to his sons landed at her feet, Denobria was shaken from her thoughts.

"Denobria," Curtis smiled with his hands stretched out. "Throw me a touchdown!"

Denobria merely kicked the ball away from her and looked off in the distance as she crossed her legs and shook them back and forth in obvious frustration. Curtis sensed his wife's tension and walked over to her and took a seat on the bench. "What's troubling you?" he asked lowly.

"Who is she, Curtis?" Denobria asked as she looked over to her husband, unable to hide the pain being carried in her heart.

"Not this again." Curtis sighed as he ran his hands over his wavy hair.

"Yes, this again," Denobria responded as she rested her head in her hand planted on the top of the bench while staring into her husband's face. "What was last night all about? I'm sleeping next to you naked and never once did you try to touch me. I've been trying to be intimate with you since your trip to Oregon, but you won't even touch—"

"I'm filing for a divorce, Denobria," Curtis stated bluntly as he leaned back and looked out towards the open field.

"What?" Denobria asked as she turned and faced Curtis head on. "You're what?"

"I'm moving on. The love just isn't there anymore." Curtis said as he looked towards the ground. "I can't, and I refuse to live a lie."

Denobria jumped up and slapped Curtis in the face several times before he stood up and backed away. "Is this is how you're going to act? Let's be adult about this, Denobria!"

"I am being adult about this!" Denobria yelled, getting the attention of several people who were out on the park with their families.

"Look at the scene you're causing," Curtis said under his breath. "Now, if you want to talk, we can talk, but not like this! Not here!"

"This is where you decided to tell me that you were running out on your family, cheater!" Denobria screamed as she stepped closer to Curtis.

"I'm not going to entertain your shenanigans, Denobria. Not at all." Curtis said as he shoved his wife aside and walked over to his sons, who were standing by watching their parents in silence.

"What's wrong with momma, daddy?" Curtis' son, CJ, asked as he held onto his football.

"She's a little under the weather, son. Sometimes—"

"Stay away from us!" Denobria screamed as she ran and stood in between Curtis and their sons. "You and your mistress will not enjoy the fruits of my labor! I've put years into this and you walk away?" she cried. "You just, you just walk away?"

"There isn't—" Curtis was about to scream aloud, but he calmed himself. "This day is over, Denobria! Over!"

"You're damn right it is—*Curtis*!" Denobria snapped as she grabbed her sons' hands and pulled them away. "And not only is the day over, everything is over!"

"Where're you going? We need to talk about this!"

"We will—in court!" Denobria said through tears as she walked away from Curtis. "I'm going home! And it's best you not show your face there until I've talked to counsel!"

"How am I supposed to get home? Where will I stay?"

"Oh, she hasn't a home for you two to share?" Denobria laughed mockingly. "What a pathetic man you've proven yourself to be, sir. Look at what you've pissed into the wind," she ended as she turned her back on Curtis and led her sons back to the family's SUV, leaving her husband standing by his lonesome.

CHAPTER SEVENTEEN
HOW QUICKLY THINGS CHANGE

It was later on in the day after Curtis had revealed to Denobria that he was filing for divorce. The tension in the air between the married couple was so volatile, Curtis could not return home to lay his head. He'd caught a cab back to his residence in order to retrieve his Mercedes along with some other personal items and valuables. Denobria followed him around with her arms folded and in angered silence as he gathered some of his clothes and jewelry and important documents before leaving an hour later without so much as saying good-bye. He knew better.

Denobria closed her door and locked it and went and sat in her office where she'd been keeping the contents she'd received in the mail a couple of days ago hidden from her husband. Her decision to not reveal the contents was a good one in her mind because she now knew what she was up against exactly. Her lawyer would definitely have something to fight with in the court room. Still, the thought of 'who is she' plagued the scorned wife's psyche. So much she'd developed an intense curiosity as to what, or better yet who, was driving her husband's desire to want to divorce her.

Curtis, meanwhile, had texted Kree and told her he was headed back to Saint Louis. He didn't divulge the full intent of his actions, merely texting that he wanted to meet her later on

213

and she'd agreed. He entered his suite and went to the bar to fix himself a drink as the sun began to set on the city. The betraying husband only wanted to be alone on this night to reflect on his own decision, one in which he believed to be the right one given the circumstances and the love he held for another as he went on with his plans for the future while taking straight shots of gin on the rocks to the head.

****

While Curtis was in his suite reflecting on what had transpired with his wife and easing his betrayal with a bottle of gin and making plans, Kree had just returned to Fox Park where she joined Jessie and company, all of whom were sitting out on a set of bleachers on the basketball court.

"What you get from the mall," Loopy asked as she sat beside Kree.

"Nothing much," Kree responded. "I got these heels and a new outfit and some lingerie from Victoria's Secret."

"I know what that's for," Loopy laughed.

Kree brushed Loopy with her forearm as she chuckled. "It drives him crazy, girl. Besides that, I just felt like getting away for a minute. Doing me, you know?"

"I understand. You're just a love bug," Loopy chided. "What you doing later?"

"I'm going home and relax."

"Jessie called Kantrell back right before you came, we all going over there later to hang out if you wanna come."

"Nahh," Kree sighed. "I'm tired. I'm going home pretty soon, but you guys have fun. Kantrell's not mad with Jessie anymore I take it?"

"They okay. Kantrell good peoples. She understands what our girl up against." Loopy remarked.

Jessie, meanwhile, was thinking of a way to earn money as she sat out with her friends. She was contemplating on asking Pepper and Simone, both of whom were polishing the chrome 28" rims situated under the snow white Hummer they'd driven onto the park, to front her an ounce of cocaine in order to flip, but she knew she would have to hang in the neighborhood far longer than anticipated in order to sell off the product and it wasn't to her liking as it would be a big risk, not to mention she had an attachment out on her for attempted murder. If she could hit a quick hustle and stab out it would be perfect. The only problem was what to do. She leaned back on the bleachers and began scheming as bass began rumbling from the Hummer parked beside the bleachers in the grass.

"*...If Ion't do nothing I'ma ball...I'm counting all day like the clock on the wall...nah go and getcha money little duffle bag boy...say go and go and getcha money little duffle bag boy(get money)...I ain't neva ran from a nigga and I ain't damn sure ain't 'bouta pick ta' day ta' start runnin'(look honey)... I ain't neva ran from a nigga and I ain't damn sure ain't bouta pick ta' day ta' start runnin'(get money)...*" Pepper and Simone were blasting Player's Circle song *Duffle Bag Boy* while sipping cognac as the immaculate SUV sat parked in the freshly-cut grass beside the bleachers, the bass from its interior vibrating the bleachers Jessie, Kree, Sweet Pea and Loopy was sitting on as they bobbed their heads to the music.

Pepper and Simone were enthralled in the song, the two of them on the passenger side of the Hummer waving their polish rags in the air with one hand and their clear plastic cups of cognac in the other as they danced away from another while yelling aloud. Life was carefree for Pepper at this point and time in her life. She and Simone were making money hand over fist with their cocaine connect coming out of Cape Girardeau.

Sixteen year-old Pepper was a boss in the making. The streets were her playground and she had the gift of gab coupled with courage and instinct at the tender age of sixteen. She'd been around major players since the age of ten and knew how to run game on those around her; she stayed scheming and today was no different. With Jessie back in Fox Park for the day, Pepper saw an opportunity to reach out and touch those in whom she despised in a subtle manner.

After her and Simone's impromptu dance routine had

concluded, Pepper walked up to Simone and asked her, "You think Jessie 'nem can beat them punks across the way?"

"Toodie and her people?" Simone asked with a wide smile on her face.

"Yeah," Pepper responded without cracking a smile.

"Oh, you serious," Simone said a she stared Pepper in the eyes while setting her rag and cup down on the running rails of the Hummer. She then looked across the court to where Toodie and her crew were posted up and sized them up. "If they go up against them two Mexicans with Toodie they should win it. How much you talkin'?"

"Nothing big. Somethin' like five stacks. I know they need it."

Simone bumped her fists together and looked up at Jessie, Sweet Pea and Loopy sitting up in the bleachers. "They be ballin', Pep," she said as she turned back and faced her friend. "And we done made money bettin' on 'em before."

"I know. I think I'ma do it, girl—just to fuck with Toodie." Pepper said through a mischievous grin. Pepper was willing to put money up for their friends in order to help them out with their troubles, but she also had ulterior motives geared towards Toodie.

Twenty-six year-old Kathryn 'Toodie' Perez was Pepper's nemesis and she was despised for several reasons, with the main reason being that she was under the belief Toodie had killed her mother down in Valle Hermoso, Mexico when Pepper was only ten years old. That act alone was the very thing that had landed Pepper in Saint Louis; and as she grew older, her hatred for Toodie matured right along with her. She would do anything to get under Toodie's skin, even kill her if she ever got the opportunity to pull it off and get away with it. For now though, Pepper was satisfied with taking money out of Toodie's pockets on this spring evening. She went up under the driver's side of the Hummer and grabbed a silk bag and skipped over to the bleachers as the song played on.

"Eh," Pepper said aloud to Jessie, Loopy and Sweet Pea,

who were just kicking back watching cars pass up and down Saint Louis Street while listening to the music.

"Sup, Pep," Loopy asked as she eyed Pepper climbing the stairs headed in her direction.

"Y'all wanna make some money?" Pepper asked as she sat beside Loopy.

"What we gotta do?" Loopy asked as she scooted over towards Pepper.

Pepper leaned into Loopy as she eyed the crew across the court and said, "Go over there, and call out Toodie for a game."

"Those girls are tall," Loopy said as she eyed Toodie and her crew, who were standing in front the bleachers on the opposite side of the court talking.

"What the fuck they gone do? Toodie the only one who can ball really," Pepper reasoned.

"I give you that, but what about the other two chicks?" Loopy questioned.

"Just double Toodie," Simone interjected as she climbed the stairs and sat beside Loopy, opposite Pepper. "She can ball a li'l bit, her other two girls barely be on the court."

"Right," Pepper chimed in as she held onto to a silk Louis Vuitton bag containing five stacks, all in hundred dollar bills. "And Toodie gone play y'all, especially when she find out I'm puttin' the money up. Y'all can take 'em, Loopy. I got y'all front right here," Pepper said as she opened the bag and showed Loopy the money. "Just go over there and call them fools out. They ain't doing nothing right now. And I know they'll play y'all for money because they gone look at y'all and think they can beat y'all easy."

"How much money is that?" Loopy asked as she scanned the money and looked over to the opposite side of the court.

"Five thousand dollars. I'm tryna help y'all out with that shit going down with Chastity, ya' feel?" Pepper responded.

"You got five stacks in that bag," Jessie asked, overhearing the conversation as she hopped up and sat behind Pepper.

"Five grand. Y'all win today? Fuck it! Me and Simone gone split a stack and y'all get three stacks apiece."

"What y'all girls think?" Jessie asked Sweet Pea and Loopy.

Loopy looked over to Toodie and pulled down on her Cardinals baseball cap and leaned back on the bleachers behind her. "All three of 'em tall. We gone have to kill 'em with the jump shot because they gone be grabbing all the rebounds look like," she said. "Me and Sweet Pea running through our stash like crazy, too. Pepper puttin' the money up so fuck it, let's do it. She say we can win, we can win." Loopy ended as she jumped up from the bleachers and began stretching.

Pepper dapped Simone and laughed. "That's that shit I'm talkin' bout," she exclaimed. "And look, y'all," she added, "talk that shit to 'em like y'all be doing them other hoes when y'all out there."

"Call Toodie a bitch for me," Simone said as she began rolling a blunt to smoke while she watched the festivities go down.

"I ain't calling that girl a bitch, girl," Jessie snapped. "I know all about them and the shit they be doing around here."

"Fuck it," Pepper remarked. "Just talk that shit y'all talk. Go over there and tell Toodie I said I got five stacks her and her girls can't beat y'all in a three-on-three full court."

Jessie really needed the money. She was near the end of her stash and needed to save up for a lawyer. She shrugged her shoulders, retied her Jordan's, jumped down from the bleachers and led the way across the court as she righted her nylon gym shorts.

Pepper and Simone were laughing hysterically as they watched their friends walk across the ball court. They were subtly instigating matters, but they didn't care. To them, taking some of Toodie's money would be like pulling off her fingernails one at a time with a pair of hot grip pliers without Novocain.

"Let's go over there and fuck with 'em, Simone," Pepper

said through laughter while hopping up from the light-grey steel bleachers.

"Tell Jessie and them I will see them later," Kree said just as Pepper and Simone began leaving the bleachers.

"Okay," Pepper said as she turned and hugged Kree briefly. "But you should stay and watch this ass whipping our girls put on Toodie."

"Tell me later," Kree said as she grabbed her keys and left the bleachers and headed towards her car.

"Hey, Toodie?" Jessie called out as she approached Toodie and her girls. "We got five thousand dollars that say y'all can't beat us in a three-on-three full court."

Toodie and her girls, who were two slender Mexicans, eyed the three people before them and burst into laughter. They had the height and weight on their challengers and saw a quick five grand headed their way.

"I know y'all three joking," Angelica Arnaz, a twenty-four year-old five foot ten Mexican with short black hair, laughed slightly as she bounced a ball back and forth, her gold herring-bone chain swaying side to side. "Toodie? You gone spot that grip since they callin' your pockets out?"

"Yeah, I got it," Toodie laughed as she folded her arms and stared at Sweet Pea, Loopy and Jessie.

"Look like Christmas is coming early, family," Jada, Toodie's other partner in crime chimed in as she went and stood before the three and raised her tattoo-covered left arm above Loopy's head. "You the tallest out your click," she said as she held her arm up in the air. "How you gone stop this here, chica," the skinny, freckled faced twenty year-old asked while smirking.

"Wait 'til we get on the court and I'll show you," Loopy scoffed as she stared at Jada.

Jada Murdella, (Yah-dah) who was sometimes called Ya Murder, or simply Ya, was a snake by all measures. She knew Loopy and Sweet Pea from high school. She was a bully back then, and was known to set people up to get robbed at this present day and time, and now that she'd hooked up with Toodie, she was more dangerous than ever. "Them high school games y'all won back in the day don't matter here in Fox Park," Ya teased as she backed out on to the court and caught a pass from Angelica.

Toodie had been watching Pepper's every move. She'd seen when Pepper had shone what she perceived to be money she had in a small sack to Loopy and read the whole play. She handed her car keys to a young male solider hanging out with her and her girls. "Get that shoe box out the trunk of my whip," she requested. "And don't even think about cuffin' some of my shit, li'l boy, because I know exactly how much in there," she snapped as the teenager trotted off.

"Yeah," Jessie yelled to the teenager as he trotted off, "go get our grip!"

"Y'all done laid up there and let that li'l wannabe boss buck y'all asses up I see," Toodie laughed as she stretched. "Might as well leave y'all currency right here 'cause me and my girls is takin' all that shit this evening."

"Like the fuck y'all is," Pepper snapped as she jogged over to Toodie's bleacher twirling her silk sack of money. "Where ya' stack, trick?"

"Don't worry about that there, li'l girl." Toodie replied. "The fuck you doing over here on this side the court anyway? You trespassing right about now."

"Last time I checked this was a public park—li'l girl! I'm on my grown woman shit so you best recognize right about now," Pepper scoffed.

Toodie sucked her teeth and brushed Pepper off as her soldier returned and handed her a Nike shoebox. She grabbed the box and pulled the lid off and scanned the rubber-banded money inside as she took a seat on the bleachers. Toodie had a real disdain for sixteen year-old Peppi Vargas, but she gave her props because she knew the youngster was about her hustle and she and Simone did body somebody a while back on her behalf. That was water on the bridge, though; because if given the chance, Toodie would kill Pepper, Simone, and anybody else on her team. She wasn't really worried about Kree or Jessie, they weren't about that life was her reasoning; but she knew of Loopy and Sweet Pea's rep, and based on those circumstances, she had to be on guard with all the people that hung with Pepper.

"Let's do this," Toodie said as she eyed Pepper seriously. "First team to fifteen counting by ones and three pointers go for two."

"Handle these chumps!" Simone snapped.

Toodie laughed as she backed out onto the court. "Yes indeed," she sang as she extended her hands and caught a pass from Jada. "Bitches get a li'l money and go to smelling they self 'round this mutherfucka. You done went from pissy to prissy, huh, Simone? Ya' chink-eyed cow. Remember you used to work for me back on Ann Avenue?"

"I remember them days," Simone answered dryly as she stood courtside. "I was broke as hell fuckin' with your ass. I went from food stamps to platinum status a week after I quit," she ended as she spit on the ground while bumping her fists together.

"When ya' get on diamond status hollar at me—broke asses. We ride Maybachs and shit. What you got? A motorcycle and one Hummer that you bought from me? Get the fuck outta here, children! And when me and my girls rip y'all outta five stacks y'all be back on Ann Avenue looking for love, but it ain't gone be none."

"If we thought five g's would...fuck that! Jessie? Handle these rookies!" Pepper said as she and Simone walked back across the court in preparation to watch the game.

****

"And we'll be able to have the same suite we always have whenever I visit Vermont?" Curtis asked over the phone as he stood behind his desk inside his office in downtown Saint Charles. "Good deal. Now, I want rose petals throughout and chilled bottles of champagne in the bedroom and master bathroom upon arrival next month." Curtis remarked before he ended the call. He waited a few minutes and then called Kree, who was just leaving in Fox Park as her friends prepared for a three-on-three challenge.

"Baby," she said happily upon answering.

"What are you doing?" Curtis asked.

"I'm headed home for the night. My friends were about to play basketball, but I'm so tired I can barely keep my eyes open. What's up?"

"Got some good news. I just booked our trip to Vermont next month."

"Really," Kree smiled. "Reminiscent of Oregon will it be?"

"Even more special, baby, I got a real surprise for you."

"What is it?"

"You asked me that the last time and I refused. Just wait until we get to Vermont and I promise, you'll be very pleased."

"Okay. I love you."

"I love you, too, Kree. See you soon. Good-bye for now."

"Bye, baby," Kree ended happily.

****

"That's all day right there, bitch!" Jessie yelled out to Toodie as she back peddled away from the rim after hitting a seventeen foot jump shot in her face. She then pointed at Simone, who had two fingers in her mouth, whistling like crazy as she and Pepper sat up high in the bleachers. "Got that in for ya' homegirl!"

"You damn right you did!" Simone yelled aloud.

The score was eight to eleven in Fox Park with Toodie, Angelica and Jada leading by three points. Jessie, Loopy and Sweet Pea were in the game, but they had to make every shot, which wasn't happening on this day. Every time Jessie or one of the Cruz cousins missed a shot, Toodie, who was the tallest on the court, would grab the rebound under the rim, denying the three a second shot. She stood like a stone statue under the goal, moving Jessie, Loopy and Sweet Pea out of the way like they were mere rag dolls. The three friends had no chance of capturing a rebound under the rim for a second shot with Toodie standing under the goal.

The only thing keeping Jessie and company in the game was the fact that Angelica couldn't run full court. She would catch a rebound and throw it out to either Toodie or Jada—and therein lay the three young women's weakness. Angelica, because of her slow-paced game, couldn't keep up most times. Toodie was double teamed always by Loopy and Sweet Pea would sometimes intercept Angelica's pass and take it down for a score.

The game went on this way for nearly twenty minutes, both parties running up and down the court, except for Angelica, who would only make it to half court before the group came rushing back her way.

After Jessie made her shot, Toodie dribbled the ball up court. She executed a crucial cross-over that tripped Loopy up at the free throw line and was going in for a layup when the improbable happened. Sweet Pea, all five foot eight inches of her, came from the backside and leapt into the air and swatted the ball away. The ball landed in Jessie's hands and onlookers cheered and laughed.

"Fast-break, Loopy!" Jessie yelled as she ran full-speed down the court while dribbling the ball. She then leapt into the air and hurled the ball down court.

Angelica was near the free throw line when Loopy caught the long pass from Jessie. She ran pass Angelica, who was bent over at the waist, and slammed the ball into the goal and began doing the River Dance as Jada ran over and grabbed the ball.

"Your cousin got lucky with that blocked shot," Jada stated as she tried to inbound the ball.

"That's skill, already. Told you we was gone rip a hole in y'all pockets today," Loopy snapped as she defended the inbound pass.

Jada inbounded the ball to Toodie and the group made their way back up court, running past Angelica, who still had her hands on her hips while taking deep gasps of air.

"Get in the game with your sick ass!" Sweet Pea laughed as she ran past Angelica and headed up court.

Angelica only turned around and watched as everybody ran past her; she was sweating uncontrollably and breathing heavily. Her mouth was gaped open and her eyes were wide and wild. Not wanting to let her girls down, Angelica took one step forward to rejoin the game, but that one step was about all the energy the slender Mexican could muster. She fell over onto her side just as the others were running back her way after Toodie had missed a mid-range jump shot.

Toodie and Jada didn't bother to help Angelica as she lay on the court. They jumped over her body and went on trying to defend their opponents. Five thousand dollars was at stake, not to mention their pride. Loopy dribbled the ball a few times and stepped behind the three-point line. Toodie tried to run up and block the shot, but Loopy got the ball off in time. She hit an arching two-pointer to tie the game up eleven even.

Jessie then intercepted an inbound pass from Jada after Toodie missed the ball, and she quickly laid it up to put her team up by one point.

"*Man, these some sorry mutherfuckas I'm ballin' with,*" Toodie thought as she ran around the court trying to catch another inbound pass from Jada.

Toodie and her team were now trailing by one, but she was determined to regain the lead. She ran around the court trying to get open for the inbound pass, still paying Angelica no mind as she lay motionless on the ground. When Jada passed her the ball, Toodie ran towards it, but she tripped over Angelica.

Jessie immediately scooped up the loose ball and took it in for a layup. "Thirteen, eleven," she yelled as she high-fived Loopy and Sweet Pea.

Toodie and Jada paused the game after the brief series of plays that had just cost them the lead and went over to the free throw line where they looked down on Angelica.

"She's gonna cost us five thousand dollars," Jada said

somberly. "She came out strong, but what the fuck is happening now?"

"Angelica, get your ass up, man," Toodie snapped as she nudged her with the tip of her Air Force Ones.

"Your girl need a tank of oxygen!" Jessie yelled as she and the Cruz cousins walked over towards Toodie and Jada while laughing aloud.

When Angelica groaned and began twitching as she lay on the ground, everyone watching the game knew it was far more serious than they'd assumed. Toodie and Jada had to hold her hands down to her sides to prevent her from punching herself in the face.

Pepper walked up at that moment and poured water on Angelica's face. "What the fuck is wrong with this bitch?" she asked.

"I ain't got a clue. Maybe she having a heat stroke," Jada reasoned.

Everyone around the two was wondering what to do to help Angelica, but Pepper, although pretending not to know what was going down, knew exactly what was happening to Angelica. She was having a seizure; but she wasn't about to say anything to anyone. *"I hope her ass choke on her own tongue and die,"* she thought to herself. *"That'll make Toodie that much easier to get to."*

"You got our money? 'Cause this here look like a forfeit," Pepper said aloud to Toodie, who only looked at her and shook her head in dismay.

"Don't you see this girl is about to damn near die out here," Toodie asked with a frown on her face.

"Not my problem, chica. We need our stacks." Pepper replied as she curled her lips and stared Toodie up and down.

"This bitch here," Toodie sighed as she whistled for one of her soldiers.

Pepper could care less about Toodie and her crew's troubles. She was thinking about the money she was going to win for

Jessie, Loopy and Sweet Pea. Toodie, Jada and Angelica would no doubt have to forfeit now; and if they decided to play the game out, they had no chance of beating Jessie, Sweet Pea and Loopy, something they'd thought they could do at the start of the game.

"I called an ambulance for this sickly mutherfucka," Toodie sighed as she shook her head while staring down at Angelica, who was laying on her side franticly gasping for air.

"Simone, you wanna go out to dinner and shit with our new money? Do some shopping?" Pepper asked. She then eyed Toodie and sniggled.

Toodie eyed Pepper for a few seconds. She thought about continuing the game, but the bet was only five grand, pocket change to her. She also knew if she didn't pay Pepper and Simone, they would get into it over something petty. Pepper would get hers one day, but not this way, and not this day. *"I'm a hit that li'l bitch where it hurt,"* Toodie said to herself before she openly agreed to pay off the bet.

No words were spoken as the group parted ways, Jessie and company following Pepper and Simone back to the Hummer to split the winnings. The three then hopped into the Durango and left the neighborhood after copping their earnings and headed over to McDonald's on Jefferson Avenue to grab a quick meal. They were sitting inside eating when Pepper and Simone rolled up in Simone's hummer about twenty minutes later. The two spotted their friends when they entered and Pepper gave Simone her order and headed towards her friends' table.

"Your ass know you can't stand being in this place," Jessie told Pepper as she approached the table.

Pepper had witnessed Toodie's sister, a young woman named Phoebe Perez, get gunned down in the drive-thru at this particular McDonald's four years ago and she had vowed to never use the drive-thru, and she wasn't too keen on entering the building either, but she did it for the sake of friendship.

"Nahh, it's cool right about now. I ain't gone be long anyway," Pepper said as she eased into the booth while Simone placed their orders. She had a jubilant smile on her face and was laughing quite often. "Angelica caught a seizure out there, y'all," she laughed.

"For real," Sweet Pea asked. "Is she okay?"

"Fuck you care about that bum-ass bastard for?" Pepper snapped. "She lucky that's all happen to her ugly ass out there. Coulda caught a heart attack or something. She be all right soon enough."

"That's good-looking on that bet, Pepper," Jessie said as she unwrapped her burger. "I can use that money for a lawyer."

"Damn," Pepper sighed as she leaned back in the booth. "I forgot all about that shit right fast, Jessie. That gotta be fuckin' with your head. You ever tried to talk to ole girl? Maybe she gone change her mind about going through with it."

Jessie rested her elbows on the table and looked down at her Big Mac meal. "I tried calling Chastity," she said somberly. "That broad don't wanna hear shit I gotta say. She cussed me out and thanked me for doing what I did to her. Said umm, said her and her husband or whatever done made up."

"You never told us that," Loopy said excitedly. "So, y'all kinda gettin' back cool?"

"Gettin' back cool? You kiddin' me?" Jessie asked in a high-pitched voice. "I hate ta' bust everybody bubble. I mean, I was happy myself when she thanked me for being the reason her and her li'l beau got back together. I ain't gone even try and play hard and shit. I was happy." Jessie couldn't help but to laugh lowly while shaking her head from side to side as she wrung her hands in frustration. "That bitch hate me, fam," she admitted.

Deep down inside, twenty-two year-old Jessie was hurt and scared. She sincerely never meant to hurt Chastity so badly. She also knew had Chastity not had her gun off safety that night she could have very well been killed. And Chastity would have had every right to do so. The realization that she could have died that night had hit hard for Jessie and she was left stunned.

"You all right, Jessie? You look like you bouta cry and shit,"

Loopy said as she chomped down on a large order of fries.

"I'm good. I need to get over to Kantrell spot tonight. Take me to pay this girl light bill first, though," Jessie said as she slid out the booth. "My life all fucked up."

"Girl," Pepper snapped, "you betta forget about a light bill and just carry your ass inside! You took a chance being in Fox Park all day like you was. You need to get back inside. You done already made money, Jessie. Just go ahead with your girls," she reasoned as she held out her hands.

"I told Kantrell I was gone do that for her, though."

Sweet Pea shook her head in protest. "Kantrell said to take care of yourself, Jessie. You gone need them dollars for that lawyer," she said matter-of-factly.

"Nahh. She been givin' a nigga a place to hide out, I been eating her food and drinking all her liquor? And it's the least I can do being she had to close her shop for the day over my bullshit."

"Whatever. We gotta pay our cell phone bills anyway," Sweet Pea remarked just as Simone whistled for Pepper.

"Y'all, y'all be careful out here," Pepper said seriously. "And Jessie, you make sure you take your behind inside after you do what you gotta do."

"No doubt," Jessie said as she dapped Pepper.

The group left McDonald's and went their separate ways once more. Sweet Pea wheeled the Durango down Jefferson Avenue headed south and turned west onto Russell Boulevard and headed towards Compton Heights where Kantrell's house was located near Reservoir Park, just off South Grand Boulevard.

"I got a bad feeling about this here, Jessie," Loopy said as she fumbled with the CD player. "We should just take this money and go by Kantrell and kick it with her," she added just as Pete Rock and C.L. Smooth's song *They Reminisce Over You (T.R.O.Y.)* began playing over the speakers.

"We right down the street from the li'l check cashing place

on South Grand," Jessie responded. "That's right up the street from Kantrell crib. Eh, I ain't heard that joint in a hot minute."

"We keep that old school," Loopy responded as she turned the volume up and nodded her head to the beat.

The trio of friends cruised down busy Russell Boulevard under the street lights bumping Pete Rock. It had been a good day for everybody, money had been made, they hadn't encountered the law and were preparing to wind the night down three thousand dollars richer.

"Right here," Jessie said as Sweet Pea approached the check cashing place, which sat off the road in small strip mall that held a twenty-four laundromat, a barber shop, Family Dollar and a Subway sandwich shop.

Sweet Pea looked over to Loopy, who only shook her head. "Fuck it," Loopy spoke out, "she ain't gone rest until she pay Kantrell's light bill."

"And you know this man," Jessie quipped as Sweet Pea wheeled the Durango into the strip mall and parked in the slots across from the check cashing place.

Jessie climbed out the back seat of the SUV and walked into the building with Sweet Pea and Loopy trailing. The check cashing place was no more than a small, brown-carpeted office that had a counter stretching from end to end, half wood and half glass, with wood paneling on the walls in the open area. There were only few people in line and one lone cashier working behind the bullet proof window.

"Aww yeah, we should be in and out in no time. They only got three people ahead of us," Jessie said happily.

"It's almost ten 'o' clock, it shouldn't be crowded," Sweet Pea remarked. "You talked to Kree, Jessie," she then asked.

"Yeah. I hit her up after the game and she text me right when we got up to Mickey D's. She at the crib chillin' and said Kantrell waitin' on us so we can play cards and grill out."

"We ain't all hang out in a while. Kree shoulda came out tonight." Sweet Pea remarked.

"I know, huh?" Jessie responded. "She all wrapped up into Curtis now. It's all good. I'm happy for my girl."

"We all are. But back to the subject at hand—Kantrell should have a fresh bottle of yak or something waiting on us when we get there."

"I know she got some weed to smoke if nothing else." Loopy said as the line moved forward.

"Eh, I asked Kree about her new dog back on the park," Jessie laughed. "She said she was hot with y'all asses for a minute."

"I still can't figure out how Riley got hit," Loopy wondered.

"Me either," Jessie quickly answered, still refusing to admit she'd had a part in Riley's demise.

The friends' light-hearted conversation was interrupted when a light-skinned female dressed in all black and wearing a ski-mask to hide her face ran into the medium-sized building toting a black semi-automatic rifle with an infrared beam. She pointed her weapon at the five customers standing before her. "Drop everything on the fuckin' floor and turn around and get on your knees," she yelled as she aimed the gun at the customers.

Loopy, Sweet Pea and Jessie were scared out of their minds and sick to their stomachs—scared over the robbery taking place—and sick to their stomachs because all three had their winnings in their pockets. They'd just been caught slipping and there was nothing they could do about the matter. The barrel on the rifle pointed at the three looked like an open garbage can it was so big. They stood motionless with their hands in the air while the other two customers dropped all of their contents onto the floor. "You heard what the fuck I said, bitches?" the young woman yelled as she stepped forward with the gun pointed at Sweet Pea's face.

"*No disparen, señorita!*" (Don't shoot, miss!) Sweet Pea pleaded.

"Miss my ass with that shit!" the gunman snapped. "Empty ya' pockets!" she demanded. "Now!" she yelled as she lurched forward with the assualt rifle.

Sweet Pea, Loopy and Jessie had just under nine thousand dollars in total. They couldn't believe the dumb luck they'd just been hit with; with the gun aimed on the three of them, they slowly began emptying their pockets, tossing stacks of hundreds onto the floor. "Oh shit," the armed robber laughed as she looked down at the money being thrown at her feet, "y'all mutherfuckas got more than what they got behind the counter!"

Unbeknownst to the robber, the cashier had seen her running up to the front door when she was crossing the parking lot and she had tripped the silent alarm. Sirens off in the distance forced the bandit to pull up. She exited the building with the stolen money and fled the scene on foot just before flashing blue lights began reflecting off the glasses of the surrounding businesses.

Jessie, Sweet Pea and Loopy all knew they were wanted. Bad enough they'd had their money stolen, to stick around and talk to the police would only add to their problems. Without giving it a second thought, they ran out the door a few seconds after the armed robber and made a beeline for the Durango.

Sweet Pea was backing out of the parking slot when three patrol cars pulled up behind the jeep. Six officers jumped out with guns drawn, ordering the occupants of the SUV to exit the ride with their hands in the air.

"That's not them! She ran towards the back of the building! You got the wrong people!" the cashier and the two other customers began yelling as they slowly approached the officers.

"Get back on the sidewalk!" an officer yelled as he pointed his gun towards the three people approaching him.

"Eh, we ain't do shit! Our asses got robbed, too!" Jessie yelled aloud as she slowly climbed out of the backseat of the Durango with her hands in the air.

The officers weren't listening to no one's reasoning. They'd just arrived on the scene and had to sort things out; for all they knew, the people they'd ridden up on were the ones who'd robbed the check cashing place. After securing Jessie, Sweet Pea and Loopy, the officers got the full story from the cashier, who'd explained that Jessie, Loopy and Sweet Pea weren't involved, but were victims themselves. The cashier's story corroborated with what the two customers had relayed to the officers and Jessie, Sweet Pea and Loopy were let off the hook.

"See?" Sweet Pea snapped as the three walked back to the Durango. "All you had to do was go your ass inside, Jessie!"

"Eh, it's not every day you get caught up in some shit like that, Donatella. Like I just knew all our shit was gone get took over paying a light bill!"

Loopy was crushed. She really wanted her money. She'd hustled her ass off to win that game only to have her winnings snatched up by a total stranger. She was just ready to drop Jessie off and go home and smoke a blunt and go to bed because the night had been ruined.

The three were backing out of the parking slot once more when officers surrounded their car again with guns drawn. They seemed to be angrier than before this time as well. "What the fuck is it now, man?" Sweet Pea snapped as she pounded her fist against the steering wheel. "Can a bitch just go the fuck home?"

"In about twenty years or so you can," one of the officers replied as he pulled the door open and snatched Sweet Pea from behind the steering wheel.

Loopy had two guns pointed on her; she was escorted from the jeep and was already being handcuffed. At the same time, Jessie was pulled from the backseat and flung to the ground.

"What the fuck now?" Jessie asked in frustration.

"You're under arrest for the attempted murder of Chastity Hubbert. You have the right to remain silent...anything you say can and will be used against you in the court of law...you have the right to an attorney..."

The officer read Jessie her Miranda rights and placed her in the backseat and threw a copy of a flyer with her mug shot into her lap as he sped off downtown with his lights blaring. Detectives arrived on the scene a few minutes later and Loopy and Sweet Pea, who were only wanted for questioning for the time being, were driven downtown to be questioned.

CHAPTER EIGHTEEN
ROOKIE SEASON

"So, Guadalupe Cruz, your friend, Jessie," Sandra Cordova, a heavy-set, thirty-seven year-old Hispanic detective said to Loopy, "you said you had no idea she had ever gotten into a fight with this woman Chastity Hubbert?"

"Si, Sandra," Loopy replied as she sat inside a small four-brick-walled interview room. "We hang together? But she never lets us know her personal business at all."

"Well, the report says that two females accompanied Jessie during this attempted homicide. Any idea who that may be?" Sandra asked calmly with a smirk on her face.

"Nahh," Loopy said as she looked over to the concrete wall to her right. "I, I couldn't tell ya' who those people were, man."

"We have footage of that fight you know?" Loopy looked over to the mid-thirties blond-haired woman with a stone-faced expression at that moment. "That's right," Sandra said as she reached into her business suit jacket and pulled out a pack of Newports. "*Cuidado de humo?*" (Care for a smoke?)

"You got some dozier up in this piece?" Loopy asked as she eyed the detective seriously.

The detective laughed aloud as she reached down into a pocket situated on the inside of her suit jacket. "You're fucking with me now," she chuckled as she slid a cell phone towards the center of the table seperating the two. "Did you not hear me say I have your ass on video assisting your weird-assed friend? Jessie can get a boat load of time over this incident."

Loopy patted her pockets and threw her hands up. "Show me the video," she said calmly. "And I'll show you that it's not me on that tape."

Sandra eyed Loopy from across the table as she leaned back and crossed her legs. "Your lawyer will see it once you're charged. Then you can see it, come back here and tell me what I already know and try and cut a deal. Or you can just tell me what I need to know today and you and your cousin can…be on your way," she said as she extended her hand towards the locked door.

Loopy's mind was working overtime at this moment. She believed someone on the scene had indeed recorded the incident, but she was willing to gamble that none of the people in the cell phone video could be made out clearly. It was nearly pitch dark at the red-light the night Jessie attacked Chastity, and the few people who'd witnessed the assault were off in the distance. The only way Jessie got made was because Chastity had lived to tell who attacked her. In Loopy's eyes, the detectives were trying to close their case quickly by getting her and Sweet Pea to flip. Loopy was willing to take the fall, however; Jessie was her friend and she wasn't about to turn state.

"Me dan mi banda roja para que pueda ir cambiar," (Give me my red band so I can go change out.) she told the detective.

Sandra stood up and stared down angrily at Loopy at that moment. She eased her chair back, grabbed the phone and walked towards the door. Before she turned the handle to exit, Sandra looked back at Loopy and said, "You're willing to go down with Jessie over something you had nothing to do with? I know you're innocent, Guadalupe. Why waste your life on someone like, Jessie?"

"Just do your job. I ain't gone make it easy for you. And if you're not charging me or Donatella I want the keys back to my ride so I can go home!"

Sandra left the room and pressed play on the cell phone and stared at the blurry, darkened images on the phone. Most perpetrators would've given up the information she needed to close her case. Loopy was a stubborn one, however; she was the type to play it all the way through, Sandra realized. She shook her head towards her captain and went over to the one way window and looked in on Sweet Pea's interview that was being conducted by her partner, who was a female rookie six years her junior.

"You talkin' bout Chava's over by the, by the taco house down in Soulard. We know that joint! I ain't even know y'all hangout over to Chava's," Sweet Pea laughed as she knocked ashes from her cigarette. "Y'all eat there all the time? That's like a police hangout or something?"

"Si! Me and my partner Sandra eat there all the time, Donatella. They have the best Mexican food in Saint Louis, I'm telllin' you."

"Nice place. Never knew it was a police hangout, though. So, you tellin' me y'all gone question the driver of that li'l Buick in y'all video and he might take the stand on my girl?"

"Yeah," Darby Jones, the thirty-one year old slender, Caucasian brunette said as she puffed on a Marlboro right along with Sweet Pea. "I mean, this will be like my first arrest for a serious crime since I got promoted two months ago."

Darby Jones was a real square in Donatella's eyes. She may have been a robbery/homicide detective, but she had not a clue what the hell she was doing if Sweet Pea had to tell it. The two hit it off well to say Sweet Pea was a possible suspect in an attempted murder case. Darby had tried to befriend Sweet Pea by telling her that their lunch had been interrupted when she and Sandra got the call to investigate an armed robbery and she was surprised to learn that she would be investigating her first serious crime.

It didn't take long for Sweet Pea to realize that Darby Jones was, in a word, nice. When she'd offered Sweet Pea a cigarette, the oldest trick in the book detectives used to warm up to suspects and lit it for her, Sweet Pea knew right then and there that she could work the woman over. The twenty-year-old hustler didn't even smoke cigarettes, but it was a tactic she was using in order to get closer to the detective and cipher information from someone she viewed as being a little dense. Sweet Pea hadn't a clue what Loopy was telling the detective interviewing her, but if she knew her cousin like she did, she knew Loopy wasn't coming off any information what-so-ever, and neither was she.

With the quick understanding that her partner was giving up information that she had tucked away in her pocket to bust the case wide open, Sandra rushed into the room and ended the interview. She grabbed Darby up by the collar and pulled her out the room and slammed the door shut. "What are you doing tellin' the suspect about our witness," she asked in dismay as she pushed Darby up against the wall just outside of the interrogation room.

"I was trying to get her to warm up to me, Sandra," Darby said surprisedly.

"You're giving her information, Darby," Sandra said lowly. "What did I tell you? What did I tell you when you were first promoted to robbery-homicide?"

"The suspects aren't our friends," Darby sighed.

"Get that through your head, rookie—or you'll be out of a job before summer ends if not dead. Recognize who you're dealing with, Darby. These aren't nice people."

"Everyone that gets arrested isn't bad," Darby retorted lowly. "Nice people just make mistakes, that's all."

"Not of this caliber. Attempted murder? That's no accident," Sandra said as she walked off. "By the way," she added as she turned around and stared at Darby from a short distance up the white, vinyl-tiled, narrow hallway, "you know where all the nice people are right about now?"

"Where?" Darby asked as rested up against the wall eyeing Sandra.

"They're home with their families having dinner. Which is

what I'm about to do."

"What about our suspects, Sandra," Darby called out.

Sandra turned around and spread her arms. "I'll sign papers to release them," she said. "Jessie is already booked and we have the witness's story. Until we can present further evidence to move things forward with Sweet Pea and Loopy, where're done with those two until this case goes to court—if it ever does at all." Sandra ended before turning and walking back to her desk.

****

A couple of hours after their interview with the detectives, Loopy and Sweet Pea were pulling away from the downtown precinct. "What they ask you, Donatella?" Loopy asked as she wheeled the Durango out of the precinct's parking lot.

"They asked me about us being on the scene when Chastity got beat, but I didn't give up a thing."

"Me either. I wonder what's gone happen to Jessie, though. She got charged with attempted murder."

"I know. And they have a witness too," Sweet Pea remarked.

"Who? That video isn't showing anything, Sweet Pea. If it did, we'd be locked up too right now."

"Not the video," Sweet Pea said as she yawned. "Dibble. He told the law he saw you and me riding around with Jessie before we left Fox Park like a hour before the fight. Pepper and Simone were right about what they saw this morning. Dibble talking."

Loopy looked over to her cousin with a serious expression on her face. The video was one thing; but the situation with Dibble was on a whole other level. "How you get the detective to tell you all that, chica?"

Sweet Pea laughed and sat upright, "Loopy, she just started talkin' to me. Gave up all that information to me and all I was doing was asking. Her partner came in and stopped the thing when she heard us so I know she wasn't lying."

"You know what that mean right?"

"What?"

"If Dibble testifies against Jessie and puts us in that car, we all could be looking at some serious time."

"What you plan on doing?"

Loopy rubbed her chin as she drove with her left hand draped over the steering wheel. "We'll need to steal us a car tonight," she said somberly as she jumped onto Interstate-70 and headed towards East Saint Louis.

Sweet Pea didn't respond. She gazed out of her window at the city skyline and bit her bottom lip. Forty years was long time. To just let Dibble testify would be foolish. Too big of a risk. No one really had money for a lawyer to fight to the case, and to test fate was not how the Cruz cousins operated. Neither cousin spoke any further concerning Dibble as they headed home.

CHAPTER NINETEEN
RIGHT OUTSIDE OF KIRK'S

The Cruz cousins pulled up to their Aunt's home over in East Saint Louis on the corner of Wimmer Place and exited their Durango and entered the home's front yard. The dope house in the middle of the block had a flurry of activity with cars parked out front of the trap with music blasting and fiends were up and down the block. The Cruz cousins stayed in a rowdy part of East Saint Louis, but they were right at home amidst the organized chaos.

Upon entering their home, the two were greeted by their Aunt, who was sitting at the kitchen table with all of their baby pictures displayed across the table. *"Dos están a salvo!"* (You two are safe!) the auburn-haired, heavy-set mid-forties Hispanic cried as she leapt up from the table and ran and hugged her nieces. *"Tuve un sueño terrible que ustedes dos se pusieron en una celda de la cárcel"* (I had a terrible dream you two were put into a jail cell!)

"We're fine, Auntie CeeCee," Sweet Pea assured as she hugged her Aunt.

Loopy hugged her Aunt, but said nothing. She left the living room and headed to the bedroom inside the small two bedroom section eight home and closed the door. She grabbed an old cell phone out of her dresser drawer and sent a text to Pepper as she began searching for a pair of dark jeans and a hoody.

She had changed her clothes and was tying the laces on a black pair of Nike's when Sweet Pea entered the room.

"CeeCee always have bad dreams when something is about to go down," Sweet Pea said as she closed and locked the door. "She doesn't want us to leave. She took the keys to the Durango and said for us to stay inside."

"We can't do that," Loopy said matter-of-factly.

"I know," Sweet Pea replied as she went to the closet and grabbed a pair of dark jeans. "I need one of your hoodies," she added.

After changing their clothes, the Cruz cousins, now wearing dark jeans and black hoodies and black shoes, each grabbed a pair of black leather gloves and a thick, long screwdriver and climbed out of their bedroom window. Their Aunt was always trying to hold them inside because she knew they were outlaws in the making. They were just like their mothers and fathers, all four of whom who had perished on the streets of Uruguay years earlier. CeeCee had brought the two up with her from Uruguay to America years earlier to give them a better life, the trip paid for by the cousins' parents, who were scheduled to join them once they'd settled a score with a rival human trafficker who'd dropped a dime on them to the F.B.I.

A botched hit, one in which the federal authorities had been tipped off, had ended the Cruz cousins' parents lives just months after CeeCee had landed on American soil. Their Aunt, Clarissa Cruz, who they affectionately called CeeCee, was all they had in life now and they loved her dearly; but the streets were where their heads and hearts were at this point and time in their lives.

The cousins walked pass the back stairs of their home, briefly eyeing CeeCee as she moved about in the kitchen while listening to a Spanish radio station before hopping their neighbor's fence and emerging onto the block the next house down. They walked down the busy street under the moon-lit night sky and walked over to the trap house where they knew a couple of the dealers.

Loopy and Sweet Pea were popular in their neighborhood.

They got down with a few of the drug dealers on their block in times past, but the two guys they'd dealt with had been sent up state on long bids. The newer dealers were cool, but Loopy and Sweet Pea never gave the click the time of day; they only sold stolen electronics to the young black males from time to time now. They walked up onto the set before the trap and spoke to a few dealers and asked if anybody had a car they could use for a while.

"Y'all ain't breakin' in nobody business with none of these whips," a young dealer named Tito Charles spoke aloud. "Give a man some pussy we might reconsider, though," he chuckled.

"Lame culo," Sweet Pea scoffed as she and Loopy walked off.

"Yeah, fuck you too!" Tito laughed as he dapped his brother. "Fuck them crazy ass Mexican bitches."

The cousins ignored Tito and soon made their way onto another block where they stole a pristine 1988 four door Cadillac Brougham and headed back across the Mississippi River Bridge towards Fox Park.

****

"I racked it one time already. All you gotta do is squeeze the trigger, so be careful how you handle this bitch because she ready to fire," eighteen year-old Simone Cortez told Loopy as she handed her a semi-automatic twelve gauge. "It got like eight rounds in it, but two blasts is all you gone need to knock Dibble into the afterlife."

"That's right," Pepper chimed in as she jumped down the stairs and pranced into the living room where she handed Sweet Pea a nickel-plated .9mm Beretta.

Tonight was better than Christmas Eve for Pepper for two reasons. For one, her girls were getting down for real by going after Dibble for ratting on them; second, she'd learned Dibble was hanging with Toodie now, seeking protection for ratting on her friends. For Pepper, if Loopy and Sweet Pea were to hit Dibble, it would be just as if she'd pulled the trigger and disrespected Toodie herself. It would be the hand she would fan with; Dibble may have been a neighborhood fiend that was cool and got along with everybody, but Pepper knew anybody that Toodie dealt with, she was down for them to the very end because she was just that loyal and carried that much pride.

Pepper was looking to kick something off with Toodie so she could go after her with no-holds-barred. She'd heard about her friends getting robbed at the check cashing place earlier and had gotten word that Ya Murder was behind the jack play, wanting to get back at Jessie, Loopy and Sweet Pea for winning that ball game earlier in the day. How Ya Murder had gotten up to the check cashing place, however, Pepper hadn't the answer, but it was a good chance Toodie was involved becuase she and Ya had both disappeared once Angelica was hauled off to the hospital.

Pepper was a young manipulator with an intense bloodlust geared towards Toodie; and if her girls held it down for Jessie by killing Dibble, she was going to go out in that water head first on their behalf against Toodie, Ya Murder and Angelica Arnaz. It was something she'd been wanting to do for the last several years and she'd now found a way to go at her nemesis unabashedly.

"That boy Dibble been on Ann Street all day and he still out there, we rode pass there right after you text me, Loopy," Pepper said as she lit a blunt. "When y'all done, toss the guns and go lay low in East Saint Louis until this shit blow over."

"Si," Sweet Pea said as she racked the semi-automatic handgun and tucked it into her front waistband and took the blunt handed to her by Pepper and toke several tokes.

Loopy was headed towards the front door with the twelve gauge draped at her side when Simone stopped her, "It's already racked," she reminded Loopy. "You see that boy Dibble, all you gotta do is let loose. For Jessie," she said as she looked her friend square in the eyes and shook her hand.

"For Jessie," Loopy said as she flipped the hood of her sweater over her head and opened the door, stepping out into the night air with Sweet Pea trailing close behind.

"How you think they gone make out?" Simone asked Pepper

as she locked the door.

"If they see Dibble, Loopy gone knock that boy flat on his ass. Let's get our shit together so we can dip out when they done," Pepper stated as she trotted back upstairs. "Shop is officially closed," she quipped as she disappeared from sight.

Loopy and Sweet Pea, meanwhile, had just climbed back into the stolen car. Loopy sat in the backseat with the twelve gauge resting in her lap as Sweet Pea pulled away from Pepper's apartment. Street lights were nonexistent for most of Fox Park. Toodie and her click had shot out nearly every street light in order to prevent the law from spying on their activities. It was an action that would work in the Cruz cousins' favor on this warm spring night in May of 2007. With all four windows rolled down on the Cadillac, Sweet Pea wheeled the car through the darkened neighborhood with Twista's song *Get Me* playing low on the radio, steadily toking on the blunt Pepper had given her as she became absorbed in the music.

"What the fuck really going on...does he bite 'cause he know he on...don't he know I already established myself as Twista Corleone...well I'm holdin' city down...ain't going nowhere here I stand...you know where I am...if you hate me(come and get me)...if you want me(come and get me)...here I am..."

Loopy was scanning the block as her cousin cruised through the darkened streets of Fox Park. A couple of times she'd thought she'd seen Dibble, but it was a false alarm each time. Sweet Pea knew Dibble moved around a lot, she was hoping to catch him up to *Kirk's*, the neighborhood corner store, but there were only a few teenagers and winos hanging out on the corner under the lone street light that lit up the area, and a small line of people were waiting to buy items from the store's walk-up window and Dibble was nowhere on the scene.

Sweet Pea cruised pass the corner store and turned onto the next block, headed north. She then hit Russell Avenue, headed west and made a sharp right turn onto Ann Avenue. She turned the music down as she entered the most dangerous set in Fox Park and she and Loopy both began searching for Dibble. It was pitch dark on Ann Avenue, the row houses standing like still ghosts in the night as shadowy figures focused in on the unfamiliar car traveling down the block.

Sweet Pea grew nearer to Toodie's main trap and it seemed as if bodies were emerging from every cut on the block. Reflections of chrome steel could be seen under the moon light and Toodie herself had emerged from her trap with a long rifle. If Dibble had been out on the block, he would not have been hit tonight. Ann Avenue was a fortress. The Cruz cousins would not have made it off the block and they knew it. Sweet Pea rode pass Toodie's trap, her face shielded by her hoody as Loopy lay down flat on the backseat, hidden from sight.

"We may have to wait and catch him some other time," Sweet Pea remarked as she turned off of Ann Avenue.

"Si," Loopy replied as she eased up from the backseat. "Let's bring these guns back to Pepper."

Sweet Pea relit the blunt she was toking on and made her way back over to Saint Louis Street. She was pulling up to Pepper's apartment when she eyed Dibble standing on the corner in front of *Kirk's Corner Store*, the same store they'd passed by just minutes earlier. He was waiting in line to make a purchase from the walk-up window with four people standing behind him and two in front. The corner had grown a little more crowded in a short span of time, but Dibble was out by his lonesome; none of Toodie's people were around.

Loopy saw Dibble on the corner as well. "Let's move," she told Sweet Pea as she grabbed the twelve gauge and scooted over to the passenger side in the backseat. "Turn left right before the store and slow down enough so I can jump out," she added as she flipped her hood onto her head and tied a white bandana around the lower portion of her face.

Sweet Pea drove the car at a steady pace with her .9mm in her lap. When she reached the corner store, she made a quick left turn and slowed the car. Loopy hopped out at that moment with the twelve gauge on full display, leaving the back door wide open as everybody scattered. She ran up on Dibble, who was not a fast runner given his drug habit, and squeezed the trigger. The back of Dibble's navy blue mechanic's uniform shirt was ripped open and he fell face forward onto the sidewalk just a few steps away from the walk-up window and out of the light that had been shining down on the corner.

The entire corner had been cleared when Loopy emerged from the backseat of the Cadillac with the long, chrome cannon. Even the cashier inside the corner store had taken cover, slamming the Plexiglas window shut before she dropped to the floor. No one was around to witness Loopy walk up on Dibble, who was squirming on the ground in the darkness and calling out for help. Loopy said nothing as she walked up on Dibble and fired another blast from the twelve gauge that shattered the back of his skull. She reemerged from the darkness and crossed under the light and jumped back into the backseat of the car and slammed the door as Sweet Pea mashed the gas pedal, fleeing the scene and leaving behind a scene of carnage as Dibble lay mangled on the concrete sidewalk in the darkness.

Dibble's murder would eventually be the spark that would lead into a bloody feud that would play out on the city streets between Toodie and Pepper. In the meantime, however, the main goal, which was to eliminate the lone witness who was able to link the Cruz cousins to Chastity's assault, had been accomplished. And now that the Cruz cousins were linked up with Pepper, their status on the streets of Saint Louis had been elevated. Everybody now knew that Loopy and Sweet Pea meant business on the streets. The cousins returned home to their Aunt's home and got high as they reflected on their treacherous deed, all-the-while hoping that what they'd done would set Jessie free.

CHAPTER TWENTY

NEVER SAW IT COMING

Kree was stirred from her sleep by her ringing phone early Sunday morning as New Riley barked uncontrollably beside her bed. She rolled over and grabbed her phone and answered. "Hello?"

"Good morning, Miss Devereaux."

"Curtis," Kree smiled as she stretched and leaned over and petted her dog to soothe his barking. "The only thing that is better than waking up to your voice is waking up beside you."

"Well, let's make it happen, baby. I got our favorite room and a couple of games, some movies. What you have planned today?"

"Well," Kree chuckled as she climbed out of bed. "I think I'll play a board game or two and watch some movies, but I haven't eaten," she sulked.

"I got you covered," Curtis laughed. "What time you be here?"

"In a couple of hours. Say around ten 'o' clock?"

"Okay, I'll run out and grab a few things for later on. See you later."

"Muah!" Kree said before she hung up.

The day had started off wonderful for Kree, but as she reflected on the matter a little more, she began wondering why Curtis was able to get away this early and on a Sunday. The move was welcomed, just far different from their regular routine of meeting on Friday nights and a day or two out of the week for drinks. She kept in mind to ask Curtis exactly what was going on with the divorce as she ran herself a bath. Thirty minutes later, she was drying herself off when her phone rang once more. She answered by clicking on the speaker phone. "What's up?" she said, not knowing who was on the other line.

"You have a collect call from the Saint Louis County Sheriff's Department from…this Jessica…to accept press…"

Kree scrambled over to her phone and accepted the call. "Jessie you in jail? What, what happened to you?"

"I thought Kantrell or somebody woulda been told you."

"Nooo. I been home since I left the game yesterday. No one has told me anything! What happened?"

"Hey, don't go to cryin' and all that shit," Jessie stated. "We talked already. I'm up on an attempted murder charge."

"Oh no," Kree cried as she leaned against her sink. "You think you can get out?"

"They set my bail at a quarter-mill. Even then, I'm gone need a lawyer to smooth this shit over."

Kree thought about Sean Bradsworth at that moment. He was a criminal defense attorney and had a good presence in the court room, she believed, given the trials he'd discussed with her in times past. The two were still on good terms also. "I'm gonna help you out, okay? I haven't enough for bail exactly, that's nearly everything I own, but I can get you a lawyer."

"For real? Who?"

"Don't worry about that. I'm coming to see you this morning." Kree responded as she walked into her bedroom and opened her closet.

"You can't come until Tuesday," Jessie replied. "They not gone have my papers processed in time."

"Well, that'll give me time to talk to this lawyer I know. You need anything? Is there anything I can do now?"

"Nahh. Just check on my place. You still got the spare key, right?"

"Yeah, is your rent paid?"

"For this month. Not sure about next month."

"Well, I can cover you for a few months. You talked to Kantrell?"

"Nahh, let her know what's up, though. Tell her I won't be in Tuesday," Jessie chuckled.

"You have a mighty fine attitude given the circumstances," Kree said seriously as she pulled out a fuschia silk skirt and matching blouse.

"That's all my ass can do to keep from going crazy in this place. Kree, you think this lawyer will be able to get me off this here?"

"He's pretty good. You'll have to fill me in on everything when I come there on Tuesday."

"Okay. I appreciate all you doing, Kree. You a good friend."

"I don't wanna see you go away, Jessie," Kree remarked as her eyes watered. "You take care, okay? We'll get through this together."

"I guess this is a bad time to tell you I was kinda responsible for killing Riley, huh?"

"What? What're you talking about?"

"Riley. I was chasing him and he ran into the street and got hit by a car. It was an accident. I never meant for him to die, man."

"Forget the dog, okay? I learned some things about myself that night. And me and New Riley are doing just fine. You just take care of yourself until you get out."

"I ain't gone lie, I'm scared as shit, Kree," Jessie whispered into the phone.

"I'm scared for you, Jessie. Let me call this lawyer and see if he's available. I'll be up there Tuesday morning."

"Alright. See you then. I ain't say this in a long while, but I love you, Kree."

"Now who's getting soft and sentimental?" Kree laughed.

"Hey, when shit get real, the real come out. I'm okay, though. See you in a couple of days."

"Okay, bye for now." Kree responded before hanging up the phone. She then dialed Sean's number and his voicemail picked up.

"Hey, darlings! This is your beloved! Sorry I'm unavailable this weekend because I am in—Vegaaasss! Don't you be so jealous now! Just leave me a message and once my little shindig is up I'll get back to you A-S-A-P! Happy three-day-weekend, huns!"

Kree left Sean a message telling him of Jessie's predicament and requested that he call her back immediately before ending the call. She dressed herself and left her home to meet up with Curtis once she'd checked on Jessie's place. She'd called Loopy, Sweet Pea and Kantrell continuously, but neither were answering their phones. Before leaving Fox Park, she stopped over to *Kirk's Corner Store* in the neighborhood and noticed police tape lying on the sidewalk just down from the store's entrance. "What happened outside?" she asked as she placed a container of Edy's butter pecan ice cream and a bag of sunflower seeds onto the counter.

"Somebody shot and killed Dibble last night," the clerk responded as he rung up Kree's items.

"What?"

"Yes, ma'am. He was waiting in line to buy something when somebody jumped out the back of a Caddy? Boom!" the clerk remarked as he threw his hands up. "Knocked his head off damn near."

Kree merely shook her head as she left the store. The last time she'd seen Dibble was when she'd given him five dollars to get high. She couldn't believe he was dead and only wondered who would do such a thing, let alone why, as she climbed back into her car, never noticing the pristine, white Maybach parked behind her Maxima. She was startled when her passenger door was opened.

Toodie slid into the front seat brandishing a chrome handgun. "Just drive," she told Kree as she placed the gun to her side.

"Please," Kree exclaimed in a terror-stricken manner. "What did I do?"

"Your fuddy duddy ass ain't done shit. It's what your homegirls did last night," Toodie snapped. "Drive this mutherfucka before I blow the toppa' your head out into the streets."

"Toodie, please. I don't, I don't know what's going on." Kree pleaded as she pulled away from the curb.

Kree had her gun tucked away in her purse on her side, but she had not a chance on going for it. Even if she did have the chance, she knew she hadn't the guts to kill Toodie. As many times as she'd placed her hand on her .380 to protect herself, when she was finally thrust into a real life or death situation, Kree now realized that she hadn't the intestinal fortitude it took to take another life. "Toodie," she cried. "I swear I don't know what this is about."

"I bet your scary ass don't—so let me hip you to the shit. See? This my 'hood. I own Fox Park," Toodie stated as she pointed towards the apartments whizzing by as Kree drove nowhere in particular. "If I was a low down bitch, which I could fuckin' well be, I'd take your ass somewhere, stick this gun in between your dick-suckin' lips and put a slug down your throat like the come your ass like to swallow. But that's not the message I wanna send today."

Kree said nothing as she drove. She was sure to turn corners in the neighborhood where she knew people would be out, the busy blocks, as she remained as calm and still as possible, not wanting to upset Toodie. "What do you want from me, Toodie?" she asked meekly.

"I want you to tell Pepper, Simone, Guadalupe and Donatella that I know what the fuck they did last night with Dibble and I don't like it. The man came to me and asked to be untouched. Word was already out, but they disobeyed," Toodie said calmly as she held the gun to Kree's side while scanning the area cautiously. "They want beef? Tell 'em they got that shit and then some."

"Okay. Okay, I'll tell them as soon as possible," Kree cried as she eyed Toodie briefly.

"Drop me off back at the store and take your weird ass the fuck on from 'round here."

Kree did as she was ordered, dropping Toodie back off at her Maybach. She then sped off the block and left the neighborhood. Pausing at a red-light, she opened her glove box and grabbed a plastic bag and vomited, knowing she was lucky to be alive, because Toodie could have very well killed her had she wanted to do so. She jumped onto Interstate-44 and drove downtown towards Embassy Suites while calling Loopy once again. This time, Loopy answered.

"What's up, Kree?" Loopy asked, having just waken up.

"She said she knows what you two did. You know who I'm talking about?" Kree whispered as she wheeled her car down Interstate-44 and merged onto Interstate-70/55.

"Fuck her!" Loopy snapped, understanding full well that Kree was referring to Toodie.

"She's mad."

"Everybody gets mad from time to time," Loopy said nonchalantly.

"She said if y'all want beef—"

"Fuck—*her!*" Loopy snapped. "You heard about Jessie?"

"Yeah. I talked to her this morning and I'm going see her Tuesday."

"Tell her that's been handled when you go, then." Loopy said as she sat up in bed and checked the time. "Me and Donatella gone be off the scene for a while so stay out of Fox

Park, this isn't any of your business."

"You don't have to tell me twice," Kree quickly stated. "Keep your phone on so we can keep in touch. I'm headed downtown."

"Si," Loopy responded before she hung up the phone.

Kree now knew the whole play that had gone down. Her friends had conspired and killed Dibble in order to get Jessie off for beating Chastity. It wasn't how she would've handled things herself, but she'd seen this scenario coming on the day the police were up to Kantrell's salon and when she and her friends had met up over to Pepper's apartment shortly thereafter. She wanted no part in the drama that was going down between her friends and Toodie, however; she was only planning on helping Jessie get out of jail. From there, all bets were off.

Kree wasn't about the life her friends were digressing into. Hers was to be a life of love, harmony and peace. She was close to realizing her dream of being with Curtis and nothing was going to stand in her way. She would do all she could to help Jessie walk on the attempted murder charge, but that was as far as her loyalty went. It wasn't a betrayal of her friends in her mind because she felt they would all understand and respect her decision. She was actually in a good position as she reflected on matters. She could work behind the scenes to help her friend go free and avoid all the impending drama that was going to go down in Fox Park.

Upon entering the valet section of Embassy Suites, Kree exited her car and opened her trunk and grabbed a can of Armor All and a bottle of sanitizer in order to wipe down the interior of her car where some of her vomit had spilled. "Let me get that for you, Kree," a male voice called out.

"Now, I know I don't come here that much in order for us to be on a first name bas—" Kree's reply was cut short when she backed out of her front seat and saw Curtis standing before her with a couple of shopping bags in his hands. "Baby," she smiled as she reached out and hugged her lover.

"Hey," Curtis smiled as he backed away from Kree. "Not

here. You never know who's watching."

"I've been wanting to ask you this all morning. How did you pull this off?" Kree asked as she placed her hands on her hips and smiled up at Curtis.

"We'll talk upstairs," Curtis responded as he walked off.

Kree could only smile in stupefaction as she returned to cleaning her car's interior. When she was done, she turned her car over to valet and entered the hotel. She was so anxious to get with Curtis she could barely contain her joy. This would be the first time they'd ever spent an entire day and night together down in Saint Louis and she was in high anticipation of this day. The incident with Toodie had been vanquished from her memory knowing she was near Curtis. She now felt safe, and back in control.

Upon entering the room, Kree was surprised to see bouquets of flowers on the kitchen counter and rose petals spread out along the floor leading to the bedroom.

"You're really turning it on aren't you?" Kree smiled as she sat her purse on the kitchen counter and walked over and hugged Curtis.

"Are you surprised?" Curtis asked as he looked down into Kree's joyful eyes. "This is a prelude to Vermont."

"I like it. But I'm curious to know what brought about this day?"

Curtis backed away from Kree and walked over to the vista window. "I told Denobria of the divorce yesterday," he said.

"Before she received the documents," Kree stated. "What happened?"

"What you think happened? The shit hit the fan, Kree. I can't go back home now. I'll have to remain here until the divorce. I don't want to rent anything yet because that will be you and I's first decision here in town."

"You're welcome to stay with me, you know? We can save more money that way."

"I know, baby. But until the divorce? I don't think that

would be a good move."

"Well, maybe I shouldn't be here today," Kree said as she took a seat at the island counter. "There's no telling what your wife is planning or thinking."

"She has my sons and is seeking representation. I left home and she hasn't a clue where I am."

"Are you sure?"

"I know my wife, okay? She wants to burn my ass in court." Curtis sighed as he folded his arms and stared out into the Saint Louis skyline.

"We had this discussion on Friday, baby," Kree said as she walked up to her lover and hugged him from behind. "I know what we're up against. And I'd rather be broke with you, than to be rich with anybody else because I love you just that much, Mister Morrow."

Curtis reached back and hugged Kree and rocked her body against his. "I love you, too, baby," he said as he leaned down and kissed her forehead tenderly. "There's no turning back now, Kree."

"Do you have any regrets, Curtis? Am I the one?" Kree asked as she looked up into his eyes.

"Ever since the day we first met in that perfume parlor," Curtis responded as he tilted Kree's chin up to his lips and kissed her with passion. "Now, I've got a game of chess that we can play before lunch. I owe you for that whipping you put on me in Oregon."

"Good luck, soldier. Set it up and I'll shower. I went to Victoria's Secret yesterday so you know what that means," Kree smiled as she leaned into Curtis' chest. "We'll be okay, baby."

"Yes we will," Curtis responded as he watched Kree sashay into the master suite.

The two lovers spent the entire day inside the suite playing chess and ordering room service. They'd watched a couple of movies while sipping wine in bed. It seemed as if Kree's role of mistress was fading into the past as time ticked by. Curtis was not returning home ever again, and the only thing that stood in her way of earning this man now was time, a short period of time at that—thirty days to be exact. What once had been a discreet rendezvous between two secret lovers was slowly morphing into everyday life. The future possibilities were boundless if Kree had to tell it. She and Curtis made love unremittingly before drifting off into a deep slumber in one another's arms, the two of them longing for the day to come where they could share their love uninhibitedly.

****

"What are we going to do today," Kree asked Curtis as she laid her head on his bare chest the following Monday.

"I have no appointments, baby," Curtis responded as he twirled Kree's hair with his fingers. "You wanna take a walk around downtown and have lunch?"

"I would love that," Kree sighed as she nuzzled closer to her love. "This time together has been spectacular. Better than Oregon."

"Only one day? Is it that special really?"

"Yes. Because this was the first time we've ever spent a full day and night together here in Saint Louis. We're advancing," Kree said happily as she rolled onto her back and lay against Curtis as she stared up at the acoustic ceiling. "Did you ever think this day would arrive when you first met me in that perfume shop?" she asked happily.

"I didn't," Curtis responded lovingly as he kissed Kree's lips while stroking her hair. "But if ever there was a love deserving, I would have to say that you and I deserve one another."

"About Vermont," Kree smiled. "You're going to ask me to move there aren't you?"

"Would you accept?"

"What," Kree laughed as she turned over and straddled Curtis. "This is a dream come true, baby," she said seriously as she leaned down and kissed Curtis passionately.

Curtis ran his hands over Kree's bare skin as he kissed her deeply. The two soon became intertwined a frenzied round of kissing that left them in an intense state of longing. It was nothing for Kree to lower herself down on her lover's stiff rod and engulf him fully. Curtis' love had a mind of its own. It readily searched for its source of pleasure, no hands were needed in order to guide it towards its stimulation, where it now sat snug inside a transfixed position of warmth and satisfaction that was unparalleled. The two lovers soon entered onto a rhythmic, slow, yet intensely pleasurable love-making session where kissing and intertwined fingers dominated the passion.

"This is all I ever wanted. For you to be mines," Kree moaned as she rocked back and forth on Curtis' member. "I love you so much, Curtis."

"Talk to me in Spanish, baby," Curtis moaned as he held Kree's face in his hands and widened his legs in order to gain deeper access to her opening before he kissed her deeply. "Tell me how you're feeling at this moment," he requested as he gazed deep into her alluring brown eyes.

Kree was moaning huskily as her body lay atop Curtis. She ran her hands along his strong jawline, licking at his lips tenderly as she ground down onto his pole that was hard enough to shatter glass. *"Soy tuyo para siempre. Marry me."* (I'm yours forever. Marry me!) she moaned. *"Soy tuyo para siempe. Marry me."*

Those two words, 'marry me', was more than Curtis could bear. He imaged in his mind the life to come with his young lover and tilted his head back and moaned aloud as he gripped Kree's rear end and thrust upwards.

Kree screamed as she felt the her lover's rod throbbing deep within her insides. The two were staring deeply into one another's eyes as they held one another tightly while making love. It was a look undeniable; one that had permanently solidified their love for one another. This look had been experienced before between the two, but with the divorce impending, and their being open, there was no denying that the next level of their planned life together was indeed underway, and neither could wait for what the future had in store for their exclusive romance that was destined for a fairy tale ending.

Frantic rhythms and palpating hearts soon mixed with moans of delight. Curtis drove deep into Kree and filled her insides, releasing a low, guttural groan as he gripped her body tightly. She lay atop him in a state of heavenly bliss as his member slowly eased from her crevice.

"That was wonderful," Kree moaned through closed eyes.

"You want breakfast again?" Curtis asked as he ran his hands through her hair.

"A western omelet and hash browns, please," Kree responded softly as she rolled over to the edge of the bed and put her feet to the floor. "We've spent the entire time in bed except for the walk to that restaurant last night."

"Well, we'll get out later today. Are you upset?" Curtis asked as he reached for the the menu.

"Seriously?" Kree laughed. "I could do this every day of my life. Look at my hair, though," she added as she picked at her curls while staring at the mirror on the wall. "I look a mess this morning."

"You look beautiful to me, baby." Curtis smiled as he touched Kree's back. "I love seeing you in your natural state. You are beautiful always."

"Thank you, but let me get myself together. Order breakfast and I'll go and pretty myself up."

"More than what you already are?" Curtis chuckled.

Kree leaned over and kissed Curtis' lips. She then leaned back and stared into his eyes and thought about the ring she'd lost. She was determined to tell him the truth on this day because she didn't want to enter into a commitment with him knowing she was hiding a secret. "I wanna tell you something while we have breakfast," she said.

"What's that look? What are you hiding," Curtis smiled.

Kree closed her brown eyes and smiled. Curtis was a sweet man in her eyes. She felt he'd understand, but she wanted to pretty herself up before she broke the news, hoping he wouldn't be too upset over her actions. "I'll tell you over breakfast," she responded tenderly as she eased up from the bed and walked into the master bathroom inside the suite's bedroom where she closed the door.

Curtis, meanwhile, had eased up from the bed and donned a robe. He picked up the hotel's phone and ordered breakfast for he and Kree and emerged from the bedroom into the living room where he poured himself a morning glass of wine. He then went to the door and unlocked it in order to retrieve the morning paper and was hit with a sight he'd never imagined.

"Good morning, Curtis," Denobria said coldly as she eyed her husband and stepped into the room.

CHAPTER TWENTY ONE
THE HARD TRUTH

Curtis was speechless. He stood in the threshold in utter disbelief watching his wife stroll by him. "You shouldn't be here," he said calmly.

"I know," Denobria said in a giddy manner. "But I just left my lawyer's office. She said if I were to witness you with said lover? I would have your ass by the balls."

"No one's here," Curtis said aloud, hoping Kree would hear the discussion unfolding in the foyer of the suite.

Denobria wasn't dumb or blind. She'd been following Curtis ever since the day she'd received that package in the mail. She'd had her assumptions after she'd talked to her husband on that day, but she just had to be sure. She'd witnessed Curtis and Kree having dinner Sunday night. It was the first time she had ever witnessed her husband with his lover, but she needed more. She'd spied the two of them walking hand in hand back into Embassy Suites and had decided to watch his car all night and saw that it hadn't moved.

Under the belief that her husband was going to work on this Monday morning, she waited outside of his room. She'd gotten his room number from the front desk after showing identification, telling the receptionist that she was his wife and had just flown into town and wanted to surprise him. She'd been laying in wait since five in the morning, basically holding her own stakeout throughout the early morning hours.

Denobria did not want to miss this moment. She just knew Curtis was inside the suite with his lover and was aiming to confront him and lay eyes upon the woman who'd stolen her husband up close and personal. When the door opened, she'd ceased the moment in order to let her position be known to both parties involved—her cheating husband, and his trifling lover.

"I'm going to own your ass when I'm done with you," Denobria smiled as she walked into the living room. "So, who is she?"

"I'm here alone, Denobria," Curtis said as he stood before his wife with his hands tucked in his robe.

Denobria had seen Curtis with his mistress, but she cared not to acknowledge his lie. "As I look around," she smiled, "I can't help but to see...two glasses, two plates, and there's a purse," she said in mocked joy as she pointed towards a beige hand bag resting on the island counter. "Burberry. Is that yours, Curtis?"

"You're going to have to excuse yourself," Curtis said aloud as he nudged Denobria's shoulder.

"Don't you touch me," Denobria hissed. "You've been going behind my back and I want to know who this woman is you've been cheating on me with!"

"I haven't been seeing anyone, okay? God! Can I just get a divorce and be on my way!" Curtis said as he went towards the door.

"You can open it all you want, but I'm not leaving until you hear me out," Denobria said as she walked deeper into the suite and stood before the vista window. "You men," she laughed. "You men are so gullible. Distasteful in your habits—and careless in your dealings."

"What are you saying," Curtis asked as he walked over and closed the master suite's bedroom door and walked back into the open area.

Denobria went into her purse at that moment and pulled out a tear-stained handwritten letter. "I never had any suspicions over your trip to Oregon," she said as she held the letter out before her eyes. "But after I read this? I began thinking that if the trip to Oregon would only take two days for 'business purposes', why did you stay the whole five days after I declined your offer?"

Curtis hadn't a clue what Denobria was referring to. The trip to Oregon was in total discretion as far as he knew. "I've got nothing to hide," he said nonchalantly. "I went and took care of business and returned home to my family."

"You took care of business, alright," Denobria laughed as she licked her lips. "Listen to this, though, my love," she said in a facetious manner. "Dear Mister and Misses Morrow," she began reading aloud as she held the letter out before her eyes, "we're sorry for any inconvenience you and your wife have encountered here at our rental agency, and, as a measure of our dedication to our valued customers, we wanted to inform you that the register agent you've filed your complaint against has been reprimanded. We take pride in our service to our customers and as a token of our sincere endeavors and commitment to quality, one of our attendants discovered your wife's ring under the passenger seat of the Ford Expedition the two of you rented during your trip to Portland, Oregon. It is our sincere belief that our commitment to service and our honesty in our dealings with each and every customer that we encounter, you and your wife included, will aide in your decision to continue to do business with our rental agency. Sincerely, blah, blah, blah," Denobria sassed as she lowered the letter from her face and eyed her husband while holding the ring in her fingertips.

Curtis recognized the ring right away. It was the one he had bought for Kree. He was dumbfounded over how his wife had gotten her hands on the item at first glance. He then thought back to what Kree had asked of him and realized she hadn't been honest. He now understood. Kree didn't want to know where he'd bought the ring to have the ring cleaned, she wanted to know where he'd purchased the gift in order to have it replaced because she'd lost it. Her actions, had led up to this very day, but Curtis was willing to bear the brunt of the storm on his lovers's behalf because he loved her just that much. It was something the two of them could get through, if only he could get Denobria to leave before the full-scope of he and Kree's relationship could be disclosed fully before his wife's eyes.

"That proves nothing," Curtis said as he stood before his wife, determined to sway her from her beliefs. "It could have been a gift for you, baby."

"Now, I'm baby again." Denobria said as tears formed in her eyes. "You patronize me, Curtis? Am I the whore you've fallen in love with? Do you think that you could tell me anything and call me 'baby' and I will succumb? You've betrayed me!" Denobria yelled as she threw the ring at Curtis. "That is her ring! Hers!"

"Denobria, you need to think about what you're doing here," Curtis replied calmly.

"What is there to think about, Curtis," Denobria responded as she grabbed the purse off the counter and unzipped it. "She has to have an I-D! Who is she," she cried as she scanned the contents quickly and came up with a chrome .380 pistol. "A gun? Who the hell are you dealing with?" Denobria asked as she stared Curtis in the eyes.

"You have a gun as well," Curtis answered with a hint of anxiety. "Just set everything down and we can talk about this later. Denobria," he said as his eyes welled up. "Please, leave. Leave and I will come to you. I will, wherever you want to meet. I will even meet you at your lawyer's office today. But please," he pleaded. "You haven't a clue what is going on with me. Just leave," he begged through tears.

"No," Denobria cried. "Does she know of me? Is this what she had in store for me, Curtis?" Denobria screamed as she held the gun out before her body.

"It was never for you, okay?" Curtis admitted. "That gun was for her own protection."

"I knew it," Denobria cried as she raised the gun to her temple, its barrel pointed to the ceiling as she wept in frustration. "My flowers, my dress, my ring, my man, my lover, *my king*," she then sang through her tears, quoting lines from R. Kelly's song *A Woman's Threat*, the song she'd been playing throughout the weekend as she spied her husband. "Why? Why you hurt me in this way?"

"Because I'm in love with her. But you don't understand the situation fully." Curtis defended.

To hear her husband admit that he not only loved, but was in love with another woman had sent Denobria off into a mindset where nothing made sense. The realization that she was on the verge of losing her man was too much to bear. "You ain't shit," she hissed as she aimed the gun at Curtis.

At the same time, Kree was in the bathroom brushing her hair. Hash browns were her favorite, but she remembered she'd forgotten to mention that she'd wanted grits with her order. She exited the bathroom butt-naked, opened the door on the master suite and emerged while brushing her hair. "Curtis, baby, I forgot to order grits with breakfast," she said with her head down while brushing her hair. "Can you call room service and have them add grits to my order, my love?"

Curtis tilted his head back and placed his hand to his forehead. "Oh my God!" he cried aloud and in utter pain and shameful regret.

Denobria was shocked into silence. It seemed as if everything was playing out in slow motion as she eyed Curtis' lover walking into the open area of the suite while brushing her hair. She was gorgeous on first glance with her long, shiny black hair and perky breasts, but when Denobria saw what lay between the person's legs, her heart sunk to the pit of her stomach.

"A man?" Denobria exclaimed in utter shock and disbelief as she covered her mouth with her free hand. "Your, your sleeping with another man?" she yelled aloud as she grabbed her stomach and sunk to the floor. "Curtis, what are you doing? What are you doing, baby? Dear God what have I done? What have I done Father and Master?" Denobria asked aloud as she eyed her man standing before her with a transsexual. "Is this the reason you haven't been with me since your trip to Oregon? This is what you want?" she screamed as she rested on her knees while looking up at her husband from across the room. "I am a woman! A *real* woman! What is wrong with me, Curtis? Ohhh," Denobria cried painfully as she bowed her head to the floor.

Curtis walked over and tried to console Denobria, placing his hand on her shoulder to soothe her, but she quickly stood up and aimed the gun. "You don't wanna do this, Denobria," he said calmly as he backed up towards Kree. "I love who I love. This wasn't the plan I had in mind, but now that you know, I ask that you respect my decision. I'm in love with her."

"In love with *her*?" Denobria said enraged as she ran her hands through her frayed, brown hair. "The whole time I'm thinking you're leaving me for another woman and I see that that is what you want?" she yelled as she pointed towards Kree. "You are in love with a man, Curtis! A man! She is not a 'her'! This is a man you say you love!"

"Denobria, just let us be, okay? Whatever way you feel about it, just let us be, please." Curtis said as he hugged Kree and turned his back on Denobria.

"I didn't know she was here," Kree said lowly as she leaned into Curtis to shield her body while being overcome with embarrassment. "I'm sorry."

"Don't worry about it, baby. We'll work it out. You should've told me you lost that ring," Curtis said as he ran his hands through Kree's hair and kissed her on the forehead in a tender manner. He then turned to his wife and was about to speak on the terms of the divorce and how things had come about with Kree when what sounded like a firecracker erupted inside the room.

Curtis took one step forward and Kree had tumbled to the floor at that moment. With a bullet having passed through his body, Curtis turned and looked down at Kree and then looked back towards his wife and saw nothing but rage. "You don't have to do this," Curtis moaned as he touched the bullet wound that had penetrated his torso while trying to maintain his balance.

Denobria was in a state of disbelief. Her mind could not let go of the sight of her husband professing love for another man. She could only imagine what all the two had done and been doing behind her back for God knows how long.

Denobria Morrow was staring the man she once loved unconditionally directly in the eyes as she squeezed the trigger again, and again, and again and again, releasing four more shots.

Curtis fell back on top of Kree and lay flat on her body face up, he was looking directly in his wife's eyes, the lone witness to her heartache, shock and rage. The last thing Curtis Morrow heard was that of his wife yelling for both him and his lover to die before one more gunshot rang out.

CLEVER BLACK

CHAPTER TWENTY TWO
THE AFTERMATH

"Kareem, how are you this morning," a nurse asked as she entered Kree's room with her medications.

"I'm fine, but, can you call me Kree, please?"

"Sure, Kree," the nurse smiled.

Kree, whose real name was Kareem Devereaux, lay on her bed in a depressed state. She'd lost the love of her life a month earlier and was saddened that she'd missed his funeral. Maybe it was for the better she reasoned as she lay in her hospital bed. The attack Denobria had instituted was nothing short of vicious. The bewildered wife had shot her husband to death and had beaten Kree into within an inch of her life; and she would've probably still have been beating Kree to this very day had not hotel security barged into the room and gained control of the situation once other attendees reported hearing gunfire and screams.

When the smoke cleared, Curtis was left laying dead atop Kree, who'd been beaten severely with her own pistol and had caught a fragment of the first bullet that had passed through Curtis' body.

Denobria had fractured her face in two different places, broken her nose and the bullet had ruptured her right silicone breast, all of those acts had landed her in the intensive care unit. 'The man' was beaten back into Kree was what she told herself after demanding that her doctor show her her image in a mirror a couple of weeks ago. The very thing she held dear, which was her feminine looks, had been taken away and she no longer viewed herself as a woman, just another feminine man who loved masculine men, which was a life she'd never wanted to live.

The incident inside Embassy Suites had made headlines across the greater Saint Louis area. Curtis Morrow had died in shame. And his reputation throughout the Saint Louis vicinity was ruined. The full story was that his wife had caught him sleeping with another man, a transgendered person, and she had become so enraged, she'd killed him. The last shot Denobria sent into Curtis had literally knocked his dick into the dirt—she'd blown his penis off completely and he'd bled to death on the floor inside the suite as he lay atop Kree.

Kree was gasping for air, trying to catch her breath as she lay on the floor underneath Curtis, having been knocked down by the bullet lodged in her breast and she was terrified out of her mind over the tragedy unfolding.

Denobria heard her cries and began pistol whipping her across the face with the empty pistol, all the while yelling, "You're not a woman!"

Those words now haunt Kree. For as long as she could remember, she'd always been acknowledged as being a woman. Those who knew the truth about her gender never even gave it a second thought, it was just the person she was in life.

Kareem Devereaux was treated as a woman, lived as a woman, and loved as woman to all who knew her. To hear the wife of the man he loved say aloud what he knew deep down inside as he sustained a severe beating, hurt more than the act itself; and the magnitude of his and Curtis' wrong doing had only entered his heart and mind when he eyed Denobria standing before the two of them with his gun.

Although the world now knew her as Kareem Devereaux, in his heart's eye, Kareem was still Kree; but nothing, not even the acknowledgement that he was percived as being woman, could repair all the wrong that had been done.

The hard truth was that Kree was having an affair, a runaway affair with a married man whom she'd seduced and whose heart she'd stolen. When she came out of her clinically-induced coma, she began to replay the nine months she'd been with Curtis and realized she'd been chasing a fallible dream the entire time. Things were just too good to be true. There could never be a happy ending given the circumstances, and she and Curtis were both walking blindly the whole time. They were so much in love with one another they'd both lost sight of reality and had underestimated a wife's willingness to confront the situation head on and it had all ended in an unexpected tragedy.

All Kree had to do was walk away that day inside that perfume shop in downtown Saint Charles. She didn't have to ask if Curtis was interested in dating her after knowing the man was married. Had she done so, Curtis would still be alive and he and his wife would still be happy, and his two sons would not be without their father, and their mother, who was now serving a four and a half year sentence after a jury convicted her of passion provoked manslaughter by reason of temporary insanity.

The Morrow family had been ruined because of Kree's actions and she was now genuinely sorry, but it was too little, too late. The damage, which was irreparable, had already been done and would stand as a testament and a life lesson for Kree, who by pursuing her own selfish desires, had destroyed a family, and at the same time, had lost what she knew to be real love.

Some good did come out of the situation, however; Jessie was freed. The message Kree had left for Sean paid off. He knew what'd happened to Kree and was willing to help her friend on her behalf. Kree had told him Jessie's full name and he went down to the courthouse and worked her case pro bono. And with Dibble unable to testify due to his untimely death, Loopy and Sweet Pea got off as well.

Chastity was unwilling to bear witness, knowing all her dirty little secrets would be exposed and she'd dropped the charges.

Jessie returned to work, and Loopy and Sweet Pea now work alongside Pepper and Simone in Fox Park. They still have beef with Toodie, but without the threat of jail time hanging over their heads, they are now able to focus on their game and hustle. What lay ahead for Pepper and company remains to be seen, but as for now, things are back to normal in Fox Park.

Kree left the hospital in bandages two days later and the first place she went was the cemetaries where Curtis Morrow and Alonzo Milton were buried to say her farewell to two of the men that had shaped her life. She thanked them for their love before returning home where she was joined by all of her friends, Pepper and Sean Bradsworth included, the following day.

The wounds would heal, and Kree would return to her old self, but she would be forever scarred on the inside and left wondering what could've been, and would she ever find another love like the love she'd shared with Curtis Morrow. Only time would tell what would become of Kree's love life, but as of June of 2007, it felt good just be able to breathe and return to a sense of normality.

Three months later, Kree was back to her old self. She wasn't dating nor looking to date as of September of 2007, only focusing on her career, her friends and her pet dog. She lay asleep in her bed, having styled her hair and doing her nails the day before after returning home from the mall where she'd purchased a brand new wardrobe for the fall. Her eyes snapped opened upon hearing the alarm clock on her phone go off and her phone was also ringing as it vibrated across the night stand beside her bed inside her tranquil home. She sat up and grabbed her phone and shut off the alarm and answered the call, knowing who was on the other end.

"Jessie, why do you keep messing with the alarm on my phone," Kree complained as she stretched.

"I *knew* your ass was gone oversleep, Kree! I just *knew* you was gone be late so I set your alarm before you left the shop last night," Jessie laughed. "Come on! It's Saturday and you know how Kantrell ass get when we late, homegirl!"

Things were indeed back to normal for twenty-four year-old Kree Devereaux and her friends after several months of turmoil, and as the old saying goes, life goes on....

...One would have to guess that the moral of the story is that in life, there really can be a happy ending, just not the happy ending we all expect.

Kree was happy just to be alive and to be able to continue on being herself.

Jessie, Sweet Pea and Loopy were happy just to be free.

Whatever mechanisms, transgressions and schemes that had led up to that tragic weekend back in May of 2007 would be absolved and chalked up to the annals of history in the lives of these four friends, the rule of the street, and the attitudes that all who were involved in this tale of deceit, love, lust and romance run amuck divulged themselves into without thinking of the consequences of their actions.

May they all live on in peace, and learn from the mistakes made, thereby earning them a right to attain their own individual happiness without being judged by others who now know their story, yet carry their own Implicit sins and secrets without judging them, lest they themselves be judged.

THE END